WOMEN LIKE THAT

Fiona Curnow

FOR SHONA

Also by this author
Before the Swallows Come Back

Writing as F J Curlew
Dan Knew
To Retribution
Don't Get Involved
The Unravelling of Maria

Women Like That is a work of fiction.

Chapter 1
1914

It was a cruel and heartless place when the navvies had arrived. Mud and machinery. Rock-face and desolation. A brutal wind howled up the valley, over the loch, and into their very souls. Rain lashed alongside it. This was a place needing tamed before it could be inhabited, but there was no taming of the weather. Tame the land. That was their job. Work it. Master it. But that weather? Christ!

Houses weren't yet built. Not that any house would be for them. No. They would be cast out like intruders, vagrants, people of no use. No worth. Apart from to build and slave and grind away at life as best they could. Shelter for them was minimal. Canvas haphazard as if thrown down by some greater power with no care. No design. But this was at least a job. Money to be made. Lives to be bettered. That was what they had been told, and when you have less than nothing the chance of something is a call to be answered. And they had. Hundreds of men and a handful of women with promises of dinner. A settling of hungry stomachs. Shelter.

Mhairi had cut off all of her hair—rough like a navvy's—baulked as she had taken the clothes from Jamie, her dead brother, stuffed rags into the toes of his boots so that they would stay on her feet and joined the people of the road. Itinerant workers. People of no importance. People who had fled their homes to look for something, anything, to lighten their load. People

1

like her.

It was easier than she had thought, this disguise, this slip into someone else. She had Jamie to thank for that. The big brother who had toughened her up, challenged her, and she would not be beaten. She worked hard and the strength came of its own accord. Muscles to rival most boys of her age.

Jamie had joked. 'Ye'll no be finding a man when it's time, wi muscles like that!'

'Oh, and who says I'll be wanting a man?' Mhairi had answered, proudly flexing her arm, poking at the muscle she had worked so hard to create. She looked across at him, a grin breaking up her face.

'Aye, well, just saying,' he said, with a playful slap to her head.

They raced up the hill, as they had done at the end of every day when they'd been offered casual work at one of the nearby farms. Their income was small, almost insignificant, but it helped to put food on the table. What they had been working on was what they were paid in: potatoes, turnips, cabbage, eggs, milk, oats. It was all welcome.

Dying bracken, brown and crispy, snapped at their legs. A wind was whipping up, shouting its presence through the trees—aspen and birch with tall, tall pine trees stretching above it all, keeping an eye out—an eerie sound, almost ghostlike. The aspen and birch swayed to its rhythm, casting off their remaining leaves. Hooded crows, rooks, and ravens cawed out their warning. Magpies mimicked the sounds, a flash of white and a swirl of the colours of petrol, barely seen in the decreasing light, but their presence was felt, nevertheless.

When Jamie and Mhairi rounded the brow of the hill everything looked wrong. There was no smoke from the fire twisting out of the chimney. Strangers stood on their land. Their mother, father and the two youngest were huddled together by the front door. A rag-taggle collection of bags at their feet.

'You're turning a family out into nothing! How can a man of the cloth do such a thing?' their father shouted. His wife bowed her head in grief. The children clung onto their mother's skirt, and she to them. They were too young to understand fully, but they could feel it. The fear. The desperation.

'You've had more than enough warnings to pay your rent or leave. You haven't paid and now it's time for you to go. Let's not make this ugly for your children now.'

'But...' their father began. But what? There was nothing to be done and he knew it. Their lives had been hard, a challenge, poverty always biting at their bellies, at the clothes on their backs, but they had their home. A place that was full of hope and love, most of the time. No more.

And that was that. Everything had gone. Jamie and Mhairi were old enough to look after themselves now. To find a job of some sort or other. Their parents had agreed that they should leave, fend for themselves. The family would survive easier with just the youngsters. Fewer mouths to feed. More chance of finding some sort of lodgings. A room somewhere. The family were heading to Glasgow, big and dirty and strange, but maybe something for them.

'You take care o yer wee sister, Jamie,' their mother called in the wind, a break in her voice, tears streaking her face. She glanced back at them every few steps until she tripped, almost fell.

Her husband caught her elbow, held her up. 'That'll do ye no good, now,' he said. 'You need all o yer strength for these two.' He nodded down at the children still clinging to her skirt. 'Come on now.'

She knew that he was right, but it broke her heart nonetheless to turn away and walk on, her family splintered, separated in a way she hadn't anticipated. Yes, they were nearly grown up. They would have moved out with their own loved ones soon enough. Started their own homes, and with luck, their own families. That would have been normal. Expected. Joyous even. It wasn't meant to be like this. Not in her wildest dreams had she anticipated this. Yet here it was, and she was powerless. A failure of a mother.

Her husband took her hand and squeezed it tight, before reaching for the hands of his children, a forced smile on his lips. 'What an adventure this is going to be!' he said.

Jamie and Mhairi turned back to take one last look at their little house. Peculiar how it had slipped from a place of warmth and comfort to nothing. The rough stone walls and thatched roof that had sheltered them, now forlorn. The patch of land that they had worked, grown vegetables on, limp and weary. A sadness had enveloped it all, as it had their lives.

They headed further into the countryside, quiet and lost in dark thoughts. Struggling to come to terms with this. Work and food were their priorities. Focus on that. First, they had asked at their neighbours', where they had put in a couple of hours most days for years now. 'Sorry. We could give you an hour, but no more.' It wouldn't be enough, so they moved on, hoping for something better. They headed north towards unknown farmland. The harvesting had been done, bales of straw gathered and packed away for the coming winter.

'There'll be tatties needing picked, if we're lucky,' Jamie said, trying to keep things positive. But the adventure soon enough became a challenge. A chore. Their feet began to blister, but they couldn't stop. Not yet. They needed shelter, at least, and work.

It hadn't been long—more than one week, less than two—before Jamie got sick. An awful coughing and a fever and he just wasn't her brother anymore, as he spat blood and whimpered. He was confused and weak and could barely speak for the coughing.

'You—Need—To stay—Away—From me. Away!'

Mhairi didn't want to. Of course she didn't. She wanted to sit by him and comfort him and do what she could to help him. To ease his cough. To lessen his fever. She sat opposite him, her arms wrapped around her knees and watched. It was the most awful thing. To watch his life bleeding out of him like that.

And all of a sudden, he was dead. Gone. She couldn't make any sense of it. Here and then not. Her brother and then a body, cold and lifeless. She stared blankly, her body frozen, her mind closed, her feelings deep in the darkest place of her soul, until day became night, and night became day once more. It was the shivering that forced her to move, warned her that she would join him soon enough if she didn't take control of this.

She pulled herself up, searched the ground for some kind of a tool. Something to dig with. It would be a sin to leave his body uncovered, crows pecking at him, food for wild things, stares of disgust from passersby. No.

She couldn't do that to the remains of him.

She scratched at the ground, hammered it with a sharp rock, scratched some more, dug some more. A rhythm to it. Death's toil. A slow and strong rhythm that made her hands bleed. That buried her thoughts. A peculiar strength took over her. It was like she was someone else, detached from him, his death. She buried him as best she could, whispered words of beauty; of what he had been to her. 'I'll always love you, Jamie,' she said as she kissed the cruel soil, stood tall, turned away, and moved off.

It was a strange moving. Almost like floating; like being something else, someone else. She knew that this was her body, those were her feet that she was placing one in front of the other, that was her breath that twisted through the cold air in a plume of disappearing white. Yes, this was her, but it wasn't. Not really. Not anymore. Half of her lay back there under the earth. This half felt empty and soulless. Push on. There was nothing else that she could do. Push on.

Chapter 2
1914

∽

She traipsed through the countryside, keeping to the small road that they had been following. It was little more than a track carved out by horse and cart, by cattle—sheep mostly—and by itinerants like her. No-one paid her any mind as she passed through villages, past crofts, smallholdings. Perhaps a curse if she got too close; asked for some food. 'A slice of bread? Could ye spare one? Just a crust.' There were the kind folk who smiled and offered her enough to keep her going. The others that spat or cursed or even threatened her with violence or the police. A vagrant. A tramp. A nuisance. No worth.

Sometimes her thoughts drifted back—not that long ago, but a lifetime in her head—to when she had been loved and cared for. Her family holding her, keeping her safe. They may have had little compared to others, but that love, that belonging, was beyond compare and she had never wished for more. But it didn't do to dwell on that. It hurt so much. A stabbing to her heart that she could ill afford. No. Her brother had said there was a future up here for them and why not then for her?

It wasn't as if she was the only one. The world had been cruel to many a poor family. Folk turned out, like hers. Rents too high. Others left destitute from the famine. Many had crossed over from Ireland to find some hope here in Scotland. Anything. When she saw them, she hid herself in the bushes, always wary, and listened for clues, for direction. Things overheard could calm an angry stomach, save a life.

She heard talk of a farmer looking for help for a while. Potatoes to pick, cows to milk. It didn't matter what the work was. There would be a roof, of sorts—straw in a barn—a bit of food, even a few pennies at the end of it all.

There were almost as many children as adults travelling and working, travelling and working. Folk of her age and younger taking on the guise of a grown-up. And when the howking was done, the work finished, they moved on; some in groups, friendships that had formed, families; some solitary strangers, like her. She hung back a little, just enough to see, to size them up, to catch talk of where they were headed to.

'Aye. Good money and months, years of work, they say.'

'Is that right?'

'Aye. So yon man was saying.'

She wasn't sure of where they were headed, these men, of what this promise might be, but there was a positivity to their talk and that pulled her on. She had nowhere to go anyway, and a rumble in her belly that needed quieting, filling. Again. A hard frost bit at the land now, at her flesh. Her skin prickled with it. Breath caught, stuttered, like it was a struggle to do even that. To breathe. Her clothes, already thin and worn, wouldn't last through the coming winter, and neither would she. This—whatever this was—had to work.

She followed, keeping her distance, but close enough to know where those men were. Keeping them in her sight. They walked quickly, as if they had a real purpose now, but she was strong and, by the grace of God, healthy, and she kept up. When they settled for the night, so did she. But that was a worry. They might move off early and leave her far behind. Her sleep was light and fitful. Always anxious. Always wary.

∽

That place. Kinlochleven. By God! A wild place the likes of which she had never dreamed of, let alone seen. Mountains high and stark. Unforgiving. Their peaks streaked with snow. The memories of trees, bare and lifeless. A bleak valley that seemed to have no purpose other than to make the winds howl and shriek their way along it. Loch Leven stretched through it, deep and dark and foreboding. Water that could snatch the life out of you and made no pretence about it.

At the building site itself there was mud and rock everywhere. Little to bring a break to your soul, a breath to your lungs. It looked and sounded like hell. She had bound her chest tight, deepened her voice, tried to keep a scowl on her face, in an attempt to appear masculine. She attached herself to a group of men and boys. Mixed herself up with them. There was a confidence to them. A knowing. That was what she needed. They were all checked in. It was easy enough. Anyone could work there. It seemed that she had become a navvy. One of the boys.

The constant hammer of metal on rock filled the air. Explosions as dynamite blew more and more of the mountain away. Sometimes navvies with it. A man at work. An accident. A body. She found it hard to get her head around that. These men though? They just carried on. Hard drinking. Hard gambling. Hard grafting.

Do your graft, earn your wages and that was that. The work was hard though, and you weren't allowed to

9

stop. Not even to catch your breath. Foremen shouting at you. 'Get a move on! No slacking.'

Chapter 3
1914

~

It wasn't just that the work was hard. It was dangerous too. That first accident she had witnessed made her stop and stare. Blood and flesh. Splintered bone. It was grotesque.

'Move along now. There's work to be done!'

'Sorry,' she mumbled.

The foreman stared hard. Like he was seeing through her. Sizing her up. Imagining what lay beneath those clothes. It was like he knew. She pulled at her cap, picked up her hammer and swung. But his eyes were still on her. That night she couldn't sleep. The canvas hut was full of men. Many sharing bunks. Snores and a filthy stench of stale alcohol and manliness filled all the empty spaces. For the first time she felt like her difference stood out for all to see. Now she was vulnerable. Exposed. Frightened.

The clattering of the night shift drowned out most of the snoring. The rhythm of it thumped through her body. There could be no sleep. Not now. He knew. She was sure of it. The foreman knew. She was at risk now. Fearful. He could use her. She had never witnessed such things, but she had heard. Young women like her for the taking. No. She couldn't allow that to happen. It was done. Her time here was done. She should never have come anyway. As if she could pretend like that; as if she could become one of them.

Before the rise of the day shift and the return of the night shift she crept out of the bunk, wrapped the blanket around her shoulders, and slipped into the night with nothing but the clothes she had on and the few coins she had managed to put aside. It would buy her bread and milk for a few days, assuming the weather didn't take her first. That cold. That bitter, biting cold that carried relentlessly on the wind.

She didn't look back until she had reached the top of the hill. Far below, the toil of men, the clatter of hammers, a shout, a chorus of some song or other, laughter. It had struck her from that first day how these men, these navvies, could raise a laugh in the direst of circumstances. She envied them that ability. That and their camaraderie. Their way of life? No. That was hell on earth, and she was glad to be rid of it. But what her future held was now a blank, and that was frightening enough in itself.

From where she stood the snake of the loch, black and treacherous, stretched its way between the mountains, cold, inhospitable, and full of foreboding. She could hear the crash of the Grey Mare's Tail waterfall in the distance. While she could hear it, she had a point to focus on. Keep the sound behind her and her direction would be true. But there was so much else interfering. So much noise in a place of such wildness.

The snow had stretched further down the mountains now, into the hills, and she was heading towards it. She had to keep climbing higher to get away from the place. Higher and into the snow. It was falling now, heavy and wet. The wind howling, the snow blinding, the cold biting, but she could not stop. She would not stop, for there lay death.

Her passage was painfully slow as she had to place each foot carefully, testing the ground, before putting her full weight on it. She could see nothing but snow, even with the breaking of dawn. There was no crack in the clouds, no sun, only a slip from black to grey. The snow at least lightened the place, softened it in its treachery. She slipped, fell to the ground, felt like crying, but didn't. This had to be done. Had to be got through. There was no place for tears at her destitution, the throbbing in her ankle. The unknown that lay ahead of her.

She was following what felt like a track of some sort; a place where feet had trodden before hers.

A few steps further on and she came upon a gathering of gravestones. She walked through slabs of rock marking where bodies lay. Her fingers trailed across letters, words. Most were engraved with "Not Known". Just a few names identified who lay beneath. But they had been known, these men. They had been sons and fathers, lovers and friends. Before this, they HAD been known. What causes a human to become that? Unknown. She was caught between sadness at the losses and anger at the lack of care. The lack of recognition. Men who had lived and worked and died and lay nameless, forgotten, in the unforgiving ground.

It began to stir something in her as she thought of the bosses, the landowners, her parents' landlord, the church; all of them seemed to her to be uncaring and cruel. They were known. Those men. Oh yes. Of that there was no doubt. But the cold was biting into her bones, and she had to move on, quicken her pace. She could see nothing now but snow, feel nothing but the burn of cold in her toes and fingers. 'Jamie, guide me out of this,' she whispered.

She had been on the move for several days and

nights. She didn't know how many. Counting them had seemed pointless. The going had been slow, difficult, treacherous. The land slick with snow, frost and ice. At least the snow had stopped falling and she had a better view of what lay ahead, could see where she was placing her feet. Purchase on the ground was still hard to make.

The surroundings were changing. She walked amongst cliffs, high and unforgiving, scree that tumbled down to unseen depths. The sound of a river, far below.

She could breathe again, think again, as the land began to level out and she felt the easing in her body, in her mind. She could focus now on the way ahead, not just where each foot was being placed. Death had stepped back. Respite had taken its place. Here and there were caves, shepherd's huts, abandoned buildings, broken walls where she could rest, shelter, but she didn't stay for long. An hour or two, then onward.

She walked on through the changing of the season, the snow and the storms lessening, the mountains now far behind. Her journey up had taught her how to survive, how to find casual work, how to beg, how to steal when she had to. And she did it all again. There was a fire in her belly now and she didn't know whether to try and dampen it or feed it. Nevertheless, she lumbered on through the blisters her leaking boots left, through mud and farmland, tracks and rough roads.

Finally, in the distance, the outskirts of a sprawling city broke up the countryside. Sliced through it. This must be Glasgow. Such places were an anomaly to her, but she had heard stories of an immense sprawl of buildings all packed close together, people too. She stood high on a hill and stared at it all. After a life in the countryside, weeks in the wild, mostly alone, now she was about to face people, buildings, strangeness.

She allowed thoughts of her parents to creep back. Perhaps they had made some success here. Found a home, a future. She would find them again. It would all be okay. But the place stretching out before her was vast. She wondered if there was a power, a strength, that ran between families; that would allow them to reach out and find one another. It would need something like that. Some kind of magic.

Chapter 4
1915

~

Such a clamour. An entirely different world to everything she had known before. Dirty, smoky, a stench through it all of human waste and sweat and decay. It was almost too much. Tenements, tall and grim, the likes of which she had never seen before. She couldn't even imagine what might lie behind those grey windows. Such a squash of humanity.

Night was falling and she wanted, needed, to find a place of relative safety where she could curl up and snatch some sleep. She kept her head down despite the pull to look at everything, everyone. Invisibility was her goal right now and recent life had taught her that the best way to remain hidden, unseen, was to act it, be it. Invisible. She turned to her left and up a quieter side-street, then another, smaller, closer to a lane, through some tenements and ducked into a close that led into a stairwell. She didn't know if she was allowed through there, but she walked on anyway, hoping that no-one would come out of a building and question her. There was little point in thinking more on it. She would either be safe, or she wouldn't. Stairs twisted up four flights. People's houses. Not for her.

The stairwell also led out onto a back green. Now she looked around. Listened. It was quiet enough. The odd shout. The odd laugh. The odd whisper. Nothing of any note.

At the back of the tenement, she could just make out a shed of sorts through the fading light of the gloaming.

She stretched her hand across the covered opening, glanced around again then tugged at the wooden door. A squeak that seemed to echo through the oncoming night. She froze. A rabbit startled by a stoat, not daring to move. She waited. Nothing.

She slipped through the opening and found herself in a coalbunker. It was dank and dirty, and the air choked heavy with coaldust. She would be even more filthy come morning but at least sheltered for now. Her exhaustion was such that sleep came instantly, despite the cold creeping through her bones. She had nothing to do, nowhere to go, just sleep. No nightmares haunted her and that was a welcome relief.

⁓

A squeak and a clatter woke her up. Her heart thumped; her mouth was suddenly dry. In the opening, through the harsh glare of the morning sun, she could make out the form of a woman, her hands on her generous hips. A floral apron wrapped around a frame that looked well-fed; well cared for.

'Well now, what have we got here, eh?'

'I'm sorry. I didn't mean nothing. Honest. I wasn't thieving or nothing,' she managed to force out through parched, cracked lips.

'Come out here so as I can get a look at you and see for myself, aye?'

Mhairi stood up, tried to dust herself down but just made matters worse, the black of the coaldust on her hands smearing across everything she touched.

The woman laughed. That was good. Mhairi felt a tangible relief wash through her. Lighten the air. Calm that heart.

'You'll have a name on ye, then? Mine's Maggie.'

17

Mhairi hesitated, trying to weigh up what would be best now. To maintain the facade of being a young man or relaxing back into herself? There wasn't much thinking to be done. She had already spoken in her own voice, and a woman would feel less threatened by another of her kind. Not that this woman looked as though she would feel threatened by anything much!

'Mhairi.'

'Right Mhairi. You look like you could be doing wi a feed.'

The joy of this. Of human contact. Of kindness. Of not pretending. This was quite wonderful. Mhairi smiled and followed the woman through the close, up two flights of stairs. Maggie stopped at a door. Pointed. 'Now, that there's the lavvy. Best nip in and out as quick as you can.' She winked and smiled. 'Right!' She led them on into a tight, cramped, flat. A smell of smoke, sweat, and stale food carried in the air. Damp clothes hung from the pulley. It was all comforting. Reassuring. People, food, and warmth.

'Turfed out by the landlord, aye?' Maggie asked.

'Aye.' The vision that came along with the question was a hard one to hold on to. The pain of it all slipped in alongside, making her feel horribly alone again. 'I'm hoping to find my family again.'

The words tumbled out. The whole story. And she was quite taken aback by how easily it had happened.

Maggie listened, nodded her head. So many stories just like Mhairi's echoed through these streets. 'As it happens, I was about to head into the march.' She caught Mhairi's blank expression. 'The rent march? The demonstration up town?'

It didn't matter to Mhairi what was happening,

where she was going. This woman just made her feel safe and that was wonderful. They sat down to a hearty breakfast of sausage, egg and tattie scones. Mhairi wolfed it down, forgetting all of the manners her parents had drilled into her. Maggie smiled, saying nothing.

'Right. That's better. No good in walking on an empty stomach now, is there? Let's be off.'

Mhairi walked with her through narrow streets and chatter. The streets became wider, busier, the chatter louder. A swell of it all around her. A buzz of something new. A power.

There were so many people thronging the streets. Thousands and thousands of them. They were shouting for fair rents. They demanded that prices go back to their pre-war level. Landlords were having none of it. Bailiffs had been sent in to carry out evictions. Families like hers left with nothing. But this was a Glasgow where women had had enough. Where they had the gumption to fight. Where they stood together and said, "No!" When they heard of an eviction coming up, they banded together, beat pots and pans just like their ancestors had done in the time of the Clearances in the Highlands. They pelted the bailiffs with flour, with rocks, with whatever they could lay their hands on. More often than not the bailiffs retreated. The roof kept over some poor family's heads for a while longer.

Mhairi listened in awe as the speakers called for fairness, for equality, for a rent-strike that would put a halt to this rampant greed.

She could just see a man climb up onto a platform of some kind. A box maybe. A cheer swelled up from the crowd. A buzz of expectation filled the air. It was electric. Like nothing she had ever felt before.

The crowd turned silent, as if a switch had been flicked, and they listened as the speakers spoke of workers' rights, of resistance, of the right to fair and decent housing, of the conspiracy of the ruling classes.

Mhairi had never heard such things, had no idea about most of it. But she had lived it.

A scream cut the air from somewhere behind. Men in uniform, batons raised, barged their way through the crowd. It seemed like they were just hitting at anyone, anything. Maggie grabbed Mhairi's arm and pulled her away. It was too late. A baton caught Maggie's head. She fell. Mhairi stared but was pushed on, pushed away in the swell of the crowd. Such a terrifying commotion. A mass of heads and bodies and fear. She recognised nothing. No-one. Couldn't find her way back to Maggie. Couldn't change direction at all. Her feet barely touched the ground as she was carried away on the tide of panicking people.

She stumbled, fell, pulled her arms over her head. Feet stamping everywhere. Shouts and screams. She thought that this was it. The end. She was going to be trampled to death. The thrumming in her head. Blackness. But something tugged at her. Pulled her to her feet. She didn't look. Didn't resist. It seemed like she was powerless. Miniscule. Anyone could have done anything to her, and she wouldn't have been able to resist at all. She allowed herself to be dragged along with whoever this stranger was, to wherever he had chosen to take her.

The crowds thinned as they twisted through alleyways and tenements. Her chest burned, heaved. Breath was hard to catch. But she couldn't stop. They couldn't stop. The stranger leading her didn't hesitate. It was like he knew every inch of this place. Every back green, every close, every piece of tumbledown building, every smoky secret. When they finally stopped, she had lost all sense of direction.

They were in some kind of back green. Dirty grey tenements turned black with soot all around. Rubbish strewn about. An old mattress, a chair with its stuffing bulging out of a wound. A rusty pram with three wheels. The giggle of some children rose above the distant clamour of the escaping demonstrators in the distance. Perhaps they were safe now. Her rescuer slipped down the tenement wall, breath heavy. She followed suit. What else was she to do?

Chapter 5
1915

He was a peculiar looking young man. Not handsome but striking in his own way. Thick black hair that flopped down over his forehead. A curl to it. The clearest blue eyes that stared like they could see right into her. A look of the Devil about him, but when he showed that crooked grin, his face shone like something very special, something very good, and the world shone with him. Despite it all—the excitement, the fear, the loss, the utter confusion—her heart was pounding in such a peculiar way. Something she hadn't felt before, tipping on the edge of fear, but not. No. It was distant from that.

He nudged her in the ribs, and she realised that she was staring at him.

'You all right there?' he asked.

She shook herself out of whatever had had a hold on her. Forced a smile. 'Aye. Fine. I think.'

'On your own?'

'No. I was with...Oh God...Maggie! She fell. I lost sight of her. Got dragged away with the crowd.' Her voice was cracking, and it was a struggle to keep the tears away. His hand clasped her knee.

'Who is it you've lost then? Sure, they'll be at home waiting on you. Where is it you bide? I'll see you home safe and sound.'

'You'll not. I...' What was she to say now? That she was a vagrant? That she didn't know where she was? No. That wouldn't do. That would make her vulnerable.

22

'I'll be getting on. Thanks, and everything, but, aye, I'll be getting on.'

When she stood up her legs were wobbling, trembling, her whole body felt like it could just fall apart at any minute. She took a deep breath. Drew on her strength. She was not some feeble girl who couldn't stand on her own two feet. She was a woman now. *Stand tall, stand tall.* And she did.

'Thanks,' she said, forcing the hint of a smile. 'For that, back there. I'll maybe see you around, aye?'

She walked off, across the green, keeping her eyes trained on where she was going. That feeling of someone staring was boring into her, but she wouldn't look back. This was done and she had to move on again. Find something. Be someone strong and capable.

He sprung to his feet, paused with his mouth open, about to call out to her. But he didn't. It was best this way. Strangers could be anyone. He had learned that he had to be careful.

She slipped along a close and out into a quiet street. There was little to see. A horse and cart rattled by. A couple of children ran along the pavement screeching in a joyous adventure-filled way. A woman pushed a pram in front of her as she took a deep drag on a cigarette and turned to her friend. They shared a joke, laughed easily. A shopping bag bounced along in the basket under the pram. Something fell out. Neither woman had noticed. Mhairi kept her eyes on the brown paper bag, like a hawk getting ready to swoop for its kill. It could be something or nothing. It could stave off a night's hunger.

She watched and waited until the women had turned a corner, then tried to casually walk along the pavement. When she reached the bag, she scooped her arm down and swept it up. Her fingers clenched tightly around the overturned top of the bag. There was a beautiful smell to it. Freshly baked bread. Bliss! She ignored everything else and walked along the street, her head held high, the bread clutched tightly to her chest. If only she knew where she was, where Maggie lived, even where the demonstration had been. If she could at least find her way back there she might run across Maggie or recognise a street, the way they had arrived. She could retrace her steps.

She made her way across another back green, along a close and onto a side-street. Another horse and cart clattered along the cobbles. Two men were having a chatter. A woman was leaning out of a tenement window, calling down to her weans. It was all very normal, like today hadn't happened at all. She wished that it hadn't. She wished that none of the past year had happened. But it had, and that was no good to her. Feeling like that. It was no good at all.

She listened for where more noise was coming from. That many people couldn't have just disappeared into nothing. But it seemed they had. She had been walking for hours and was still none the wiser. Still hopelessly lost. She could ask someone. But ask them what? The policemen hadn't been at all friendly. Quite the opposite. One of them might recognise her as having been in amongst it all. She might be in trouble.

Her feet were aching, as was her head. She decided that the best thing to do was hide away again. Find a safe place, eat her bread, and hide. A door swung open. Laughter escaped. Laughter and a familiar stench that reminded her of Kinlochleven, of the navvies. It was a drinking house and that meant danger. She turned her back on it and walked away.

'Well now. What have we got here, then?'

Two men blocked her path. A panic took hold of her body, of her mind.

'Well? What have you got to say for yourself, then? Speak lassie.'

'How's about a wee kiss. Aye. A wee kiss for the both of us and we'll let you pass.'

'Och, don't you mind him. Tis just the drink talking. But what's a pretty young thing like yourself doing out here at this time of night? It can be right dangerous hereabouts, aye.'

She tried to push through them, but they closed ranks.

'Tsh. That's a bit rude. Just trying to be friendly. Make conversation.'

'Please. I just want to go home.' She bit back tears, again. Tried to show strength, again. But it wasn't so easy. 'Let me through!' she demanded, with a stamp of her foot and a glare.

They laughed, nudged each other and parted just enough to allow her to walk in between them. Their bodies brushed against hers as she walked through. It was disgusting.

She strode on, until she heard their voices disappear into the sounds of the night. An indistinct hum of strangeness; of other lives; of everything and nothing. Around one more corner and she ran. No thought given to it. No destination in her mind. Just away. Just far away from those men, that place. She ran until the fight for breath was too much. The pounding in her chest, too much. She walked now, calming her breath, her fear.

25

There was a church in front of her, just across the street. No, her experience of men of the cloth hadn't been good, but these were meant to be safe places, so she had been told. "If all else fails, Mhairi, you can always turn to the Lord", her father had said time and again.

She stepped onto the cobbled road. 'Watch out there!' someone yelled at her. A man driving his horse and cart. She jumped back. 'Sorry...'

'You nearly got yerself killed, lass!'

She closed her eyes and tried to calm herself again, before looking left and right and walking back onto the cobbles. They had become shiny and slick in the light rain that had begun to fall. A leerie was walking along the street, stretching up to the gas lights and setting them aglow. The gloom lifted. A limp brightness slipped across the wet cobbles, lit up the nearby walls.

The church now seemed bigger, more imposing. She climbed the steps and reached for the door. It was slightly ajar. She listened to the peacefulness of it all. Soft footsteps. Hushed voices.

The minister opened the door wide and stepped out, almost knocking her over. 'Oh. I am so sorry. I didn't see you there. Too busy huddling myself against the rain! Can I help you at all?'

'Yes. I need directions. I got a bit lost.'

'Right. And where is it you need to get to?'

'I'm not from hereabouts. I don't know the name of the place, but it's where that big meeting was today. The demonstration.'

The minister seemed to bristle, wrinkled his nose in a sort of sneer. She sensed distaste but carried on, nevertheless. 'I just happened to be there, and I got separated from my friend. If I could just get back, I

26

could find my way home again.'

'I see. Well now. It's quite a way away, but easy enough to find. Follow along this road, take the second on the left and follow it straight for about...' He looked her up and down as if sizing her up. 'For about an hour, I'd say. And you'll see it there. No doubt you'll see the mess too, right enough.'

'Thank you so much!' She smiled and turned to go.

'Go with God and be careful. The city is no place for a young woman such as yourself late at night.'

Chapter 6
1915

Mhairi kept her gaze to the ground and found the place, just as the minister had said. Despite the dark she was quite sure that she recognised the street she and Maggie had walked along to get there. There was barely a soul to be seen, anyone able to shelter would surely have done so on a night like this. Her clothes were soaked through, and she had begun to shiver.

Now she was looking up, looking around, taking stock of all that was there. Not wanting to miss a turn off they had taken, a landmark that might call out to her. And there it was. That same little alley that she had followed. The close. The stairs. The lavvy. The door.

There was no light seeping under the door. She put her ear to it. No sound either. Perhaps they were asleep. She had no idea of the time, but it must be late. Too late to chap the door. She debated with herself about what to do. There was the coalbunker that she had spent last night in. No. It was colder out there, and if her luck was in, someone, maybe Maggie, might come out to go to the toilet. Best stay here where she might be found.

She picked at some more of the bread. It was soggy now, but still food. Still satisfying. She curled herself into a ball to try and warm herself up, not expecting sleep to visit her. But it came anyway.

She was startled awake by someone prodding at her with their shoe. 'Ye canny be biding here. Move along now.' The woman stared at her, a heavy, challenging scowl across her brow. Unwelcoming wasn't a strong enough description. The woman was seething displeasure.

Mhairi took a deep breath; tried to hold her nerve. 'I'm sorry. I came to see Maggie, but it was so late, and I didn't want to disturb her so...'

'Family, are ye now?'

'No. No, I'm a friend.'

'Ye'll no have heard then.'

'Heard what?'

'I tellt her. I tellt her often enough, but she wasnae having it. It'll get ye in trouble, I says. An right enough. Trouble, it came. Aye. Trouble an all o its friends!'

'I'm sorry, I don't understand.'

'She's in the gaol, lass. Trampled by the boots o her ain folk, picked up by the polis! Would ye credit it, eh? Nice woman too, but I tellt her. Aye. I tellt her. Had polis up here, the lot, banging away on that door o hers. That's how I found out, see? The polis. Aye.'

'I'm so sorry. I...'

'Now you be on yer way. I've had more than enough trouble the day. On ye go now.'

Mhairi turned and walked slowly back down the stairs. A heavy weight pushed on her shoulders. She glanced back up. The woman was watching her. There could be no harm in asking a question of her. 'You wouldn't know of a family called McIntyre wi two wee kids that came here a year or so back, would you?'

'I wouldnae. Naw. Best try the Sally Army up at the Gallowgate. Aye, that's best.' The woman turned and pulled her door tight behind her, the noise of it bouncing down the stairs. Mhairi cursed herself for not asking more. Was Maggie all right? Which gaol was she in? Could Mhairi help in any way? Then she checked herself. Of course she couldn't help. She was an outsider. A young woman lost in a world of strangeness. It was none of her business anyway. A fleeting moment of kindness, of friendship, now gone. This world felt very cold and alien now. A place of fear and darkness.

By nightfall Mhairi was none the wiser about her family. The people that ran the Salvation Army were kind. Helpful. They had taken her details, made enquiries, checked whatever lists they could call to hand, but everything drew blanks.

'Not to worry. We'll keep looking for you. It can take days, weeks, even months to find lost souls. And I don't want to give you false hope. There is the chance we may never find them for you, but God willing. Yes, God willing.' Her smile spread warmth and hope. That was good enough for Mhairi for the time being. 'Now, let's get you a bed for the night, at least.'

The air in the shelter was full of hopelessness and despair. The beds full of folk with less than nothing. Mhairi was grateful for the shelter, but she didn't belong here. She didn't feel like she was one of them. Her situation was temporary. She would either find her family or find a way out. A job. Something. She was more than this.

But this was such a hard time. The war was taking its toll on everything. Wounded soldiers, widowed wives, orphaned children. Homelessness and poverty were rife, and she felt guilty taking up the time of these people, taking a bed, accepting their food. Their charity. Days turned to weeks and with their passing her hope for something better waned too.

One of the younger Salvation Army volunteers had taken a liking to Mhairi; spent that little bit more time with her, encouraging her, even sharing a seemingly inappropriate laugh with her. She felt almost like a friend. Early one morning she came hurrying along the beds and gave Mhairi a hug, a grin on her face. Some good news, at last?

'You've found them?'

'No. No, I'm sorry. No news on that front. But I have heard of a job. A fine house up in Kelvinside. They need some help. It would be a live-in position. I thought it would suit you just fine.' She gave Mhairi a change of clothes, helped her smarten herself up, boosted her confidence. 'You'll be grand. You'll see. Just grand. On you go now, and good luck to you.'

'You are a pure star, so you are. Thank you. Thank you so much!' Mhairi smiled at the world now. Life seemed to be smiling back at her.

Chapter 7
1915

Mhairi found the address that she had been given easily enough. This was a part of Glasgow with wide streets, the houses grand and separated by large gardens, high walls and gated entrances. This was a different world of wealth and opulence. She felt like an intruder, an imposter, as she stood at the entrance just staring up at it. Such a beautiful grand house. From the wrought iron gate set in its own little stone archway, to the pathway with shrubs on either side, to the wide steps that led up to the double-fronted door with its highly polished brass knobs and bell. There were bay windows, curtained with heavy velvet drapes, on both floors.

'Right Mhairi!' she whispered. She pushed on the bell and almost jumped back at the sound. A deep resonance that boomed her arrival. Her presence. She heeded the advice she had been given. *Deep breath. Shoulders back. A friendly but respectful smile, a toning down of the accent.* That last one would be hard. How was she supposed to change the way she had spoken for her entire life? She would try though, if that's what it took, she would try.

The door opened silently but briskly. A man stood there, the look on his face as he eyed her up and down, one of distaste. His clothes were fine. A black woollen three-piece suit with the hint of a pinstripe running through it, a highly starched white cotton short, a claret silk tie. His shoes held such a shine to them that she imagined he could see his reflection in them, if he had a mind to. His hair was turning grey, thinning, his eyes held no welcome.

'Right. You'll be the girl, then,' he said. He was pointing at her with a silver-tipped cane. 'Impossible to get decent staff these days. Bloody war! Women doing men's jobs and women's? Well. Children it seems!' He looked her up and down again, shook his head. 'Wait there.' He pointed to the side of the house with his cane. 'And I'll take you down to your quarters.' He reappeared from the back of the property. 'Come on then! We haven't got all day!' She gulped at his brusqueness and followed him round the side of the building.

It was winter, but she could imagine what it would be like come spring and summer. The ivy clad walls, the apple trees, the rose bushes. There was a summer house at the foot of the garden, with windows all the way round. Her attention was caught by a figure sitting in a chair inside the odd little structure. If buildings could be such things, this one felt friendly.

It was an octagonal affair with a steeply pointed roof; a brass pineapple on its tip, turned green with age and weathering. The windows were set in semi-circular frames. It was painted white, now slightly flaky, as if in need of a fresh coat of paint. Plant pots stood on the concrete surrounds. Whatever had been planted in them was now dead, perhaps sleeping through the winter. It was at complete odds to the formality and unwelcoming air of the house itself. Different worlds in such close proximity.

'This way! This way!' he barked.

He led her to a basement. A damp-smelling affair. There were two small doors. Her room and one other. Nothing was said other than an instruction to get dressed and wait. A maid's outfit lay across the single bed. It was a little on the large side, but it was okay. It would do. She tightened the belt of the apron as best she could. There was no mirror so she couldn't check herself. In fact, there was very little light. A candle had been placed in a clay holder on the wooden bedside cabinet. Two empty drawers below it. The window was a narrow strip above head height, which saddened her. She would like to have been able to sit and look out at the garden in her free time. There was no curtain, and she doubted the need for one anyway.

She paced the length and breadth of the room. Four paces by three. Her fingers touched the ceiling when she stood on her tiptoes and stretched as high as she could. It was off-white, as were the walls. The concrete floor was bare but also painted off-white. It gave the place a peculiar feel. No definition to it. The edges blurred into one another. It made her feel dizzy. Uncomfortable.

She took a seat on the narrow metal bed, which squeaked as she sat. She bounced gently up and down, ran her hands over the mattress, pushed down on it. It was better than anything she had slept on before. She smiled at her luck and waited. There was nothing else to do.

She would love to have been able to explore what was above her, what was around her, but she didn't dare move. This felt like a place where orders were given, and rules were followed. She wasn't at all sure how that would go. Taking orders had never been something that came easily to her. Rules? Well, they were for the breaking. For challenging. "It'll be the death o you some day! You mark my words," her father had said. Her mother had agreed but turned her back to smile at this daughter of hers who had such a spark to her. Something that she thought might save her, rather than the opposite.

At last, a sound. Footsteps drawing closer. Mhairi jumped to her feet in expectation. Swiped at her apron. Did her best to appear confident. Acceptable. This was all so new to her.

The handle turned and the door squeaked open. She held her breath, fixed her demure smile.

The man with the cane looked through her. Her smile slipped. There was no need for it, and she certainly didn't feel it! She hadn't been introduced. Had no idea of whom she was in the presence of, nor who her employer was. Was it him? This austere man? She had been expecting something different. A welcoming, at least.

'Right!' The man with the cane barked. 'On you come. I trust you'll have more gumption about you than the last one. Useless. Utterly useless!'

Mhairi followed him to the rear of the basement and up a small flight of concrete stairs.

'This is only to be used when you are on duty. Do I make myself clear?'

'Yes. Of course.'

'Right. Well then.'

He led her through to the kitchen. It was a huge affair with cupboards galore, a Welsh dresser piled with fancy looking plates the likes of which she had never seen.

'Break anything and it comes off your salary.'

She instinctively clasped her hands behind her back.

'If anything should go missing, likewise! The

responsibility is yours, and yours alone.'

As he went on it was sounding as if she were the only employee; that the running of this house would be down to her, and that was quite terrifying. She could swing a hammer as well as the next man, but this? She was to light the fires before the mistress rose. Breakfast would be taken to madam's bedroom on a tray at precisely eight o'clock. Tea, toast and jam, and if available, two lightly boiled eggs. She would then clean and dust every room before preparing luncheon, which would be served at one thirty. Weather permitting it would be taken in the summer house.

'Why the devil she insists on that is beyond me, but there you have it. My daughter on a plate! Dinner is at seven o'clock, and, if instructed, it will be taken in the dining room. The mistress will let her preferences be known in ample time. I am seldom here, and I am entrusting you with the welfare of both the house, and its occupant. Do I make myself clear?'

She wanted to say, "no!" She wanted to say, "I can't do this." She wanted to say, "who are you, and who is madam?" How she wished she had spent more time with her mother, learning about such things. But no, she had been the archetypal tomboy and now, it seemed, was payback time for every tree climbed, for every adventure had. But she wouldn't change it. Any of it!

A lump caught in her throat as visions of Jamie flooded her head. Yes, they had been poor, but it hadn't felt so. The air had been clean, the river pure, the surrounding forests alive with wildlife, birdsong their lullaby. They had had such wonderful adventures, exploring, playing hide and seek, taking on the guise of adults, prey and predator. More often than not they had returned home mud-stained and breathless, holes in the knees of their trousers, catches on their jumpers. There was no chastisement, just an order to get cleaned up before tea-time.

Mhairi was brought back to her present reality by the harsh clatter of the man's cane on the immense kitchen table, old oak, scarred and stained. She jumped. It seemed he hadn't noticed her or the jump. Again, looking through her, looking past her. She was invisible.

He tapped at Mrs. Beeton's Everyday Cookery and Housekeeping Book. 'Everything one needs to know can be found in there, apparently. I suggest you digest every word.' She hurried behind him as he strode out to the entrance hall. Again, he used his cane to point. This time to a fur-trimmed, fur-lined Ulster coat that was hanging on a brass peg. 'Do I have to spell it out?'

She gulped, realised what he was instructing her to do, slipped the coat off its peg. The weight of it took her by surprise and she almost dropped it. She gathered herself and turned to hand it to the man. He was standing with his back to her, his arms outstretched in some kind of expectation.

'Come on, come on. I haven't got all day.'

I am meant to dress you? Is this for real?

He gestured towards a Fedora that hung beside the coat.

She stretched, handed it to him, assuming that he would put this on himself. He did, but with a shake of displeasure. The relief was palpable when he closed the front door behind him, and his footsteps slipped into the distance. It struck her that he didn't appear to have a limp. Was the cane for effect? Did rich people do that? She had no idea.

Chapter 8
1915

∿

It was now mid-afternoon, and Mhairi was at a loss as to know what she should do. She decided that she should introduce herself to madam, whom she assumed to be the figure in the summer house. She took her time walking down the garden path, a mish mash of crazy paving which seemed to be somehow artistic, as if it had had been created with beauty in mind above functionality, that twisted down to the happy little structure at the foot of the garden.

She glanced through the windows. The figure—the woman—was still there, a blanket wrapped around her shoulders, a book open on her lap. She was staring out at the border of shrubbery that lined the high stone walls keeping the outside world at a distance.

Mhairi tapped lightly on the door.

The woman turned slowly, smiled softly, and beckoned her in. Her black hair was tied tightly back from her alabaster skin, her cheek bones angular, her dark eyes sunken. She had the look of a phantom about her.

'Do you see them?' she asked quietly. 'I do love them so. Their bright red chests proclaiming them to be something so special, and the most beautiful celebratory of songs. Quite wonderful!' She turned her head to face Mhairi. 'Come close. Let me get a good look at you. We are to become the closest of companions, after all.' She stretched her gloved hand out.

Mhairi gulped and took the woman's hand.

'There now. You see, I don't bite!'

'I'm sorry. I didn't mean...'

'I know. It's dreadfully off-putting, this whole appearance of mine. Accident, you see. Left me just a tad maimed! But I remain me inside. I do hope my father didn't frighten you too much. He has a way of making sure that no-one stays here for long. I do hope that won't be the case with you. I think that we are going to become great friends.

'You shall call me Connie, when we are alone, Constance when in company, Madam when my father is in earshot. My father is Edward, but you must NEVER call him that. His is Sir. Were you to call him Mister Fotheringale he might faint, Edward and he would at once have you dismissed. As for Eddie, well, that would also involve a flogging. And a public one at that!'

Connie laughed, before wincing at some unseen discomfort. 'Some water. Could you? And the medicine. This beastly influenza!' She gestured towards an ornate little wooden table, inlaid with ivory and what appeared to be gold. In the centre was a crystal jug with a matching tumbler by its side.

Mhairi was almost afraid to touch them. Afraid that she might drop something. Break something. She filled the tumbler and handed it to Connie.

'And the medicine, if you don't mind.' She pointed to a small glass bottle which Mhairi passed to her.

Connie unscrewed the cap, swallowed a mouthful of the tincture, followed by a sip of water. 'That's better,' she said after a few minutes of peculiar silence. 'Thank you.'

There was so much that Mhairi wanted to ask. About

39

her duties, about this house, about Mister Fotheringale, but, most of all, about this enigmatic young woman who seemed to have been through some awful tragedy.

'Tell me, do you read?'

'I can, aye. Sorry, I mean, yes!'

Connie dismissed her apology with a gentle wave of her hand. 'We are in Scotland, after all! I find it rather endearing. Aye! I should begin to use the word myself, if for no other reason than to annoy my father! I am sorry. You were saying.'

'My mother taught me to read.'

'Splendid! I find it so tiring these days. My eyes don't quite work as they should. Could you?' She handed the open book, "A Room with a View," by E M Forster, to Mhairi. 'I am enjoying this so, such clever writing, but you should start at the beginning, that way you can enjoy it alongside me.'

Mhairi felt awkward and incapable, her words stilted, and she was sure, boring, but before long, and with encouragement from Connie, she had learned how to read with expression, how to put on voices for the different characters. It became a time that they both looked forward to; enjoyed. It became something special.

Mr. Fotheringale spent most of his time at Westminster, where he sat as a member of parliament. His absence was relished by both young women. They had spent weeks following the same pattern. Mhairi would do the required chores and then hurry to Connie, whether she was in her room, or the summer house, the latter being the most common, even in winter. They would wrap up in blankets. A small paraffin heater would take off most of the chill anyway. Connie only took to her room if the weather was particularly cold, or she was feeling poorly, and such occasions were, thankfully, becoming less and less frequent.

She had been a sickly child, a seeming magnet for every disease and epidemic going. Illness was simply a part of her. Her mother had molly-coddled her; kept her safe; kept her away from others. Her father had spent little time at home, and when he did, he had no time for anyone other than his wife. A woman he adored. The child was merely something that had happened, been expected, but not wanted. Not by him. But then her mother had died, and her father became someone else. A bitter man who resented the child even more. A confusion of emotions. Connie was a part of him; a part of his wife, but as he stared at her he saw only loss. He hired staff to look after her. To keep her out of sight. He used doctors to medicate her. To keep her quiet.

Mhairi made regular trips to the local bookshop, or further afield if the book Connie wanted was perhaps a little bit on the sensitive side. Something inappropriate for a young lady.

'You must ask Lizzie for something raunchy. Something to set one's mind athrill! Something to fly us away from this humdrum existence.'

'I can't ask for that!'

'But of course you can! Lizzie knows of my literary tastes. She will guide you with the utmost discretion.'

41

Chapter 9
1916

~

The weather was glorious. A bright spring day bursting with the promise of summer. The apple tree in the garden was heavy with blossom, its fragrance enticing birds, insects, and humans alike. Connie's chair had been placed in the tree's shade and Mhairi sat on the grass, enjoying the touch of it, sensing the growth of it, as if she could feel it pushing and swelling through the earth beneath her.

'I hope I'm no speaking out of turn, but, well, seems to me that you spend all o your days here. You don't see anyone or go anywhere. It's no right. Well, to my mind anyway.'

Connie pulled her hand up to her face. 'It was decided that that was best.'

'Best for who?'

'For me. For the people who might have to look upon this. And Father says...'

'Father says! That's just daft, so it is. I'm no so sure that's the Connie I know talking. No-one should be the boss o you.'

Connie laughed softly. 'Oh, but he is my father, after all.'

'Pff. In name, aye, maybe. Nothing more that I've seen.'

'You could be right, but...'

'But nothing! You're a grown woman with a mind of her own. Let's you and me go for a wee walk together. Put your bonnet on, and we'll tie a bonnie wee scarf about it, and you'll look them in the eye and say, "Aye? I've been in the wars. And what about it?" What do you say?'

'I don't know.'

'Aye, ye do.'

Connie reached for her bottle of Laudanum.

'You don't need that,' Mhairi said.

'But father insists.'

'Does he now?' Mhairi said, raising her eyebrows. She took the bottle and put it back in its cupboard.

⁓

Connie slipped her arm into Mhairi's so that the damaged side of her face was away from others. Hidden. They walked out onto the street. Her step faltered at first. It had been so very long since she had left the confines of that house. Connie had often wondered if there was a purpose to anything anymore. If there was any reason for her to be alive. Now this felt quite exciting, if somewhat nerve-wracking.

Mhairi and Connie walked around the block and passed barely a soul. Those that they did pass paid them no heed. The next day they went further, and a little further still, until their walks were lasting an hour or more.

'You know, I have no idea about anything anymore. Outside of my books, I know nothing. What is going on in your world, Mhairi? What should I know about?'

Mhairi took a deep breath, blew it out slowly. 'There's no so much that I know of either! Poor folk where I come from getting turfed out o their homes by rich folk. More poor folk working the skin off o their hands for less than a family needs to stay alive. Is that what you want to know about?'

43

Connie stopped, grasped Mhairi's arm tightly. 'Yes, Mhairi. It is! We should buy a newspaper. We should learn more.'

'I'm thinking most o the papers don't write about such stuff.'

'How far are we from Lizzie's bookshop? It's nearby, is it not?'

'Aye. Just around the corner and up the hill. Are you up to it?'

'Indeed, I am! Onwards!'

∽

Connie smiled as she walked through the door of the bookshop to the tinkling of its bell.

'Connie! I can't believe my eyes. Is that really you? How wonderful!'

'Lizzie!'

They embraced, held each other at arm's length, and embraced again.

'You look...wonderful!'

'No, Lizzie, I look absolutely frightful but thank you for the attempt at making me feel less awful about it. Of course, you know Mhairi.'

'Indeed, although I didn't know your name until now. Mhairi, delighted to formally make your acquaintance!' She held her arms open.

Mhairi stared, unsure.

'One cannot become friends without a confirmatory hug. Come on dear girl, a hug, if you please!'

As they embraced a pleasant aroma of old books and cinnamon wrapped around Mhairi. There was something timeless and reassuring about it.

'Come through to the back and we can drink tea, or gin.' She raised her eyebrows and grinned. 'And chat.'

She skipped to the entrance, flipped the sign to "Closed". 'There! You have my undivided attention!'

The shop was floor to ceiling with shelves at irregular angles piled high with books. The new book section was more orderly, but the second-hand one seemingly made no sense at all. Mhairi knew from experience that in Lizzie's head this was all in perfect order, and she could locate any obscure book that graced her shelves within seconds. There were also piles of newspapers and magazines, and to the rear of the shop, in a corner you wouldn't know was there unless you'd been shown, artwork, artist's paper and paints, canvases, easels and brushes.

'I am very pleased to see that little has changed!' Connie said.

'Indeed!'

'Are those...?'

'Yes, my love. They are yours.'

Lizzie slipped a sheet from the largest canvas that sat propped up on an easel to reveal an impressionist oil painting of a small summer house in a garden bursting with colour.

'You have such wonderful talent. I do think it a crime that it lies, wasted.'

Mhairi was staring at the picture. 'That is the most beautiful thing I have ever seen. It's your garden, aye?'

'Yes. Yes, it is.'

Her mother had been the artist, but it had soon become clear that Connie had equal talent, if not more. Connie's father didn't approve. Yet another memory of his wife that he didn't consider necessary. He had insisted that she stop. She let it be believed that she had, but continued in secret, at Lizzie's.

45

Connie turned away from the paintings and walked on. Lizzie shrugged. 'One day,' she whispered to Mhairi. 'Let's you and I make sure of it!'

Mhairi, grinned. She liked this woman. These women.

There was a small room at the back with an old velvet settee worn into the shape of its user, a cracked leather wingback chair with brass studs and curved wooden claw-feet. The oak table was strewn with an assortment of papers. In the corner there was a sink and a small cooker.

'So, what's it to be? Gin or tea?'

'I haven't had a gin in years.' Connie replied. 'Not since—well, you know when.'

'And I've never had one,' Mhairi said.

'Then I think the young one needs to be initiated into the pleasures of drinking too much and not giving two hoots! And as for you and me, well, we shall pick up where we left off!'

They all laughed, although Mhairi wasn't quite sure at what. It was simply infectious.

The first sip made Mhairi wrinkle her nose. The burn that swept through her was slightly unpleasant, but by the end of the first glass she was enjoying it. The taste and its effect.

They had been happily sipping and chatting and laughing when there was a knock at the back door.

'Hmm. To ignore or not to ignore, that is the question!' Connie said, laughing.

'Lizzie, let me in, will you?'

'Ah, the adorable young Robbie must be allowed entrance!' Lizzie said.

The voice sounded familiar to Mhairi, and she

couldn't quite believe it when that young man walked in. The one who had pulled her from the stramash at the demonstration. And again, her heart fluttered, and she was quite sure that she was blushing.

'Robbie, this is Connie and this, Mhairi. Don't worry, they're friends. You can trust them.'

'Aye,' he said slowly, looking into her eyes. 'Met you before up at the demo, right?'

'Aye, you did, right enough. Escaped from the polis, then?'

He grinned, raised his eyebrows. 'It'll take more than a handful of them to catch me, so it will.'

'I'm glad.'

'Aye, well, me an aw!' He laughed. Was he blushing too?

'So, what have you got for me?' Lizzie asked.

Robbie swung a canvas satchel from his shoulder. 'A few things for distribution, if you could?'

'My pleasure, as always. And how is Hannah?'

'Working away. You know her. No rest until the enemy is defeated! Anyway, I'd best run, or she'll be throwing a tantrum at me. Nice to meet you again Mhairi. And you...'

'Connie.'

'Aye, right, Connie.'

He turned and was gone.

'Is that the delightful aroma of an attraction?' Lizzie said with a grin on her face.

Despite her best efforts, Mhairi's blush deepened.

The night wore on and Mhairi couldn't remember having experienced so much laughter and positivity. Not even with her brother. She hoped that this would be repeated.

47

'I fear we have something of a trek ahead of us, Mhairi,' Connie said as they stepped out into the warm spring night.

'I cannae walk right,' Mhairi said with a giggle.

'I'll hold you up if you'll hold me up.'

'Sorted!'

Chapter 10
1916

≈

When they finally reached the house, a light was on.

'Oh darnation! I wasn't expecting *him* to be here yet. Be prepared for a jolly good earbashing! We must try and sneak in unnoticed.'

Despite their best efforts at stealth the gate squeaked open. They both giggled.

'Shhh,' Connie whispered.

'Are ye talking to me or the gate?'

The giggles burst into laughter. The front door opened, and they hurried around the side of the house.

'The summer house! We can pretend. He never goes in there,' Connie whispered. 'Can't stand the place! Frivolous nonsense, he says!'

In truth it had been built for his wife as a studio. She had loved it so. Her own little sanctuary. A place where beauty was created, where the outside world simply didn't exist. Even Connie hadn't been allowed to enter without express permission. The place had held a deep fascination for her as a child, and now it was hers. But all Edward could see were heartache and loss.

Connie and Mhairi ran across the lawn and into the summer house.

'Safety! My sanctuary!'

'Will he no come an check?'

'Oh probably, but we shall deny everything! We must be quiet and demure like young ladies are supposed to be. And on no account any laughter whatsoever,' at which they both giggled.

It wasn't long before Fotheringale's heavy footsteps could be heard approaching the summer house. He burst in, the door clattered against the wall threatening breakage, but it held.

'What the devil do you think you're playing at?' Edward said in the tone of an angry schoolmaster.

'I'm sorry, Father dear. What on earth do you mean? We're simply enjoying the gorgeous evening scents. The honeysuckle is quite divine at this time of night. Not to be missed!'

'You!' He pointed his cane at Mhairi. 'Are on your very last warning. Such foolish behaviour should not be encouraged. Inside! Now!'

'Yes, sir. Sorry, sir.' She bowed and backed out of the door, biting on her lip, stifling a giggle, feeling like a naughty child.

'And as for you! Anything could have happened out here in the dark. Have you completely lost your senses?' He stepped closer and crooked his arm for her to take. 'Come!'

She stood up, took his arm, and smiled.

'Do I smell...alcohol? Have you been drinking?'

She took a deep breath, focused on her words, her diction. No slurring was to be allowed to slip out. Her voice was as confident as she could muster, her head held high. 'No, no. It is just the medication.' In truth, she hadn't taken her medication for a very long time. It blurred her thinking; made her feel weak and incapable. She had asked Mhairi to dispose of the bottles in secret. Her father must not know!

'Hmm,' he said.

'And how long are you home for?'

'It is a fleeting visit, I am afraid. London beckons

tomorrow.'

'Oh, that is such a pity.'

'Indeed! I am not at all happy about leaving you in the company of that young woman. I smelled trouble when I first saw her. I should have listened to my inner concerns.'

'There is no need to worry. She was simply following my instructions.'

'Hmm. You should know better, as should she. The air still holds a chill at this time of year, and we know how susceptible you are to illness.'

He walked Connie up to her room and bade her goodnight.

The house fell into darkness and silence. Mhairi found it difficult to sleep. The room was spinning, as was her head. Finding this job had been such a blessing and she loved it. Well, when *he* wasn't there. Thoughts of what she would do, where she would go, if this ended swarmed around in her head. She should make more of an effort to find her family. The Salvation Army still had no news, but she might turn something up herself. She chastised herself for being lax. Yes, this past year had been unexpected and mostly joyful, but what of her own family? Surely, they were out there somewhere, perhaps wondering about her, and not knowing of Jamie. That was wrong of her.

The next day she talked it through with Connie.

'Well, of course you must find them. And I shall help, on one condition, that if we do find them you will not leave me. Please do not leave me.'

What a wonderful feeling; to be so cared about by someone like this. Mhairi felt truly blessed.

Connie's father had installed a telephone. It meant

that he could call every evening to check up on her, which was unfortunate, but it also meant that it was easier to search for Mhairi's family. More avenues were open to them if the Fotheringale name was used. Her father had connections, and they opened doors.

But again, nothing came of it. Pounding the streets of places where the poor were housed was something Mhairi would only do on her own. This wasn't a place for the likes of Connie. She felt guilty as she walked through narrow streets with dirty tall tenements keeping out any chance of sunlight. Women with gaunt sunken eyes. Their children ragged and grubby playing in the dirty street. Smiles breaking through grimy faces.

'Got any spare change on ye? For the weans, like.' A woman called from the doorstep where she sat, her hand out, her feet bare and blackened, two children clinging to her tattered skirt. Mhairi looked back, but their eyes didn't meet. It was as if the woman knew there would be no response. No kindness.

Mhairi turned back, knelt down beside the woman. 'I'm so sorry. I've no got a thing on me, but I'll be back. I promise I'll be back.' She squeezed the woman's hand. Still no reaction. What sort of a life was this?

Mhairi knew of the poverty, of the hardships, after all it had once been her life. But not like this. Not this awful destitution. When she was young her parents had been able to provide comfort and love. But after the turning out she had felt it too.

Now it was as if she had stepped into someone else's skin. When she had started working for the Fotheringales, settling in, their life of plenty had somehow become hers and she chastised herself for allowing it to be so. For forgetting. She began ensuring that she carried some change with her, some small items of food, things that might make life that little bit easier for the unfortunates she came across. It wasn't enough, but at least it was something. A smile brought to someone's face, a settling of a hungry belly, if only for a short while.

It was disheartening as each day of searching revealed nothing of her own family. She couldn't bear the thought of them living like this. Cold and hungry and desperate. She had never actually placed them amongst this hopelessness, telling herself it would be different for them; it had to be different.

She had just crossed Argyle Street when she spotted him, Robbie. He looked as if he were trying to dodge someone.

She caught his eye and waved. He winked at her and nodded ahead of him. Did he mean that she should follow? It seemed so.

He turned into a close and she went in after him. They climbed two flights of stairs. He chapped on a red door, quietly, like he was a bit unsure, but he smiled at Mhairi and squeezed her hand. That smile lifted her up, calmed her down.

A woman answered. A scowl on her face. She ushered them in, looked left and right, up and down the stair, closed the door quietly, carefully, as if it were something precious. She pulled Robbie into the kitchen and whispered.

Mhairi could just make it out, though. She always had been good at that. Eavesdropping. Her ma and da. The minister. The factor. She chastised herself again. She should have known something bad was coming. The warning signals had been there. The quiet threats, the quieter whispers between husband and wife, the fear of visitors, of strangers. She should have done something, but a young woman like her, barely out of childhood. What was she to do anyway?

~

'Are you mad? Bringing a stranger in here?'

'She's grand, Hannah. I bumped into her at the meeting last year and she's a friend of Lizzie's. One of us.'

'And you're quite sure of that?'

'Aye! She helped me dodge the polis down there.'

Mhairi tried to distract herself by looking around the room they had left her in. On the walls there were posters and pictures of marches, demonstrations, folk all gathered together. Others of women holding their fists high. "It's time to make a change" "Capitalism has failed" "For the many. Not the few". Lots of pictures of the same face. A man who looked proud and strong. Mhairi wondered who he might be.

Hannah looked just like the posters. Big navvy boots on her feet, dungarees, a man's shirt with rolled up sleeves. Her fingers were stained with ink and nicotine. Her face had smudges on it. Her shoulder length brown hair was tied back with a red scarf. Hannah and Robbie came back in, him grinning, a wink Mhairi's way. Hannah was frowning. No sense of welcome there. She brushed past Mhairi as if she were invisible.

Hannah rummaged through the dishevelled table, peering under piles of paper, muttering under her breath. 'Where the devil did I leave it? Robbie? Have you seen my tobacco tin? I swear it was right here!' She found it under an open newspaper, *the Forward*, sighed, sat down, and rolled a cigarette. Mhairi had seen the

54

navvies do it often enough. Never took to the idea herself. But it looked good on Hannah somehow. She lit up. Threw her head back and blew out a long trail of smoke. Mhairi felt strangely drawn to her, like she was sucking her in with each drag of that cigarette. The power of this woman!

There was a whistle from the street below. Hannah tugged the curtain aside, glanced out and hurried across to the flat door. Two older men and a woman came in.

'What is it?' Hannah asked.

'They've got Donald. He's being charged with sedition.'

Hannah shook her head, looked to the sky.

'But it gets worse. They're conscripting him.'

'He won't fight. He won't kill another human being.'

'Aye, and he'll either get shot as a coward or be killed by the so-called enemy.'

Mhairi had no idea about any of this. The way of things, war, conscription, any of it. Her previous life of day-to-day survival had consumed every minute, and now her days were filled with novels and romantic ideals. She felt ignorant and embarrassed in this company.

These people wanted to make a difference; to help those who had little or nothing; to lift them up. They printed posters and leaflets about the working-class struggle, about internationalism, about their brothers abroad, the injustice of the war, about poverty and rent strikes and the unfairness of it all.

They gave her books to read, took her to meetings, and her head was filling up with so much new knowledge. But more than that, she felt like she belonged. She had a purpose. And it was a mighty fine one to her eyes.

Chapter 11
1916

Connie had fallen; slipped on the frost that had covered the little path her mother had made many years ago, from house to summer house. It was clear that she had broken her ankle. The twist to it. The agonising pain. There was no way that she could put any weight on it. She had managed to slither up to the steps at the back of the house, sat on the bottom one and heaved herself up one step at a time. She had almost made it to the safety of the kitchen when her father came back. He found her in a crumpled heap in the doorway. Tears had stained her face.

'Good God! What the? —'

He settled her in bed and telephoned for the doctor. By the time Mhairi returned Connie was heavily sedated and fast asleep.

'Where the devil were you?' Fotheringale bellowed. 'I pay you to look after her, to ensure that she has everything she needs, and it ends like this! Get out and never let me see your face again!'

Mhairi stared. Disbelief washed through her. Then anger. 'My wages. You owe me for the work I have done.'

'I owe you nothing. Now, pack your bags and get out before I beat the living daylights out of you!'

She opened her mouth to respond, to explain that Connie had given her a day off. Every Wednesday for the past six months had been hers. But there was no point. No point at all. Men like that did what they wanted, when they wanted, and that was that. And she knew it.

It was bitterly cold, and she was thankful for the lambskin coat that Connie had given her. She pulled the collar up high and thrust her hands deep into its pockets as she walked down the steps.

'Not so fast, young lady. That coat.' He pointed his cane at her. 'It is ours, I believe,' he hissed.

'It was a gift!'

'I call it theft. Whom do you think the officers of the law will believe?'

'Your daughter!'

He scoffed. 'It is well known that my daughter has lost her mind, poor thing.' He grabbed at Mhairi, pushed her to the ground, stood over her with his cane prodding at her chest. 'Now. The coat if you please!'

She stood up, wiped herself down.

His hand was outstretched in expectation.

She slipped her shoes off, clenched them tightly in her hand, grinned at him, and ran.

'You little—Get back here, right now!'

She bolted along the street, knowing that he could never match her for speed, nor the ability to slip away into unseen places. A skill she had practised with Robbie and his comrades on many an occasion.

She stopped behind an old stone wall that surrounded the graveyard. Trees, tall and silent. Shadows stretched by the light of the moon. Gravestones, cold and abandoned. Lives left behind. It was as creepy as hell, but it was deathly quiet, and right now, that meant safety. No running feet in pursuit of her. No shouting voices. No whistles from policemen alerting others to the chase. No. She had won this one and it felt good!

She rested her hands on her knees and panted like a fox having escaped the hunt. There would be a few of them hereabouts scavenging around for scraps and delicacies. And there, as if on cue, the gentle trot of a shadow amongst the gravestones. Another. The foxes stopped, aware of her presence. She smiled at them.

'On ye go. I'll no hurt ye.'

It was too cold to stay out there for long. She waited until she was absolutely sure that there was no-one on her tail before heading back out onto the street. Again, she checked up and down the street before heading towards Hannah's. It seemed like the whole world was sleeping. A silence filled all of the spaces. It was so heavy; so intense, that she felt like an intruder on the night. She shuddered. At last, she turned into the street where Hannah's tenement stood. Her back against the wall; her body pushed into the shadows; she glanced up. There was a light glinting between a crack in the curtains at Hannah's flat. Good!

Chapter 12
1916

~

Mhairi climbed the cold stone steps with a sense of something exciting beckoning her. Yes, she had lost one way of life, some semblance of security, but the events of that day had proven just how fragile that life had been. She wasn't one of them, and it had been made crystal clear she was as dispensable as an unwanted object. A piece of garbage.

She hoped her instincts had been right and she would be welcomed here, as she tapped quietly on Hannah's door. Robbie welcomed her in with that lopsided grin and the customary twinkle in his eye.

'Ach, working for the rich didn't suit you anyway!'

'No, but it was at least a job, and a roof!'

Robbie nudged her in the ribs. 'Aye, well, sure Hannah will let you bide here with us, won't you, Hannah?'

'What?' Hannah shook her head as if that would give the question clarity. 'Yes. Yes, of course. What's another body to the pile?'

'Great!'

And so it was. A new home. A new life. Mhairi had found work at a tearoom through one of Hannah's contacts. The woman seemed to know everyone! The pay was minimal and the hours long, but it was something, at least. A stab at independence. Despite Hannah's protestations she managed to contribute a small amount for her place in the flat.

'It's not as if you're taking up a space that I would

rent out now, is it?' Hannah had said.

'That's no the point. I want to pay my way.'

'If you insist.'

'I do!'

Mhairi kept in touch with Lizzie, sometimes making the drop-offs in place of Robbie; sometimes alongside him. He took her hand and squeezed it. She turned to him and smiled. That beating in her chest.

He pulled her close, his breath warm on her neck and tugged her into a stairwell. 'Can I kiss you?' he asked. 'Aye,' she mumbled, barely able to form words. With that first kiss her legs had buckled, and with everyone thereafter. She didn't know what it was that he did to her, but it was quite magical. They did their best to keep it hidden but the looks, the sly touches, the electricity would surely be picked up on soon enough.

A new maid had been hired at the Fotheringale's. Connie wasn't happy about it, but since venturing out with Mhairi, and stopping the medication, she had grown in confidence. She took it upon herself to go out on her own, despite her father's protestations. They all met up at Lizzie's for a drink and a laugh on occasion.

'So how are things between you and the dashing Robbie?' Connie asked.

Mhairi smiled and blushed. 'Just fine!'

'Have you set a date yet?'

'Actually,' she looked somewhat sheepishly from Connie to Lizzie, and back again. She couldn't quite believe how quickly she had fallen for him, and he, in turn, for her. Smiles and laughter that filled her. The most wonderful feeling that consumed her. When he had asked her to marry him there wasn't a moment's hesitation. Of course she would. 'We have! Just a quiet

61

wee registry thing.'

'And are we to be invited to this quiet wee registry thing?'

'Aye! Course! But if ye come wi yer father in tow there'll be trouble.'

They all laughed.

∽

Lizzie, Robbie and Mhairi leafleted around the streets of Red Clydeside, as it had become known. Connie joined them when she could. They felt like their time had come. Working people at last had a voice. Things could change. The need to be careful was always there, however. That charge of sedition was a devil. An easy excuse to lock away deemed troublemakers.

They were at one of the now regular meetings. Speakers from as far away as Russia! Words that lifted their spirits. People read Hannah's leaflets. Conversations were started about them. An electricity filled the air.

'Run!' Robbie suddenly called.

Mhairi looked behind to see a swarm of police, batons raised, charging through the crowds.

As they ran, Connie stood tall, her fist raised. What an experience! No, her need was not like the majority of people here, but she had grown to care, and this fight had brought back that spark. That zest for life. It was quite remarkable, and she was relishing it.

She was duly arrested and taken to the police station along with many others. A night in the cells amongst such strong women thrilled her. There was a positivity running through their veins and she felt it feed her.

As anticipated, her father's lawyer secured her release the next day. *Hush, hush. Sneak her out.* She was taken to his office where he was waiting with that aura of entitled fury flying around him.

'Sit down! You are not to speak. You are not to make any attempt at communication. You are not to do one single thing unless directed to do so. Do I make myself clear?'

She stood up, smiled at him. 'And just how are you going to force me to do that, Father dear?'

'I shall have you thrown back in jail with the rest of those idiotic rabble-rousers!'

'And I shall shout at the top of my voice. I demand the vote! I demand e—'

She was silenced by the sting of a slap across her face. 'You—you beast!' She stared hard, held her head high. 'I demand the vote! I demand equality!' she yelled in his face.

He stormed out of the office and locked the door behind him.

She threw open one of the windows and sang the Internationale as loudly as she could.

Her father returned with a doctor and two others in white coats.

'You can see quite clearly. It saddens me greatly, but my poor daughter has, once again, lost her mind, and I can no longer cope.'

'Indeed, indeed.'

Connie backed into a corner, her eyes wide, staring at the needle in the doctor's hand.

'You promised!' she hissed. 'You promised not to do this again.'

'You leave me with no choice. Such behaviour! It is for your own good. You shall see.' He shook his head and nodded towards the doctor. 'Proceed.'

The men took hold of her. The needle pierced her skin, and she was gone. Her mind blank, her legs incapable of holding her up. She was strapped to a stretcher and taken, via a discreet ambulance, to the asylum that she had been in before.

When Lizzie heard what had happened to her friend a sense of betrayal, of hopelessness, wrapped itself around her. It was with the heaviest of hearts that she reported what had happened to Mhairi.

'And he's done it again? Got her locked up?' Mhairi said.

'Yes. The man has no sense of family, of duty, of righteousness, of humanity even!'

'Aye. No the best o people an that's for sure. So, what do we do?'

'I fear there is nothing to be done. She was committed once before by him, and she will not be released until his say-so.'

The mood that had fallen on them matched the heavy grey clouds above them. Their world had turned again, this time to the dark side. Life seemed to be pushing them down. A hammer to a nail. They could find no pliers, no release. Their friend was in the very worst of trouble and they felt powerless.

Chapter 13
1917

~

Mhairi and Robbie's wedding was a quiet affair. A simple registry office ceremony, followed by drinks and snacks at Lizzie's. But Mhairi wasn't drinking. She already knew that she was with child. She hadn't told Robbie yet. She hadn't told anyone. The slight swell of her belly, the tenderness of her breasts, were private things, for now. Things just for her and her unborn child. But now? Now perhaps was the time.

'Robbie,' she whispered in his ear that night. 'I'm with child. You're gonna be a da.'

He sat bolt upright, the grin so bright that it shone, even in the darkness. Tears fell and he felt no shame, no embarrassment. These were joyous tears. Tears of the most magical thing in the world. Him and her. And now one other.

She sat up beside him. A sliver of moonlight broke through the curtain and split the night. A piece of beauty just for them. A confirmation from the heavens that this was a most wondrous thing.

He reached for her belly with trembling hands.

She laughed softly. 'It'll no hurt you, and you'll no hurt it.' She took his hands in hers and placed them gently on that tiny swell. 'There now. Say hello to your wean.'

He leaned over and kissed her belly. 'Hello, wee one,' he whispered.

They fell back on the bed, hands and lips caressing, searching. He pulled back suddenly. 'I'll not hurt it will

I? I'll not hurt you?'

'No. No. It's just fine.'

～

How short that pure joy. He had been conscripted. It had always been expected, hanging there in the air. His age, his fitness. He would be sent to fight. But it was something he didn't believe in; something that he had stood up and shouted against.

They had talked about it. The three of them; Mhairi, Hannah, and Robbie.

'You could be a conscientious objector, but that has its own consequences,' Hannah said.

'Aye. I'd thought on that. But I can't say I'm religious. I can't claim ill-health. And now there's the wee one to think on. I need to provide for her. I need to be a good father. Not someone branded a coward. Not someone folk spat at. How can I do that to her? To the two of you?'

Mhairi smiled at how he talked about their unborn. It was a girl to his mind and there was no changing it. 'You'll be no use at all if you're dead!' she said.

'Aye. Christ! What have they done to us? Madness. Utter madness!'

Two short weeks after their marriage, he was away. One of a line of young men terrified of what lay in store for them. They had seen it enough on the broken minds and bodies of those who had returned, on the weeping faces of wives and parents, children and lovers. A hell had descended upon them, and it stayed.

Robbie wrapped Mhairi tight in his arms and squeezed, as if he were trying to blend into her. For them to become one. Inseparable.

'You'll see,' he whispered in her ear, pulling on the tiniest scraps of strength that he could gather. 'This'll

66

all be over, and I'll be back, right here beside you, and we'll make the world a better place. I love you, my bonnie Mhairi. More than anything, I love you.' He closed his eyes and tried to swallow his tears but failed. That grin, that light-heartedness that defined him, were buried somewhere deep and he couldn't bring them to the surface. Not now.

'Don't you dare go an die on me, Robbie. Don't you dare,' she whispered into the cold air.

The whistle of the train called all the soldiers on board. Brave men, frightened men, confused men. The cry of those left behind. Some cheering, others weeping.

'I love you, Mhairi!' Robbie called from the departing train. Steam and the sound of the engine, the clatter of wheels on the track, so many voices adding to the clamour. So many broken hearts. Mothers and lovers, sons and daughters.

Mhairi jumped up and down to try and catch a last glimpse of him. 'And I love you, Robbie!' she called at the disappearing train. She stroked her hand over her belly. 'And I love you.'

Hannah wrapped an arm around Mhairi's shoulders and pulled her close. 'He's got the gift, that one. Nothing's going to stop him coming back to you. You'll see.'

Hannah's embrace was strong and comforting, but it wasn't enough to break down the walls of Mhairi's heartache. The air was filled with a tangible sorrow. Those left behind staring in disbelief. Some proud, smiling, others fearful, and more still empty and lost. Mhairi didn't know that grief had a smell of its own until then. It was heavy and harsh and dirty, catching at her throat, making it hard to swallow.

Time dragged by and the life inside her grew. She could feel it now. Little kicks and strokes. A piece of him that she was growing inside her. It was a magical thing, but alongside it there was a fear that she couldn't shake. She tried for her baby's sake. Positivity had to bleed from her to it. She had to do better.

Chapter 14
1917

Months of just surviving in mud that wasn't like any mud of this world. It came from hell: earth and blood, bones and flesh. A hand protruding from the filth: a leg, a head, something unidentifiable. It was thicker and more putrid than anything Robbie could have imagined. A wetness the likes of which he had never known. The stench of gunpowder and death sickened him; squeezed into his very bones. Trenches full of dead bodies squirming with maggots. It didn't matter to him whether they were the so-called enemy or an ally. To his mind, all of this carnage was a monstrosity, and he hated that he was a part of it.

The breaks away from the madness almost made it worse. There was no release. No escape from it. They would breathe for a few days and then die again.

Young lads like him who were going through this hell, putting their lives on the line. And for what? Few of them knew nor understood. This was simply about survival now. Kill or be killed. And if you didn't kill to order? What then? A bullet from your compatriots. The death of a coward, a traitor, a deserter.

Robbie was huddled in the trench amongst many others, most of whom he knew, but he chose not to remember their names, blocking them out, forgetting them. And those he remembered he tried to keep distant from a face, from a man. It was the fear. A nameless death was that little bit easier to deal with. You couldn't be thinking, *Johnnie died* and mourning it.

Someone died. Just someone.

Yet another shell hit their trench. That sound. That constant bombardment. That terror. Beside him a young soldier began shaking uncontrollably. A peculiar jerky shake. Nothing human about it.

Robbie stretched across, squeezed the man's knee. 'Stop. You have to stop. Else he'll get you, aye.' Robbie nodded at the captain. 'You can't let him see that.'

His compatriot didn't respond at all. No sign of him having understood. Taken in the words.

Robbie had seen it. The execution of men with shell shock like that. The twitching that wouldn't stop, the legs that wouldn't walk like they should, the swaying, the screaming, the incoherence of it all. Men who looked like they were drunk. Men who were no longer men at all.

It would affect the other soldiers, they said. It might be contagious, they said. He might be faking it, they said, looking for a way out. A ticket home. A way out of this hell. And who could blame them? Not Robbie. Not any of the other squaddies who were rotting away in this field of death.

Another young soldier was crouched at Robbie's left, his head tucked down between his knees, his foot twitching. That command from the captain. The point of his hand. "Over!"

The young soldier screamed, jumped up and clambered out of the trench the wrong way. Backwards. Away. He slithered through the mud, and the fallen, through row upon row of barbed wire tearing at his flesh. Bullets flew. Shells exploded. That noise. That damned noise! But he kept on. He was crying. He was mumbling, 'I can't do this. God help me. I can't.'

'Soldier! Get back here, right now!' his captain bellowed through the mayhem.

There was no point to the call. The man had become nothing that made any sense. No longer human. No longer capable of thought. He carried on, inch by godawful inch.

'You!' The captain pointed at Robbie. 'Get out there and bring him back. I'll have no deserters in my ranks! After him!'

Robbie stared.

'God damn you! After him or shoot him.'

Robbie shook his head.

'I'll do neither, *sir*,' he said

Another shell hit the trench feet away from where they stood. Limbs, flesh, and guts splattered against the mud walls, the soldiers, Robbie. He swiped at his face. Pieces of another human. He vomited. And in one movement, no thought, he clambered out and ran. Ran and kept running. Everywhere around was heavy with smoke and fog and death. Burnt stumps that used to be trees. Black mud that used to hold life. Bodies that used to breathe hung limply across barbed wire, across pieces of wood, across each other. Some breathing their last breath, simpering, whimpering like dying animals.

Robbie stumbled upon the so-called deserter, still slithering like a snake, his elbows dragging him on. Robbie snatched at his jacket, pulled him to his feet. A face that held nothing. A blank terror. Robbie pulled himself together as best he could and dragged the man along in his wake.

After what seemed like forever and no time at all, somehow, they had stumbled upon the shelter of some trees, blackened, but some still standing in this place

71

where nothing lived. This was a miracle, surely? Somehow, they had survived. There was nothing to hear but the thumping of their hearts. The thumping of the fall of shells. The crack of gunfire. The scream of men. But it was distant. Strangely, peculiarly, distant.

Chapter 15
1917

~

Mhairi and Lizzie had reached the grounds of the asylum. 'Are you quite sure about this?' Lizzie asked.

'Aye! My man's missing. My wean's about to drop. My best friend's been put away in this place for no reason other than that she's a woman. I'm no having it!'

'I think you are truly wonderful,' Lizzie said, holding her in an embrace. 'Truly, truly wonderful! Or perhaps mad.'

Mhairi laughed. 'Aye, well, I'm in the right place for that eh.'

'Right. Here goes!'

The asylum was set in secluded grounds contained within a high stone wall. Little could be seen other than by peeking through the enormous wrought-iron gates.

Mhairi hunched herself up as if in excruciating pain, clasping her belly.

Lizzie pulled on the bell. 'Help? Can someone help us, please?'

A woman dressed in what appeared to be a nurse's uniform came striding down the gravel path, her crunching step announcing her arrival.

Mhairi bent further, clung to the rails, while Lizzie pleaded. 'My companion is with child, and I think her time has come! Can you please help her? I fear something awful might happen otherwise. I am no nurse and know nothing of such things.'

The nurse's severity slipped, and she smiled. She unlocked the gates and ushered them in, offering her shoulder as support for Mhairi's arm. Lizzie took the other. Mhairi cried and screamed as if in agony. Inside she was buzzing with excitement. They were doing something. They were fighting against wrongdoing in their own small way. This, to her, was so much more than simply rescuing their friend. This represented everything. The struggle.

'It might not be the best of places to start one's life, but, God forbidding, it will be the only time your child comes inside an asylum! Ours is, at least, a decent enough place, with comforts and safety,' the nurse said.

She led them through the heavy front door, through another, and along a corridor that smelled of disinfectant and wax. A rather unpleasant waft of overcooked vegetables and meat crept out of the back rooms. Kitchens perhaps. Or dining rooms. Did they have such things? Neither woman knew nor had any desire to ask.

The nurse deposited them in a small windowless private room with a single bed and a chair by its side. 'You sit yourself down, dear, and wait just a few minutes while I fetch the doctor, or a nurse who knows about such things, for I don't!'

With that she was gone. There was a peculiar silence about the place.

'Go! Go!' Mhairi whispered.

'Sure?'

'Aye! Hurry now!'

Lizzie had planned what to say if she was found. She had been looking for the ladies' room. That was all. An easy mistake to make in an unfamiliar place of this size.

She had noted a door with a plaque declaring "Office" as they had entered. She hurried across on tiptoes, eyes scanning, ears attuned to anything that might be a danger. She reached the office door—cold solid wood—and listened intently for what might be on the other side of it. Nothing, it seemed. More silence. Where was everyone? She gripped the brass handle and turned it, slowly, slowly. A soft click and the door swung open. There was a smell of stale cigar smoke, mixed with a cologne. Nothing cheap. Whoever spent their time in this office was a well-to-do smoker. Or the recipient of some rather expensive gifts.

There, on the wall, clearly marked, she found the key cabinet. The keys for the main gate and front door were her objectives. Everything was obligingly orderly. Everything clearly labelled. Splendid! She found the keys she needed quickly enough and slipped them off their fobs. There were spares for each which meant more noise as they tinkled and clanked annoyingly through the stillness, but there would be less chance of an alert being raised before they had completed their escape mission.

Now, to find the list of patients, records, or some such thing. She guessed that they would be in the filing cabinet behind the desk. She pulled open the drawer as slowly as she could. More squeaks and intrusions into the night; the files were helpfully marked as patient records. They were so obliging! A quick finger through the files and she found what she was looking for. Constance Fotheringale. She scanned the paperwork and found the room number. Below it, the reasons for the incarceration of her friend. It wasn't why she was here, but curiosity got the better of her.

Temporary insanity

'That bastard,' she mumbled.

Footsteps. Voices. They were drawing closer. She held her breath. Thoughts zipping around. She could hide, but if she were to be found, that would be that. No. She would brazen it out. She had rehearsed for exactly, precisely, this moment.

As the door opened, she strode towards it. She smiled, pulled her hand to her chest. 'I am so dreadfully sorry. I was looking for a powder room. I thought, perhaps, there might be a more private one in here.'

The man stared. 'And you are?'

'I am so sorry. My companion is in the throes of childbirth, and we came here seeking refuge. She is in one of the rooms across the hallway.'

The man relaxed, softened. 'Yes, yes. The young lady is quite well. A false alarm. It is quite common amongst young mothers. She can rest for a few minutes while she awaits transport. I have asked one of our porters to assist in getting you back to the station.'

'You are so very gracious. Thank you.' Lizzie bowed as she left, pleased with how she had appeared to defer to his apparent superiority whilst chuckling inside at his pomposity; at their hoodwinking of him. Of all of them.

'Yes, yes,' he said, dismissively.

Chapter 16
1917

~∞~

The "deserter" still hadn't spoken. Odd mumblings, soft cries. It was probably best that way. There was less chance of discovery, assuming he kept everything low and under his breath, as he was now. They had to keep themselves hidden from both sides. Ironically, their survival was probably more likely were they to be found by the Boche. That should mean incarceration in a prison camp. Hellish, but survivable. Their own side would probably have them executed as deserters. A firing squad made up of poor sods like themselves. What a thing to live with!

Robbie had no idea of how far they had come, in which direction they were headed, even of how long they had been travelling for. The smell and the sounds of war clung to everything still, but it was more distant now. This was a dead place. No wildlife. Blackness all around.

'Thanks,' the deserter whispered through the emptiness. 'I... Couldn't... Couldn't...' He gripped Robbie's arm but kept his gaze to the ground.

'Aye. You're all right. We're all right.' He wasn't. They weren't. But sometimes you had to lie just to get someone through. Just to get yourself through. That was what life had become.

They trudged on in silence. There, through the mist, a small building. Two. A farm, perhaps. A smallholding. It seemed deserted. Quiet. Still. Nevertheless, they instinctively dropped down, squirmed across the earth

77

like wild things. Slowly, slowly.

Robbie stood up, his back against the rough stone walls, pieces of sandstone crumbled against his touch. His compatriot copied his every move, as if a shadow. Robbie peered through glassless windows. There had once been people here. A family maybe, animals, something precious and life-giving. And soldiers. Boot prints smothered what once had lain here. What once had grazed here. What once had lived here. They reached the door which sat ajar, drifting on useless hinges. One looked to the other in question, and each nodded their agreement. Some sense of common understanding holding them together.

Robbie motioned for the deserter to stay put. He toed at the door, pushing it just wide enough open for him to slide through. Little more than a squeak. Quiet enough. He stopped. Listened. Nothing. He beckoned for the deserter to follow, and they pushed the door softly closed behind them. There was no sense here of anything living, human or otherwise. Perhaps insects, spiders. Who knew if even they could live in such places?

What they needed more than anything was rest. Proper, undisturbed rest. It had been so very long since either had experienced it. Such a simple expectation that had been denied them since they had set foot in this godforsaken place.

There was a bed, a blanket. Sleep

～～

When Robbie awoke his companion was no longer there. The door was wide open. An unexpected streak of sunlight glared across the stone floor. Robbie felt an instant relief. His chances of survival were better on his own. That was soon washed over by guilt. The man was lost. Even more so than Robbie was. He doubted his survival out there. And once that connection had been made, man to man, a commonality, a kinship, and damn it, a responsibility, there was no breaking it. To Robbie's mind they had become a part of each other.

There was no warmth to this sun. Building up in the distance, heavy cloud threatened rain. Perhaps a storm. Robbie hastily wrapped the blankets around his shoulders like a cape. They were a treasure out here. A hope to cling on to. At least he could be warm.

He couldn't call out. It was too dangerous, and he didn't know the man's name anyway. He skirted the building, the barn. No sign. He strained his ears. Nothing other than the distant sounds of war. It sounded very far away. Another world. Wouldn't that be something? Another world. Anything would be better than this one.

He circled the area a couple of times. It was futile. The man could be anywhere. It wouldn't even make sense to imagine where he might have gone. When man has been put through that, when insanity is right there, knocking on the door, when nothing makes sense anymore, when you are less than a man, a shell, there is no sense to be made of anything.

Robbie walked blindly on, the sounds of where he had come from always at his back. That was all he could think of. *Get away from that.* He hoped that his comrade had had enough sense left to think likewise. As he walked, he was now scanning for soldiers from both sides, and his comrade. And all the while images flashed through his mind. The bodies, the flesh, the horror of it all. Then, Mhairi. Mhairi and their child. He didn't know, but he could be a father now. A baby that he had made with the woman he loved could now be a reality. A beautiful reality. He could picture her. She would have her mother's looks, but his eyes, maybe even his smile. She would be the most gorgeous wee thing. And he smiled. And it felt so strange, so alien. That smile.

He was now in a valley that seemed untouched by it all. There was the hint of birdsong, trees, and the air felt different. Clean. He wanted to drop his guard. To breathe it all in. To be thankful for it. To immerse himself in this moment. This peace. This tranquillity.

He stopped, suddenly aware of a different sound. Mechanical. An engine. He threw himself face down on the earth. Held his breath. He pulled the blanket over himself and lay as still as he could, grateful that it was the colour of stone.

Chapter 17
1917

~~

Lizzie and Mhairi had gone back to the asylum later that night. It was two o'clock in the morning. Nothing lit up the sky or the earth. No stars, no moon, no lights. Nothing. It was a time, they assumed, when everyone would be asleep, or at least, switched off. They crept along the single-track road that led to the gates. Silent forest to one side, the asylum grounds to the other. Lizzie clutched Mhairi's arm. A sound. Steps.

Mhairi smiled. 'It's just deer, or cattle, or some such.' she whispered.

'Are you sure?'

'Aye! Wheesht now.'

They dropped the bag of clothing they had brought for Connie behind one of the pillars, unlocked the gates, pausing briefly to listen, before going through. The building in front of them was in total darkness. They tiptoed onto the grass and made their way up to the entrance as silently as thieves. The front door opened just as easily.

They had practised this in their heads, remembering the exact location of Connie's room, how many steps it would take to reach. Each door number was marked with an embossed plaque. The feel of it under fingertips confirmed that they were outside the correct one. Lizzie slipped the key in the lock and turned it. A dreadful squeak blared through the silence as the door opened. Each woman took a deep breath, held it, clutched each other's arms, listened, waited for longer than either of them wanted to. It seemed no-one was any the wiser. They slipped into the room and closed the door behind them.

Mhairi stood by the door, on guard. Lizzie tiptoed across to the bed. She clasped her hand across the mouth of the sleeping patient.

'It's all right, Connie. It's me. Lizzie.'

No response.

She tried to wake her, softly shaking her shoulders. 'Connie! Connie! Wake up!'

Still nothing.

She tiptoed back to Mhairi. 'I think she's been drugged. Dead to the world. This makes things a whole lot more difficult!'

'Aye. Right. So, we'll be needing to carry her, then?'

'Yes.'

'Just as well she's as thin as a sparrow on a winter's day!'

Lizzie looked back at Mhairi, a question on her brow. Smiled at the sweet words.

They heaved Connie up, stuffed a blanket and pillow under her sheet in the guise of a sleeping body. Shrugged. It had to do. They wrapped one of Connie's arms around each of their shoulders and held tight.

'If she wakes up halfway out, we're done for!' Mhairi whispered.

They dragged her out, closed the door behind them, slowly, slowly. Both women wanted to rush; to get out of there as quickly as possible, but they controlled themselves. Kept to the plan. They locked the door behind them. Propped Connie against the wall. Stopped. Listened again. Still silence. They made a basket of their crossed arms and scooped Connie up.

That was better, easier.

It seemed to take an eternity to reach the front door, but they remained caught between wanting to hurry and needing to be silent. Continued stealth was the way. At last, they were out and through the front door. They locked it behind them, crept again to the gate, keeping to the silence of the grass. Still Connie was oblivious to it all.

'What the devil have they given her?'

'No idea, but we need her awake before we try and get on the train.'

They collected the bag, pulled off the road and into the woods. Dressing a dead weight wasn't easy, but they managed. Just. The change of clothing in itself seemed to bring more to Connie. She at least looked alive in the colourful skirt and blouse borrowed from Lizzie's wardrobe—not the quality, nor style, that Connie was used to but needs must! Anonymity was preferable to ostentation. They stuffed the asylum's shapeless shift into their bag, hoisted Connie up, and carried on. It was a slow and difficult walk, as each step seemed to add more weight to Connie's body.

'Seriously, how are we going to get her on a train, like this? It's not as if we can hang around, is it?' Lizzie said.

'We just have to hope that the station is quiet and the ticket office staff no that observant!'

'Oh, lord!'

'A wee place like this? Sure, it'll be fine.'

Lizzie chuckled. 'That's you sounding just like Robbie. Sure. The Irish in him.'

Mhairi hung her head.

'Oh, I'm sorry. Stupidly thoughtless of me.'

But there was no time for self-pity; no sense to it

either. They had a job to do, and it required their full attention.

~

It was like a piece of magic. The world had smiled on them, and no-one had looked twice at the three somewhat dishevelled women, one of whom couldn't even stand. Mhairi waited outside with Connie while Lizzie bought their tickets. They sat on a bench in the small waiting room. A woman came in, looked briefly their way, nodded and smiled, as she sat down opposite them.

The blast of a train startled them.

'That'll be me, then,' the woman said.

'Yes, us too,' Lizzie replied.

The train pulling in was like a weight lifting off their chests. They clambered in, found an empty carriage—more magic—and propped Connie up in the corner. That was okay. To fall asleep on a train journey was perfectly normal. At last Connie began to stir. Peculiar mumblings trickled out of her mouth.

'What have they done to her?'

'Connie, my love, you're safe now. It's us. Lizzie and Mhairi. You're safe now.'

Lizzie hugged her, wiped the spittle from her chin. Mhairi stared in disbelief. This was horrendous. She had heard of such places but never imagined that her friend could end up like this. That her father would allow her to end up like this. He was a beast. She knew that, but this?

'Will she come out of it, do you think?' Mhairi asked.

'One can only hope. When the drugs wear off, we'll be able to see.'

'Christ!'

'Connie, my love. I know you're in there somewhere. You're coming home.'

Connie at last opened her eyes to the glare of a bright morning sun, low in the autumn sky. It burned. Her hands were trembling as she lifted them to shade her eyes. She slowly turned her head but didn't seem to register anything. It was as if there was no thought behind those eyes. No feeling. Nothing.

⚭

At last, they were in Lizzie's shop. They had decided this was the best option. It was a place off the radar to most. A quiet little bookshop that had a secret purpose. To raise awareness, to lift voices and opportunities, to offer something different. It was a place Connie's father would never dream of entering and they were quite sure he had not the slightest inkling that Connie frequented it. It was set back in the street, as if hidden by design. Its obscurity was one of the reasons Lizzie loved it so much. Most importantly, it was a place where Connie would feel at home. Safe. A small intimate space that she knew well; that held only good memories.

Chapter 18
1917

~~

It seemed so improbable that it felt like another miracle when Robbie spotted a familiar figure resting against the trunk of a tree. The deserter was silently crying through a blood-stained face, as if he had no energy for anything more than simple tears.

Robbie walked towards him, slowly. A step. A pause. Another step, his hands held high in a gesture that said, "No threat". The man was trembling, staring at his hands.

'Can I sit?' Robbie asked.

There was no sign of understanding, of recognition even. Perhaps he was now too far gone to respond. Too far into that place where no man should have to go.

Robbie sat down beside him, slipped a blanket over his shoulders.

'I'm Robbie,' he said. He pointed to his chest, eyes expectant, waiting for the customary response. 'We escaped together. Do you remember?'

There was still nothing.

'Can you tell me your name, at least?' He pointed to the soldier. Repeated the action. 'I'm Robbie, you're who?'

The soldier swiped at his tears. Stared at Robbie. 'Coward. Deserter,' trickled into the strange air.

'Less of that. There's some things a man shouldn't have to do. And back there?' He pointed angrily to where they had come from. To where the trenches stood. 'That was one of them. Now what's your name?'

The man still wasn't responding. Perhaps he didn't understand. Perhaps he didn't want to. Robbie tried again. 'This?' He drew a circle in the air all around them. 'This is madness. No man should do this. You're no coward. What's your name, now?'

'Andy,' he mumbled, his face to the ground.

'Andy, is it? Right. Pleased to make your acquaintance, Andy.' Robbie held out his hand and smiled.

Andy touched the outstretched hand so lightly it could barely be called a shake, but it was something. He managed a grimace that was almost a smile, in return. Andy wasn't a man at all. He was a boy. Eighteen years old by a few months. What was this all about? This war.

They rested in silence. A peculiar normalness was in the air. Trees, birds, even some flowers stood in the autumn chill, wilting now, bit still there, holding on for as long as possible, not succumbing to death. Not yet. It seemed that they had stumbled upon an oasis in this land of nothing. Any scent of nature was minimal. The air still carried smoke that wasn't allowing much else to break through.

Andy was following the flight of a distant bird. 'Hawk,' he whispered, pointing at the bird.

'Aye,' Robbie said. 'That would be a grand thing, the freedom of that, so it would!'

They both watched the hawk—a beautiful break in their reality—until it became a speck in the sky and disappeared. Robbie kept chatting away about his life before this, about Scotland, Glasgow Celtic, and politics. There was no response, but nevertheless, he carried on. Whether there was understanding or not wasn't the point. This was doing Robbie good, and he guessed it could only be beneficial for this poor young man as well.

'I have a wife. The bonniest wee lassie. You should see her. And there's a wean on the way. Maybe even here now. I don't know. I don't even know.' He choked on that last sentence. Sometimes it was hard. No. it was always hard. This wasn't life of any description, and he missed it all so much.

They sat in silence until the light faded, and it felt safe to be moving on. But which way? Robbie didn't know and there was little point in asking Andy. His understanding of anything was deeply hidden in a place unreachable. They stayed together, both deserters who drew a feeling of relative safety from one another. A shared existence, a camaraderie. The world felt so big yet so small. It was best not to think too much on it. A man could go crazy with too much thought on anything out there. It was survival. Think on survival. That was all.

Chapter 19
1917

Hannah had picked up the envelope. Closed her eyes. Tried to calm her breathing. It was addressed to Mhairi. She had seen too many of these, and each one was heartbreaking, but this was addressed to one of her close comrades. To her friend. And it would be about one of her closest friends, Robbie. She fought back tears and with shaking hands, placed the letter on the table. It wasn't hers to open. She wished that she could simply destroy it, burn it, have the history that it carried removed. This hadn't happened.

Mhairi was resting when the pains started. She cried out as they became more intense. 'Hannah! It's—it's coming!'

'Just hold on. I'll get help, okay? Just...just wait,' Hannah said. This was very far from her comfort zone, and she felt incapable of offering the right kind of help. She ran down the tenement stairs and across the landing. There was a woman there. Someone who knew. Someone who was known for her wisdom in such matters. Hannah pummelled on the door.

'I'm guessing it's the lassie's time, is it?'

'Yes! Can you—'

'Well, of course!'

She grabbed her bag, which was always there, ready for the next birth. It was such a privilege to be able to do this. To bring a new life into the world, especially now, when so many were being taken.

Mhairi's labour had lasted all day and into the

evening. Her screams could be heard throughout the tenement and the ones on either side.

Hannah had thought about running to Lizzie's but didn't want to leave Mhairi. She paced up and down like an expectant father. Finally, as the church bell struck midnight, the cry of a child replaced the screams of her mother.

'How is she? Let me see? Let me see my baby!' Mhairi said in a croaky exhausted voice.

As the tiny pink and purple mess was placed on her belly she wept. These were tears of joy. The most joy she had ever felt. A love she didn't know she was capable of swelled through her. This was the most beautiful, wondrous thing. It could only have been bettered by Robbie being there by their side.

Hannah hid the letter. It could wait. But for how long?

Mhairi fell asleep soon enough and Hannah was left to comfort the child. She did her best. As she rocked the child and held her close, her thoughts were only of how to tell Mhairi. When to tell her?

Come morning and the rise of noise; the chatter of birds, stirring of neighbours, the decision was made for her.

Mhairi sat up, a panic fluttering in her breast. 'What's wrong? Is there something wrong with her?'

'No, not at all. She's just perfect, and she slept most of the night.' Hannah tried to smile and make-believe that everything was just dandy. But she couldn't and instead of smiling she cried.

'Hannah?'

'Oh Christ! This dammed war!'

The envelope said enough for Mhairi to gulp, take a

deep breath. She stared up at Hannah. 'Is this? Is it Robbie?'

Hannah just stared. She had no words.

Mhairi's hands were shaking as she opened the envelope. It was done with such care, as if it were a precious thing of beauty. She slipped the buff paper out. Paused. Looked up at Hannah. Opened it.

Sir or Madam,

I regret to have to inform you that a report has been received from the War Office to the effect that (No.) 2079—Rank Private—Name Gallagher R G

She read as far as "missing, presumed dead", and scrunched it into a ball, threw it across the room.

'No!' she shrieked. 'I will not have this! My man is alive. I know he is!'

The baby stirred, began to cry. Mhairi held her close. 'It's all right, Rosie, your mammy's here, an your daddy is too. Right here.' She closed her eyes and held a picture of him in her mind. That crooked smile, the twinkling eyes. She could feel him, and she wanted to share that with Rosie. Who knew if such things were possible?

Hannah managed a smile. 'Rosie. That's a beautiful name.'

'Aye. Robbie chose it way back when. He said she would be like her ma; a rose, so beautiful an sweet smelling, but wi a prickle that kept her strong an true. That's what he said. My Robbie.'

Mhairi began to cry again, threw her head back, sniffed hard. 'No! None o that. We'll be just grand, wee one. You'll see.'

'I don't doubt it one bit,' Hannah said.

Chapter 20
1918

～

Connie had stayed in the seclusion of Lizzie's shop for weeks now. Partly to build her strength back up, physical and mental, but also to stay hidden from her father. This was a place of safety and comfort where she could find herself again. The converted boxroom may have been cramped, but it was hidden, secure, and it was hers.

'Why would your own father do something like that?' Lizzie asked.

'Oh, that's simple enough. When my mother died in the fire, and I survived he blamed me. If I hadn't been there, been alive, they would have been safe, and she alive. No-one to rescue. On top of that there's reputation. He simply cannot abide the idea that his daughter is somewhat rebellious. Disreputable to all of his chums. No. It is so much easier if I am locked away. Forgotten.'

'But he is your father!'

'Yes, well, blood runs thin in my family. Anyway, enough of that. We have happier events to tend to.'

Lizzie smiled. 'Indeed, we do. She is such an adorable little thing. You know me. I am not in the slightest a baby person, but for Rosie I have made an exception.'

'And Robbie? Do we know any more?'

'Sadly no. Still missing presumed...'

'Poor Mhairi. I cannot imagine what she must be going through. Pure hell.'

'Yes, but she is putting such a brave face on it all. She

refuses to believe that he's gone. And who knows? She may be right.'

As if on cue there was a gentle tap on the back door. Lizzie rose to answer it.

'No, no. Let me,' Connie said, getting to her feet with gusto, striding to the back door. She pulled the door open and held the broadest smile on her face.

Mhairi returned the smile, but beyond it, to those who knew her, deep in her eyes the pain shadowed any joy she wanted to show to the world.

'Rosie, this is your godmother, Connie.' She looked intently at Connie. 'You will, won't you?'

Connie squealed. Held her arms out for the baby. 'Nothing, absolutely nothing could give me greater pleasure.' She wiped a tear from her face. 'Hello, my beautiful little girl.'

'And how are you?' Mhairi asked. 'A lot better than last time I saw you, I guess.'

'Good as new! Well, almost...'

'That's great. Cabin fever must be getting to you though, aye? I mean, we love Lizzie, but...' She turned to Lizzie and grinned. 'No offence.'

'None taken. I've been saying as much myself, but there's a good deal to be taken into account.'

'Yes, not least my father!'

'Look at us standing here on the doorstep,' Lizzie said. 'Come in. Come in and sit!'

They settled into their usual places. Connie and Mhairi on the settee, Lizzie in her chair.

Mhairi turned to face Connie. 'That man can't be allowed to ruin your life. How many times, eh?'

'Sadly, that's just it. He can, and he does.'

Rosie began to stir, to whimper.

Connie panicked and held the grumbling baby out to her mother.

Mhairi laughed and nestled Rosie against her neck, gently patting her back. 'Hush now, wee one. Hush now.'

Rosie settled back into innocent sleep soon enough.

'I have a plan,' Mhairi said, now whispering above the baby's head. 'I'll bet your father wouldn't look twice at some poor person. Somebody dressed in rags an tatters, like so many. I'll bet that to him they're all faceless. A nuisance.'

Connie grinned. 'You are a genius!'

'Aye, well, it's been said!'

They laughed in that light, familiar way of times gone by.

~~~

The disguise was easily taken care of, and a couple of days later they ventured out, all three of them in other people's clothes garnered from the rag and bone man, soot smeared on their faces, messed up hair. It would have been funny had it not been so tragic. All three of them felt a tinge of shame at dressing up like this.

They walked through the park, Connie proudly pushing the pram. She was relishing this new role of godmother, especially when the child was content, quiet. The ground was sprinkled with swirls of blossom, a warmth to the sun. The laughter of children as they ran and chased each other through the falling blossom.

A young couple strolled slowly along the path, arm in arm. The man in a uniform that he wore heavily. He had been there, seen war, and was returning. The woman had eyes for nothing, no-one else. It was a feeling Mhairi knew so well. He would be going soon. She stared, realised what she was doing, closed her eyes to the pain. Turned away.

'We should go to the tearoom. Wouldn't that be jolly?' Connie said, trying to distract her friend from what was obviously on her mind. Robbie.

'Connie, we'll no get across the door looking like this, even if I used to work there.'

Connie laughed. 'Ah. Yes. Point taken! Perhaps we should just sit on the grass awhile.'

'That we're allowed to do.'

Mhairi picked Rosie out of the pram and settled her on her knee. Robbie's eyes stared up at her. She wouldn't think on it. Go there. Her man was coming home and that was that. He would hold Rosie, and bounce her on his knee, and coo softly in her ear.

The women's trips out had become regular, their destination a little further each time—history repeating itself—until they found themselves in George square. People had gathered. Speeches. Cheers. The place was still alive with political activity. With hope. They knew what might well happen soon. The police. The crowd brutally dispersed. This was no place for Rosie.

'You can stay. I know you miss it,' Mhairi said. 'I'll just head back wi the wee one. It's fine.'

'We wouldn't hear of it, would we Connie?'

'Indeed no! Another day.'

Chapter 21
1918

~

Spring turned to summer and there was no further word on Robbie. Summer to Autumn and hell was descending. Spanish flu had come, and people were dying worldwide in their millions. Four thousand in Glasgow alone. A cough, a fever and death. As if enough tragedy hadn't been faced through the last four years of the war. A state of anxiety wrapped around almost everyone. A temperature and terror. A cough from a nearby person and run. Get away from it. Hide from it.

October fifth; it was such a special day. Little Rosie was one year old, and despite it all, Hannah had arranged a small gathering. Her flat was always busy anyway, even with the flu epidemic. People coming and going, collecting leaflets, discussing politics, strategy. They had lost friends and comrades to the flu, everyone had. And once one had fallen it spread with such terrifying speed. A hint of feeling unwell, a sneeze, meant no entry, no socialising, and they adhered to it.

Everyone knew little Rosie, and today there was cake, such as they could manage, and presents.

The guests were under strict instructions to keep the atmosphere light and happy. Mhairi and Rosie were the centre of attention, and it was all very lovely. The effort, that had been put into it, undeterred by the times and hardships.

Despite their best intentions, talk soon centred on politics, on the war coming to an end, on what it was bringing home with it, on what they still had to fight for.

'That war! All o those men living in such unsanitary conditions. A breeding ground for a pandemic.'

'Aye, it was bound to happen. And look what they come home to, eh? A life not worth living. Shameful, so it is.'

'All the more reason to keep going. We cannot allow this to stop the fight!'

'I think I'll just take Rosie out for a wee stroll, a bit of fresh air,' Mhairi said.

'Splendid idea, I'll come along,' Connie said.

'You sure?' Mhairi said.

'Of course! A godmother has her duties after all!' She grinned and Mhairi reciprocated.

They wrapped themselves up against the wind that was whipping around the streets, lifting up swirls of autumn leaves and tossing them through the air. Mhairi smiled as Connie leaned into the pram and tucked Rosie's blanket around her chin.

'There now. Snug as a bug!'

Connie took Mhairi's arm and pulled it tight against her body. 'How are you doing? And I don't want to hear, "just fine", because I know you're not. Not really.'

Mhairi laughed a soft laugh that held no humour. 'Aye. Well. It's all gone mad, eh? Sometimes I think it best to pretend.' She nodded at Rosie who was now sound asleep. 'For her sake.'

'There is that, but what about you?'

'It's so hard. Every day I worry. What if? And then thoughts turn to dreams of my man coming home. I imagine that this'll be the day that he'll chap on that door and stride in all smiles an, well, you know.' She sniffed, wiped at a tear.

'Yes, I do.'

'I keep thinking I see him. Every man in uniform that's about the same height, the same build—and there's plenty o them in Glasgow—I see him. And my heart stops and for a moment—just a wonderful moment—it's all over, and I can breathe again.'

'Oh Mhairi, love...'

'Do you think—do you think he'll be back? I mean, I do. Course I do. But there's no sense to my thinking. It's all just wishful. It's all just what I want. What I need. You know?'

'If anyone is going to survive that hell, it's Robbie. I'm quite sure of it. But I can't lie to you. It might not happen. So many men...'

As if on cue two soldiers rounded the corner. Both women gasped. A momentary glimpse of hope. Of expectation. But the strangers walked on by, oblivious.

Chapter 22
1918

◦‿◦

Robbie couldn't quite believe how easy it had been to evade capture and the inevitable firing squad that would have followed from their side; imprisonment from the other, if they survived at all. They had been on the move for months now. How many, he wasn't sure. Their direction had been haphazard. They knew that they wanted to head north—the English Channel, home—but avoiding any sign of conflict was paramount to their survival, and their direction had been dictated more by veering away from any sound of battle, that acrid smell of it, than knowledge of where they might be headed.

Time had passed. The weather had warmed and cooled again, and the air felt different, hopeful somehow. Perhaps it was the gold and crimson of the fallen leaves; the impossibility of beauty in such a time, but there it was. Buds had opened, blossom bloomed, leaves unfurled and stretched, fledglings had hopped on the ground searching for morsels that would sustain them after their parents had left. Lessons learned. And now the circle complete. Leaves turning, life carrying on.

They were resting in the shade of an oak. Familiar but oh so foreign. In the distance a woman and a girl were tending a herd of goats, moving them on with the help of a dog and soft whispers that neither men could hear.

'I hope they haven't been touched by it at all. A wee

sanctuary in all o this madness. No missing brother or dead father. Just life going on,' Robbie said.

'Aye. Imagine that.'

Robbie grinned. 'Imagine.'

They sat in silence and watched as the shapes lessened and became indistinct, then nothing. Somewhere beyond the brow of that hill they imagined a small farm. An idyllic cottage. The softness of a family settling down and relaxing in the comfort of each other. A life very different. Shadows stretched and the sun slipped. It was time to be moving on. Wordlessly they rose, gathered their blankets, wrapped them around their shoulders, and walked on.

That brief encounter with a life lost had touched them both deeply, each taken back home to a time so distant it was hard to catch on to. For Andy it was his family's business—his mother up to her elbows in flour. His father likewise. His sister out front, pristine in her white apron and bonnet, selling their bread and rolls, cakes and pastries, to their customers. It had all been so easy back then. So normal. And yet he had grumbled. He hadn't wanted to follow in his parents' footsteps. Something better was calling him. What a fool! He would give the world to be back there, baking, selling. A simple, wholesome life. But could he ever? He didn't know. This was a different world. A cruel, cold place. Hell, he could barely put a voice to his words. What good would he be to anyone, anywhere?

Robbie's thoughts were very different. He missed the meetings, the hustle and bustle of Hannah's flat. The sound of the printer. The constant chatter about a different, better world. Most of all, of course, he yearned for Mhairi. The touch of her hand, her smile that swelled his heart, her soft whispers as they made love. And then there was his daughter, Rosie. He may never have seen her, but the picture in his head held strong and true. He knew exactly what she would look like. He could feel that impossible softness of her skin. The smell of her. It was all there in his head. One day. One day...

Suddenly an intrusion broke through the night's silence. Both stood up tall. Listened. Hearts thumped. Breath caught. That awful panic. A vehicle. No, vehicles. Many of them. Coming their way. There was nothing to do but fall down, lie as still as death under their blankets, and pray.

Chapter 23
1918/1919

~

On November 11th the war had finally ended. Mhairi, Hannah, and Connie had been celebrating like everyone else, but theirs was a more subdued affair. All of their thoughts were with Robbie. Could he simply have vanished off the face of the earth? No word, no sighting, no body. Nothing. They had witnessed the return of soldiers, many of whom were barely recognisable as the men who had left. But it would do. It would be better than nothing. Mhairi was quite sure that whatever state he might be in she could nurse him back to something like the man he used to be.

There was little in place to help these brave men. These returning soldiers who had walked through hell itself. Now they were faced with a lack of accommodation, jobs, help with readjusting to civilian life, support for those whose brains had become something else, something lost and confused, something angry and desperate. Missing limbs and broken souls. But enough help just wasn't there, even having enough to eat was a luxury for many.

But the war was, at least, over, and Lloyd George was a hero and remained Prime Minister. The result of the hastily called general election looked like it would do little or nothing for normal people.

Sickness, poverty, homelessness, desperation. The people of Glasgow were angry. This was no land fit for heroes, as had been promised. The fuse was lit and by God, did it explode!

Hannah and Lizzie helped where they could, heads together plotting, distributing leaflets, joining in protests, shouting for justice. Mhairi and Connie spent more time in the background. Writing and printing the leaflets. It was safer for both of them. Safer for little Rosie too. As the protests grew larger, so did Mhairi's frustration. It wasn't just that she wanted to be more a part of it all. It was also that faint hope—closer to a dream—that somehow Robbie would be there. Perhaps he had lost his memory. She knew that many had. But if there was any semblance remaining of the man who had left, he would have that calling burning deep inside of him for social justice, and hope beyond hope, for her.

A strike had been called for the working day to be reduced from fifty-four hours a week to forty. That was surely a reasonable request. No, a demand. Not only would it improve the lives of many, but it would also offer much needed employment to these returning soldiers. On Sunday January 26th, 1919, ten thousand protesters marched from St Andrews Halls to the City Chambers. Hannah and Lizzie had been amongst them.

'You should have seen it!' Hannah exclaimed on their return to the flat. 'I wrote down a quote from one of the speeches just for you!'

'Just for me, or perhaps a wee bit for the leaflets as well?'

Hannah laughed. 'Oh, am I that transparent?'

'You wouldn't be you if you weren't!'

'I'm not sure if I should take that as a compliment or a chastisement! Anyway...' she rummaged in her bag for her trusty notepad. 'This was from Mr Cameron of the Discharge Soldiers Federation. He said that his organisation was, "Backing the workers this time and looked for the workers to back them. They had fought for their country, and they now wanted to own it." With soldiers demanding change alongside us, how can we fail?'

Demonstrations continued and the strike spread. By Friday 31st January—Bloody Friday, as it became known—sixty thousand workers had downed tools.

'I have to go to this one. The whole o Glasgow'll be there an more,' Mhairi said.

'But you need a babysitter?' Hannah said.

'Aye. Come on, I've been so good!'

'Right! Connie, are you quite happy with this?' Hannah said.

'Of course I am. Rosie and I will only be on our own for a few hours. Don't go getting arrested, though.'

'Thank you, godmother of the highest order!'

Chapter 24
1918/19

~∾~

Was it possible to shrivel into nothing? To become invisible? A part of the earth? The ground beneath Andy and Robbie shook as the trucks rolled by. Neither looked. A terror ran through them. This was something consequential. A long procession of vehicles with a purpose. Whether they were retreating or advancing, neither knew. Neither cared. They just wanted them gone.

A shout split the night. The vehicles slowed. Pulled up. The sound of booted feet jumping to the ground. Running now. Someone was running and they were being chased. A single shot. The slump of a body falling to the ground. The retreat of the booted feet. Engines roared and left. An eerie silence was left in their wake in the stillness of the night.

'We should check. The man might still be alive.'

Andy nodded.

A hint of daylight was creeping in, lighting their way. The sky slipping from black to grey. They edged slowly on their stomachs, towards where they thought the person had fallen. The grass was soft and sweet, a covering of morning dew lifted its scent, even at this time of year. It could have been beautiful.

'We mean you no harm,' Robbie called, just above a whisper, to the hump on the ground. He glanced back to Andy who nodded his head again. Still few words, but at least an understanding. So it seemed to Robbie, anyway.

It was a woman, and she was still alive, but barely. A bullet hole pierced her chest and blood spilled out across her clothing. She was a civilian, and that was shocking enough, but a woman! They had assumed that, like them, this person had been a deserter. A man, like them, who could take no more. A man executed for it. They were very wrong.

She tried to speak, her mouth moving, but no sound came with it. A trickle of blood slid from her mouth down to her neck. A splutter, a twitch of her legs, and she was gone.

Now they were caught in an awful quandary. This woman was probably loved by someone. Probably local, or else why would she have been executed here? Left as a message. A warning. They didn't know but wanted to do something that was right. That was proper. That was human.

Robbie hoisted her up and carried her in his arms like a child. It would have been easier to hoist her over his shoulder, but she deserved more than that. Some dignity in death, at least. It wasn't as if she was heavy anyway. Little more than skin and bone, much like themselves. They had become quite expert at scavenging: nuts and fruit, leaves, small creatures caught in a roughly made snare, but it wasn't enough to maintain them, and any excess flesh they wore had been used up long ago. But it had kept them alive.

They headed over the brow of the hill where the woman and girl had gone yesterday. As their imagination had suggested, it was a small farm. It looked comforting. A soft gentle place, strangely untouched, that stood in its own peaceful world.

'What now?' Andy asked as they reached the fence

that surrounded the little white house, the vegetable garden, the flower patch. How unlike what they had held witness to over their time in this foreign place. A deep silence covered the land, the house, everything quiet.

Robbie smiled at the words. At last, Andy had spoken, unbidden. 'We don't know who might be here. We should leave her here and go. Agreed?'

'Aye.'

Andy opened the gate with trembling hands, and Robbie lay the woman down on the small path that led to the front door. They would like to have done more, have known more, but their own survival was paramount. They crept away, the rising sun glinting above the cottage setting it on fire, sure that no-one was any the wiser to their presence.

The creak of an opening door.

Chapter 25
1918/19

~

When the protesters walked towards the City Chambers the atmosphere was electric. So many people speaking with one voice. The numbers and the feeling grew. Lizzie linked arms with Hannah and Mhairi, who linked hers with a stranger. The man smiled.

'To revolution!' he called.

'Aye.'

'What do you think? The Socialist Republic of Scotland?' he said.

'I reckon that could be coming,' she replied.

'There's even more folk here than at Parkhead on a Saturday afternoon!'

Mhairi laughed. Her eyes were scanning though. Always scanning. For Robbie. For a familiar face that could be her parents, her sister, for she hadn't given up on them either. So much loss amidst so much hope.

The crowd was enormous, so tightly packed, that it was difficult to see anything beyond capped heads. So very many. Above them all someone raised a red flag. A cheer rang out, rippled through the crowd.

A hundred thousand people packed the square. The police charged into them. They struck out with batons. Men, women and children fell to the ground, including Mhairi. The stranger helped her up. She picked up a stone and hurled it at the charging police. Bottles had been taken from a lorry stuck on North Frederick Street. They were hurled too. Sheriff MacKenzie came out of the City Chambers and began to read the riot act. "The King orders all assembled to immediately disperse." The paper he was reading from was snatched out of his hands by a demonstrator. The Sheriff continued nevertheless, from memory.

Lizzie and Hannah found each other in the mayhem, but there was no sign of Mhairi. Bloodied and battered bodies lay on the ground as people began to disperse. Some semblance of calm began to return as the crowd thinned.

As Lizzie and Hannah walked through the square one more time, they finally spotted Mhairi. The stranger was helping her walk. Her head had a stream of blood trickling down its left side, and she was limping heavily.

'A bit the worse for wear, but she's all right. Perhaps not the best place for a young woman, eh?' the stranger said.

Hannah opened her mouth to respond with a caustic comment, but Lizzie pre-empted it and kicked her on the shin. 'Thank you for your help. It was very kind of you,' Lizzie said.

'One for all and all for one, eh?' he responded with a wink.

'We can manage from here.'

Lizzie and Hannah slipped their arms around Mhairi's waist. 'Are you all right there?' Lizzie asked.

'Aye. I'm fine. A bit sore is all.'

They drifted towards home amongst the rest of the demonstrators.

'That man. The one that helped you. Do you know him from somewhere?' Hannah asked.

Mhairi shrugged. 'Dunno. Maybe.'

'Hmm.'

'You don't trust anyone, eh?'

'No. No I don't! Infiltrators and government spies are everywhere.'

Following not far behind. That man.

Chapter 26
1919

～

Robbie and Andy froze, glanced at each other. They would have to face this. It was the least they could do. They turned back around.

'I'm so sorry,' Robbie said. 'Do you speak English?'

'Yes,' the woman replied. 'What is this?'

'This—this woman was killed last night close by. We thought. Well, we thought she might be from here.'

The woman ran to the body, slowly turned it over. There was no need. She knew as soon as she had seen them, as soon as she had seen the body. But she wanted to see the woman's face. An awful confirmation of her worst fears. It was gaunt and scarred, barely recognisable as the woman she had loved for so many years. 'Simone. Simone, mon amour. Qu'est-ce qu'ils vous ont fait?' She threw herself across the lifeless body, still warm, still soft, still so lifelike, and wept.

The girl stepped out of the doorway, pulled her hand to her mouth. 'Non! Non, non, non. Maman!' She walked so very slowly towards the body, as if she found it difficult to put one foot in front of the other. Both of them were now huddled over the body, weeping.

Robbie and Andy didn't know what to do. This was so much more than awkward. Should they stay and explain what they had heard? Or should they quietly leave these people to their grief? They hovered at the gate, quietly waiting for something, but they weren't sure what that might be. A sign? An escape? Something.

It was a peculiar thing. As if a switch had been flicked

that changed everything. The woman and the girl stood up, as one, no tears now. 'You will help us, oui?'

'Aye. Aye, course!'

'We must take her inside. Clean her. Dress her. Make her beautiful again, before she leave this world and live in the earth.'

Robbie and Andy followed behind the woman, carrying the lifeless body inside and laying her on a bed draped in white cotton, as directed.

'You go dig, oui? Everything is out there you need.' She pointed to a shed at the far end of the garden.

They walked out in silence, past the kitchen table that was set for breakfast. Three plates, mugs and sets of cutlery. Both men stared, allowed a feeling of trepidation to slip in. Was there someone else around? A man? Were they in danger? There was no need for worry. The family had never broken this habit. It had been six months since Simone's disappearance, but a place would be set, food would be ready for her return. The tradition would remain.

The house was as beautiful inside as out. The kitchen was full of dried herbs and flowers. The whitewashed walls, the polished wooden floors with a scattering of homemade rugs, the wood-burning stove, the tiny windows with jars of flowers on each sill. This felt like a place of love, and now they had brought tragedy.

Time slipped slowly by as they dug a hole beyond the vegetable plot, deep enough and large enough to carry the body. All around silence. Just silence. It was as if everything knew; the goats, the dogs, the birds, silent.

At last, the woman came out, inspected Robbie and Andy's work, nodded. They lowered Simone's body, wrapped in a shroud, into the grave and covered her with eternity. Robbie and Andy stepped back as the women said their prayers, their final messages. And it was done.

The older one beckoned them back inside. It didn't matter that they were now desperate to leave. The right thing to do was stay, and they did. She filled a pot with water. 'You will take café, yes?'

'Um, yes. Thank you.'

'Now you tell. How this came to be?'

'We don't know much. It was night. There were many trucks, soldiers. They stopped and the woman, Simone, ran. They shot her as she ran. I am so sorry.'

'Those bâtards! How I hate! And you? Why you here with no-one? No army?' Her eyes narrowed. 'British soldats, oui?'

'Yes.'

'You leave? Déserteurs?'

What to say now? Admit it, or lie?

'Yes,' Robbie answered. He wasn't ashamed of what they had done. Not in the least.

The woman nodded. 'Is all finish now. This war. Is finish and still they kill. What people do this?'

'The soldiers? They were leaving?'

'Oui.'

'And where are we?'

She smiled. 'Belgique. La chaîne anglaise est juste ici. Juste ten kilometres, there.' She pointed north. 'We give food and sleep, then you leave, oui?'

'Thank you. Thank you very much, but we should go now.'

'Non, non. Look! You must be little strong, little clean, then go.'

Neither Robbie nor Andy slept because, despite their

exhaustion, neither was sure of what this was, where they were, who these women were. This war had turned people into something else entirely. They knew it. They had seen it. They had been it.

Before sunrise they crept out and ran across the field, not looking back. They were heading north but not feeling safe about it. Not yet. Maybe not ever. They would reach the water and see what transpired. A boat? A fisherman? Something?

There was a peculiar stillness to everything. No sound of machinery, or battle, or even people. They felt strangely alone in this place, as if the world had stopped. As if there was nothing but them. They ran until they found a place to hide until nightfall, a dense copse of trees, with large roots that twisted above ground, offering seclusion. When the sun began to set again, they moved on, keeping to the shadows and trees. Ten kilometres was no distance at all. They would be there soon enough. One night's travel should do it.

Chapter 27
1919

~≈~

The press had called the demonstrators in Glasgow terrorists. The government feared a workers' revolution. The Sheriff of Lanarkshire requested support from the armed forces. Tanks and ten thousand armed troops would be deployed the next day from four Scottish regiments and two English. The Scottish soldiers were confined to Maryhill barracks. Out there on the streets the government feared there was a danger that they might end up siding with their fellow countrymen, the demonstrators. The gardens had been ruined, fences broken, and smashed glass was strewn across George Square. The City Chambers had been turned into a fortress.

Barbed wire was rolled out, and armed soldiers swarmed the streets. They were ordered to guard power stations and other infrastructure sites from damage. Machine guns were placed on the roof of the Post Office.

And this was peacetime Glasgow.

Hannah's flat was a hive of those seeking revolution, change, something better. The air was thick with smoke, with discourse, with voices all in agreement, that there was a better way and, at last, they could see it happening.

'Aye, to be sure they're feared o us now!'
'An uprising, no less!'
'What is democracy if not this?'
'Decisions are to be made by us, the people.'

115

'And how are we to divide it all; share it out?'

'After all o that we need a world o cooperation. A world where folk share and care, no matter who or what they are faced wi.'

'Aye. We didnae fight o'er there to come back to this!'

'You didnae fight!'

'Naw, but you ken what I mean, aye?'

'What gives them the right to wield power o'er us, eh?'

And at the centre of it all, Hannah, reigning supreme. It invigorated her, lifted her beyond this place.

The atmosphere was electric, but it was no place for a mother and young child. Hannah pulled Mhairi aside. 'I know you love it all, but...well...little Rosie? Perhaps this isn't the best place for her anymore?'

'Are ye kicking me out?'

'Of course not, but maybe Lizzie's would be a better option for a while. This place, well, it gets so crowded now, and it could be dangerous.'

Mhairi didn't argue because she knew that Hannah was right. It didn't matter how much she enjoyed everything that was happening, it was no longer a place for a child. She packed what little they had and said a sad farewell to the place that had been home.

'Oh, Mhairi, no need to be sad. You know that you are always welcome.' Hannah hugged her, stood back, smiled. 'Always!'

And with that, the door closed.

Mhairi pushed the pram along cobbled streets, Rosie sitting upright glancing at everything that was passing her by. The wonder of it all. Mhairi smiled at her innocence, her trust. Underneath that her thoughts were flying. It wasn't as if she had nowhere to go, but this just felt so familiar. Right now, she was rootless

116

again. A vagrant. Nothing. She laughed at herself for thinking such ridiculous thoughts, tickled Rosie's chest, to which they both giggled, and headed towards Lizzie's.

'Well, hello, again.' The stranger smiled. That man. 'The square,' he said in explanation. 'We met there.'

'Aye, course. Sorry. I was miles away.'

'Somewhere nice, I hope.'

'Eh, no. No really.'

'You're Mhairi, aren't you?'

'Em...' More peculiar words from this man. She couldn't remember having told him her name. Perhaps he had heard one of the others say it. Yes, that must be it.

He leaned towards the pram.

Now she was really ill at ease. The intrusion of this stranger irked her. Alarm bells ringing. She glared at him.

'I don't mean to frighten you. You have a nice face, that's all.'

She glared harder, pushed past and didn't look back. An uncomfortable feeling had taken hold of her, and she didn't like it. She took a circuitous route, twisting and turning, ducking into stairs, waiting and listening. It was commonplace these days. Even more so than when Robbie—No. Ditch that thought. There was no room for thinking like that, bringing it all back. The pain of her loss.

At last, they had reached Lizzie's. She checked left and right along the street. She was quite sure that no-one was following her, but she double-checked anyway. She took the path to the rear of Lizzie's building and knocked softly on the back door—such a feeling of relief—and was welcomed with open arms, literally. Hugs from Lizzie and Connie, and reassuring words that set her back at ease. These were her people; this was her place. And it was all right.

'Of course, you two must have my bedroom. I shall be supremely happy sleeping down here amongst my books,' Lizzie said.

'Naw, that's too much. Really!'

Lizzie tossed her blond curls back. 'Nonsense! Now, that's settled, let's set to work.'

The living quarters now flowed into the shop, where they had spent all day rearranging the second-hand books, tidying and restacking, until there was enough room for a bed and a chest.

'It was about time I got round to that!' Lizzie said as her eyes took in this new space. 'I'm not sure that I'll ever find anything ever again in all of this organised normality!'

They laughed.

A quick trip to the second-hand furniture store, a smile to the delivery-cart driver, and Lizzie returned with a bed, a cot, and a wardrobe and chest.

They swapped the furniture around and made Lizzie's old room as child friendly as they could.

'There now. Quite the modern woman's room, wouldn't you say?'

'I don't have the words. You two are just the best!'

'Right. Time for a quick drink before bed, I think.' Lizzie walked across to the kitchen cupboard and reached for the gin.

'Naw, no for me. It's too late an I just need my bed,' Mhairi said.

'Utter poppycock!' Connie said. 'It is never too late

for a bedtime tipple!'

'You'll be the death o me!'

With Rosie settled and fast asleep they toasted this new arrangement. Drank to their future happiness.

'You remember that stranger, at the demo?'

'Yes. What of him?'

'Well, he bumped into me again, and I don't know. It just makes me feel on edge, you know?' Mhairi began to cry. Softly, almost silently, and it took a while for Lizzie to notice.

'Oh, my love,' Lizzie said, reaching for her hand, squeezing it reassuringly. 'I'm sure it will all be fine. You'll see.'

'It's just...' She spread her arms around the room. 'This. This isn't our place. Me an Robbie's. And—an that man. I don't know. Something wrong about it all. Oh God!' She swiped at her face with her sleeve. 'I hate this! I hate all of this!'

'Well, of course you do. It's a nightmare. But you are so very strong, and you'll pull through. You'll see.'

'I'm, sorry,' Mhiari said to the air, and then to each of her friends in turn.

'You have absolutely nothing to be sorry about. But I do think I would be a tad concerned about that man being a lunatic. Some random stranger who has taken a fancy for you.'

Mhairi managed a laugh. 'He did say that I had a nice face.'

'Well, there we have it!'

'He didn't follow you, did he? Should we be on high alert?'

Despite them trying to lighten it all with a laugh and frivolity, sleep didn't come easily to any of them. This

119

stranger had caused an unsettling. Hannah had warned of infiltrators, government spies. He could well be one. Or someone working for Edward Fotheringale, which was equally concerning.

When Rosie woke with the dawn Mhairi jumped up and picked her out of the cot.

'Good morning, my precious wee angel.' She held her up high above her head and jiggled her. Rosie giggled. This was a fine start to the day.

Chapter 28
1919

~~~

'You see that?' Robbie said, nodding at the vision in front of them. There, glinting through the trees; water, stretching for as far as they could see, the horizon invisible, blue on blue. It had to be the sea. The English Channel. This part of their journey was almost at an end. Or so they hoped. They had seen no soldiers. No sign of an ongoing war. And beyond it all there was a quiet. A stillness. They knew nothing other than what the woman had said. The war was over. The Germans were in retreat. It felt like that, sounded like that, but they couldn't be sure. And even then, they had to be worried about coming across any of their own troops.

But did they? It had been such an awful situation. Their comrades were being slaughtered. They couldn't know the outcome of it all. Who had survived. Who hadn't. Their desertion might not even have been reported. It might be perfectly safe to walk up and say that they had been separated from their squadron in the mayhem. It might all be okay.

They sat down in the safety of the woods.

'Now?' Andy said.

Andy's words remained few, but Robbie, at least, understood their meaning. He grimaced, shrugged. 'Christ, I'd swim all the way back to bonnie Scotland, if I could. My wee lass, and the wean.'

'You have a picture?'

'Aye. Aye I have one.' He reached inside his jacket and tenderly pulled out the much-fingered photograph of the two of them. He stared at it, remembering that day. It was the day she had said "yes", and he would have done anything for her. All she wanted was a photo of the two of them to keep it all alive. Real. That's what she had said. They had found a small photographer's studio. A sweet old man who grinned at their happiness.

'That's you an me all tied up and bound together, so it is.'

It hadn't lasted long at all. Damned war!

∽

'Can I?' Andy asked.

'Aye. Sorry. She takes me to the very best o places, so she does.'

Robbie handed the photo over. Slowly, carefully, as if it might break.

Andy whistled. 'Beautiful!'

'She is that. And she's all mine. What a thing, eh?' He held his hand out for the return of the photo. 'Listen. I know we're nearly home and everything but, if anything happens to me will you find her? Tell her I loved her more than anything. Tell her I'll always be by her side.'

'There's no need. You'll make it. We'll make it.'

'Aye, but just in case. Promise me you'll take this photo. Don't leave it to rot in a field of nothing. Don't let it be forgotten.'

'Promise.' Andy didn't have one, a sweetheart, or a photo. At least, not that he could remember, and he would know such a thing, surely. He would be able to feel it somewhere deep inside. But everything was messed up, his feelings, his memories and he had no idea of what was real and what was imagined. He was

122

just existing. That was all there was to rely upon. Today. Now. And that was challenge enough.

Robbie sat in quiet joy for a few minutes, remembering love. Remembering something real and pure and beautiful, because now he thought that he could. It was safe enough to let that in again. That other life.

They hunkered down for the day. A gentle chorus of song rose and swelled as the birds sang their joy at the dawn. It was a magnificent thing to hear that again. Not the awful sounds of war. That. Simple beauty which had been denied them for so very long. Now they heard it. Now they felt it. And it was quite wonderful.

A light rain had begun to fall. It was the kind of rain that looked like nothing, but left you drenched in no time at all. It seeped through all of their clothing, right through to their skin. It didn't matter. Both men thought they could withstand anything nature chose to throw at them now.

They woke as the sun set, damp through but content enough with it. The endless chatter of birds as they settled for the night, the rustle of disturbed leaves lying on the ground. No. Wait! The sound of feet. Marching feet. Not again! Surely not again! They strained their eyes through the tree trunks that had kept them safe, pushed themselves hard against them, trying to become them.

English voices drifted through the damp air. What to do now? Show themselves? Make up some story which might last them until they got back on home territory? Risk court-martial? Because that's what it would be. And it was a terrible thing. A few minutes of accusation and a death sentence. They knew. They had been told.

No. They would trust no-one for now. They would find their own way. Somehow.

The footsteps and the voices grew fainter again. Neither dared to speak until relative silence reigned once more. Nature above man.

'We need to get to the coast proper. See what we can find. A boat, a friendly fisherman,' Robbie whispered.

Andy nodded.

They crept from tree to tree, ever vigilant, until they reached the beach. The sound of breaking waves washing their minds, their thoughts. A constant in this world of unfamiliarity. That calming. But this was a different thing. Fear swept up the beach alongside the lapping waves. Beauty mixed with terror. Something awful had happened here.

Both men felt it. That need to go. To just leave this all behind and go. This was it. They stood tall and stepped out. Nothing but sand and water, glinting in the setting sun, but there, in the sea, a shadow. Something foreign. Andy nudged Robbie. Fear slipped to hope. They both recognised it. The impossibility of a boat bobbing about on the waves. They took a quick glance left and right and ran down the sand dunes, across the beach, and into the water.

It was only a rowing boat, but that didn't matter. It was afloat, and that was enough. They clambered over the side and into the boat. It was whole, intact, and there were oars. They needed nothing else. The evening was cold but calm enough and the going relatively easy as they rowed with every ounce of energy they had. No words passed from one to the other, just a steely determination. That commonality that pushed each of them on for the other. A strength that coursed from one body to the other: one mind to the other. *We can do this*.

As the light disappeared with the settling of night they couldn't see land anymore. There was nothing but the dark. Nothing in front of them, nothing behind. This was now all about instinct and they kept going, trusting that something inside them would know; would guide them. The air was still, the water uncommonly calm for a winter's night. The sky was clear, awash with stars.

Andy pointed. 'That there's the North Star.'

'Aren't you just full of surprises? You're sure, now?'

Andy nodded. 'My dad taught me.' And with that simple sentence came a flood of images, of memories. His sister. He had a sister! Younger than him. A pretty young thing. Too pretty for her own good, their mother had said. He could see her smile, hear her giggle. And then she was gone and wouldn't come back. What did that mean? He bit his lip to hold back the fears that were building up in his head. No point. No point to it. Here, in the middle of the night, in a dark restless sea, he had to hold himself together.

'But are we sure it's just north we want?' Robbie said. 'We might end up in the middle of the North Sea.'

Those words brought Andy back, settled him, as he focussed on the stars once more. As he stared, they seemed to multiply. A myriad lights that heaved and swelled, as if they themselves were breathing.

It seemed the gods were smiling on them, as there, in the distance, the lights of a habitation glowed faint and steady on the horizon, a ghostly outline of civilisation, blurry, indistinct, but real, and it could only be Britain. Surely. A peculiar quiet drifted beside them, between them. The dulled rhythm of the oars, the soft splash of water, the wash against wood, and the weight of their breath. But they had made it. They would be home soon. Home. Imagine that?

Chapter 29
1919

~

Mhairi was walking along the road to the park where she liked to spend as much time as she could outside with Rosie, weather permitting, and this was a beautiful day. The sky was clear, the sun holding little semblance of warmth, but its brightness made it feel temperate. A gentle breeze prickled at their skin, making Rosie giggle. Mhairi pulled Rosie's bonnet down over her ears, tucked her scarf tighter round her neck. 'We need to keep you all snug, wee one.' Rosie was just beginning to walk on wobbly legs. This new skill was one that she wanted to practise all the time. She stretched her arms out, asking to be picked out of the pram. 'In a wee a minute. When we get in the park.' They had just reached the entrance when the sound of someone in a hurry behind them made Mhairi pause.

She went against her better judgement, turned to face the heavy footsteps, and gasped. The immaculate double-breasted cashmere suit with a perfectly folded white handkerchief arranged in its breast pocket, brogues polished to such a level that they held a reflection, the tilted Fedora, that silver tipped cane. That air of entitled arrogance. It was Edward Fotheringale.

An awful feeling of unwelcome panic grabbed her, tied itself around her chest, squeezed at her breath. No! She wouldn't allow him to do this to her. Not anymore. She was strong and out of his control, and she would be safe enough here. There were people all around.

Ordinary people who offered her some protection. He wouldn't dare do anything out here, in public. Surely? His reputation, after all, was everything.

Fotheringale's informant had been keeping an eye on her for months now in the hope that she would lead him to Connie. There had been nothing solid to go on. Other women had been in Mhairi's company, but none that matched Connie's description. And she had always managed to slip away when he thought he was about to tail her home. But this was a regular. This little jaunt with her child.

At last, he had found a way in. A chance to find out where Connie was for himself. One never could rely on others, frustrating though it was. He was a busy man after all. But this was remarkably enjoyable! He reached out and snatched at Mhairi's shoulder. His grip painful. His face held a horribly smug smile. A self-satisfaction.

Mhairi shouted. 'What do you think you're doing, eh? Hands off!'

Heads did turn. He dropped his hold. 'This needn't become ugly,' he whispered venomously, with a smile glued on his face. 'My daughter's disappearance. I know you were a part of it all. Where is she?'

'I have no idea what you're talking about,' she said. 'Leave me be or I'll get the polis on you!' Mhairi felt something heavy, substantial, slip into her pocket.

'Thief! The woman is a thief!' Fotheringale called, glancing around, drawing more attention from passers-by. 'I saw you slip my fob watch into your pocket,' he called loudly for all to hear. 'It was my father's before me. Pure gold. Worth a small fortune to someone like you.'

People had stopped now. Stared at this disturbance. Muttered to each other. The attention of a passing policeman had also been drawn.

Panic now. Blind panic. All bravado slipped through Mhairi's trembling legs and into the gutter. She didn't dare put her hand in her pocket. It would be in there. Of course it would.

'Officer? I say! Over here. Perhaps some assistance?' The policeman recognised the honourable gentleman. Blew his whistle. Ran across. 'Turn your pockets out, miss, if you don't mind.'

There was no other choice. She did as instructed. The gold glinted as it tumbled towards the ground.

Fotheringale scooped his hand down to catch it as it fell. A leery grin passed from him to her as he looked up. She was beaten, and he knew it.

'We're pressing charges. I assume, sir?'

'Indeed, we are! Thieves and criminals have no place on our streets. We didn't thrash the damned Boche for this to happen on our precious soil!'

'Now, let's not make a fuss, miss,' the policeman said as he clipped handcuffs around her wrists. A small gathering of onlookers stared, some tutting, others shaking their heads in disapproval.

'My child? Have a heart. My child!'

'Yes, yes. We'll sort that out down at the station. On you come now.'

She turned to Fotheringale and screeched, 'I'll see you in hell!'

～

They sorted it out all right. No discussion. No agreement. As Rosie was taken away, the cries of mother and child grew further and further apart until

129

neither could hear the other.

The hell became Mhairi's in the shape of a dark, dank cell. She screamed and screamed until her voice grew hoarse.

Mutterings and complaint from her fellow inmates.

'That'll do ye no good, lassie. No good at all.'

'For Christ's sake shut it!'

'Leave her be.'

'Aye, well, best deal wi it like the rest o us.'

The pain she felt was unlike anything she had imagined. Her heart had been wrenched from her chest, ripped into tiny pieces, and thrown away. Everything good had gone from her life, and she was powerless to do anything about it.

~

'Do we have an address for the woman?' Fotheringale enquired at the station.

'That we don't, sir. I doubt her name is even genuine. Women like that...' He shook his head.

'Oh, I could be of some assistance there. Her full name is Mhairi McIntyre, formerly of my employ.'

'Ah. Revenge theft, was it?'

'One could say she left under an extremely dark cloud, so, yes, I imagine that to be the case. And after I had shown her such kindness as well.' He pulled a patronising smile.

'Well, she'll need to be getting used to life behind bars now.'

'Quite! And should you find an address for her I would be most obliged if you could pass it my way, so to speak.'

'A gentleman like yourself wouldn't be wanting to grace the home of someone like that.'

130

'There is that, but I believe there may be other items of mine hidden there, or thereabouts.'

'Is that so? Very well, sir. If you could wait just a minute, I'll see what I can do.'

The policeman returned shortly after with a piece of paper gripped in his hand. He handed Mhairi's address across to Fotheringale.

'Much obliged, I'm sure. Good day to you.' He tipped his fedora and left, a feeling of accomplishment swelling in his breast.

Chapter 30
1919

~

Lizzie and Connie were becoming worried. It was late and there was no sign of Mhairi.

'Do we raise an alarm?' Connie asked.

'I think you should stay here, in case she comes back, and I'll check with Hannah. You never know, she might have got caught up in a conversation too exciting to remove herself from!'

Both women laughed.

'Yes. That's probably it.'

'Right. Stay here and keep guard. I won't be long.'

There was now a part of Connie that was beginning to resent this molly coddling. They cared deeply, and that was wonderful, but she didn't need it. This constant care. Not anymore. She felt like a child, and she was very far from that!

~

The address for Mhairi that Edward Fotheringale had been given was Hannah's. She stood with her boot pressed hard against the door which only allowed the narrowest of openings.

'Yes?' she snarled. She knew fine who he was but pretended otherwise. A small triumph, but a triumph, nonetheless.

He smiled the well-practiced smile that he used for public occasions, for dealing with people of less import than himself, for looking down politely on his constituents. 'Good day.' He tipped his hat. 'I am looking for the residence of a Miss Mhairi McIntyre. She is

132

registered as residing here, so the police have informed me.'

'Oh, really? Well, they must be mistaken. I have no idea who this Miss Whateverhernameis—'

'McIntyre,' he replied slowly, testily, as if he were speaking to an imbecile.

Hannah was enjoying this in a perverse kind of a way. To be able to annoy him—which she clearly was— was amusing. 'I really don't know the woman. Now, if you don't mind?' She moved to close the door, but his cane had been thrust between door and frame.

Davie and Brian appeared in the hallway. 'All right there, Hannah?'

'The gentleman was just leaving.'

Fotheringale's smile broadened. 'Not so fast, young lady. Now, if you'll just step aside and allow me to see for myself, I'll be on my way.'

A man like that, she knew that she had to keep her cool, but it was so very difficult. She hated everything that he stood for. The privilege, arrogance and entitlement of his type were bad enough, but she also knew all about him from Connie and Mhairi. He was one to be wary of, but she would not allow him to cross her threshold. Davie and Brian now stood behind her, their arms crossed, their stance defiant, immovable.

'As the lady said, I believe you're leaving,' Brian said.

'I see. It's like that is it? Well, I shall return with law enforcement.'

'On ye go, pal. On ye go.'

They knew that he would be true to his word. Any material that could be classed as seditious would need to be packed away and stored in the back green. Although she hated to do it, the posters would also

133

need to be taken down and hidden outside. You have to know when to bow down. At least when to pretend to.

Within minutes of his leaving there was another tap at the door.

'Not back already, surely?'

Hannah opened the door to a breathless Lizzie.

'Did I just see—'

'Yes, you did.' Hannah pulled Lizzie close, kissed both of her cheeks.

'Dear God! What was he after?'

'The pretence was that he was looking for Mhairi. He is under the belief that she stole from him. Would you credit it?'

'I don't think for one minute that he was after Mhairi. He'll be looking for Connie.' Lizzie said. 'So, Mhairi isn't here then?'

'No. Should she be?'

'I was rather hoping that she might be. She went out for a walk with Rosie, hours ago, and we thought she might be here.'

'No. No, I haven't seen her at all.' She turned to Davie and Brian. 'Boys?'

They both shook their heads.

'Right. That's not good. First, use the network to get word to Connie that her father is on the prowl. Careful mind. He'll have eyes on, that one will.' She turned back to Lizzie. 'Where else might she be? Any ideas?'

'No, but there was that stranger who was worrying her.'

'That was nothing, surely?'

Lizzie shrugged. 'I don't know.'

'I don't think there is much we can do for now, other than wait and ask everyone to keep their eyes peeled.

I'm sure she'll be just fine. Meantime, you should leave. That pathetic excuse for a man will be back, and we don't want him making any connection to you.'

'No, we don't.'

'Keep me posted.'

'Likewise.'

They hugged and kissed each other's cheeks again, with slightly more intensity than usual. An unsettling had crept in and was sitting heavy.

Within the hour Fotheringale had returned to Hannah's flat, complete with two police officers. They stood guard as he searched through the flat, rifled through Hannah's clothing, bedding, bookcase, cupboards. Everything.

She could tell that he was losing his temper by the change in colour of his ears. The red fury, as Connie had described it. It was peculiar how he managed to control everything else, but not that. She managed to stifle a laugh.

'Are you quite done?' she finally asked.

'For now, yes. But you mark my words.' He pointed his cane at her. 'This is not over!'

'Yes, it is,' Hannah replied. 'And you can put that thing away. I believe it to be something of a threat. Officers?'

They shuffled uncomfortably, looked at the ground. 'Ahem. Well. We'll be off, then.'

Chapter 31
1919

～

An unwelcome panic crept up Robbie's legs, all the way into his head. 'My feet are wet,' he said. He stretched down and felt water in the bottom of the boat. Too much for it to have been made by their inexperienced rowing. 'Christ! We must have sprung a leak somehow. We'd better get a move on! Here, you row, and I'll scoop.' He handed his oar to Andy and began frantically scooping out handfuls of sea water. Both felt the return of an anxiety they hoped had been left on foreign shores, but they had been through so much worse than this. By comparison it was nothing. Nothing at all.

Robbie reached inside his jacket, took out the picture of Mhairi and held it out for Andy.

Andy shook his head. 'No! You're making it alongside me.'

'Take it, man!'

Reluctantly Andy accepted the picture and tucked it into his breast pocket. It was the right thing to do. Out here, in this blackness, anything could happen.

Andy's fingers cramped; his grip slipped. One of the oars fell into the sea. It was the slowest thing as it was dragged away. He screamed, scrambled with his one remaining oar.

Robbie stretched over. There it was. Just an arm's length away. He stretched again. His fingertips touched wood, but he couldn't quite grab hold of it. He stretched further. His balance was going.

'Careful Robbie.'

One more lunge and he would have it. But this was one lunge too far and his body fell into the black water. Andy reached out and snatched at Robbie's leg. His trousers were sodden and slippery. No purchase given.

'No!' Andy screeched as Robbie disappeared into the blackness. Andy could just make out the splashes from Robbie's arms as they fought with the pull of the water. Then he could see nothing at all. He paddled furiously with the one remaining oar, but it was futile. His head was full of confusion. He had no idea of where Robbie had fallen in. Where the oar had slipped. How far he had moved, if at all. Nothing. There was nothing to see. Nothing to hear. In a heartbeat, Robbie was gone.

They had almost made it. The famous white cliffs stood tall and proud like a beacon, glinting with the softly golden morning sun when it began to rise. They would have been safe. Andy just lay in the boat, unable to do anything. The gentle rocking, the slap of water on wood, the shriek of gulls, the awful buzzing in his head. How could life do this? Be so very cruel? What was the point of it all? Nothing. Not a damned thing.

Chapter 32
1919

~~

Mhairi had been sent to Calton prison in Edinburgh, where she was isolated from those who could help her. It was an awful place, so cold and damp. The discipline doled out was harsh. Exercise was almost non-existent. One hour in the morning, and that was it. Letters were never sent, nor received. She had given up asking for anything, because nothing was forthcoming.

Her grief didn't diminish any, but it lay deeper inside of her. The woman she had become was silent now. Any conversations were had in her head. Conversations with Robbie, with Rosie, with Connie and Hannah and Lizzie. All there in her head. She told them everything. Clung on to the essence of them. They had been real.

In protest at her imprisonment she was refusing her food, such as it was, the diet less than basic, porridge then soup, then porridge again. If the milk served with it wasn't already sour, it was on the turn. The decision had been made to force-feed her. The hell of that. The pain. The total humiliation. She heard talk of a transfer to an asylum.

Mhairi remembered that place. The awfulness of it. The state they had put Connie into. This would be worse. She was a mere prisoner, not a woman of standing. This would be hell, but there was something in her that wanted it. Drugs that would remove all feeling from her, all sense of normality.

No! Get yourself back, Mhairi. You are better than this!
She fought with the demons in her head, pulled

Rosie and Robbie to the fore. They were still a part of her. She had to pull herself together. It felt like defeat as she accepted the slop she was given, as she followed their orders. But she knew inside that she was winning.

～

An air of desperation had taken up residence in Lizzie's flat. They knew of Mhairi's arrest and sentencing; of Rosie being taken from her. It was an awful quandary. Yes, Connie was the baby's godmother, but were she to show herself, there was no doubt in her mind that her father would have her locked up in an instant. Returned to that asylum. Left to rot in a drug induced state of incapacity.

'There must be something we can do. He is not infallible. Not untouchable,' Hannah said. 'The man must not be allowed to win!'

'We are all in total agreement there, but what can we do?' Lizzie said.

'Have him killed!' Connie said with uncharacteristic venom. 'By God, he deserves it!'

Hannah smiled. 'A pacifist is a pacifist, Connie, my sweet.'

'Oh, I know, but... It makes my blood boil. He's my own father and he's a beast, and he makes me hate, which I don't appreciate in the slightest!'

Hannah wasn't one to let something drop, some injustice stand. She had spent her life fighting for the rights of the down-trodden, of those abused by power, by the ruling classes who believed that they could do whatever they saw fit. When this terrier had the bone between her teeth, she wasn't letting go.

'I've been having a chat with some comrades.' Hannah said. 'I hope you don't mind, Connie, but there are some doctors amongst our number, trustworthy ones. We've been chatting, and they agree that, if there are several medical practitioners prepared to state, on record, that you are beyond reproach and absolutely sane, he cannot override them all.'

'It's a risk,' Lizzie said, looking intently at her friend. 'Is it one that you can afford to take?'

'I believe it is one I cannot afford not to take!'

～

They put their case before a judge. Yes, Connie was sane. Yes, she had a perfectly legitimate claim to the child. The problem was that, according to their records, little Rosie had already been adopted. A new name. A new family. A new life.

'Surely that can be overturned, given the circumstances?'

'That really isn't possible, I'm afraid.'

'But—'

'This is out of my hands. I'm sorry. Now, if you don't mind?'

This wasn't going to be put to bed with one closed door. Unfortunately, every other avenue they tried had the same result. The child was gone and there was nothing to be done about it.

'Now that I officially have my sanity, I can, at least, visit Mhairi. The poor soul. So far from home. So alone.'

'You cannot possibly go alone,' Lizzie stressed.

'Oh, but I must. Don't you see? I owe it to her, and to myself.'

～

The noise and the smell were enticing. Steam engines and whistles, and the chatter of people. Connie wondered where they were all going, these fellow travellers. What was the purpose of their journeys? She was about to step on board the train. The gap between the train and the platform was a tad daunting. A slip and she might fall on to the tracks. *Oh, come on Connie. Foolish thinking!* She shook her head, confidently stepped up, turned left, and walked along the carriages, looking for an empty compartment. She would prefer to travel alone. Undisturbed. The best she could manage was a compartment with one other occupant. A man in uniform, an officer, who was looking out of the window, an air of sadness surrounding him.

She decided to take her seat on the opposite side, but one place back from the window. It would have seemed inappropriate somehow, intrusive, to sit directly across from him, much though she would have preferred the window seat. She stretched to place her overnight bag in the rack above. As she stepped back the train began to move, a sudden jolt, and she stumbled slightly. Her foot landed on his. She felt herself turn scarlet. 'I am so sorry,' she said, her hands clutched to her chest in humility.

He looked across at her with the glimmer of a smile. 'It's nothing,' he replied in little more than a whisper.

He was staring.

She was staring.

He had burn marks across his face. Recent ones that ripped through an otherwise very handsome face. A curl of chestnut hair escaped from under his cap. His eyes were an intense deep brown. His cheekbones defined the angular shape to his face. There was a seriousness about him. A dark, heavy seriousness.

'It seems we have both been in the wars,' he said

softly.

She lifted her hand to her face. 'Sometimes I forget,' she said.

'I don't.' How could he forget that? A mortar attack that almost wiped out his squadron. The screaming of men in agony. His men. The screams turned to grunts and moans, whispers, the odd plaintive cry. 'Let me die. Dear God, let me die.' Then nothing. That awful stillness as he lay beneath the bodies of the men who had saved him, listening to their lives seeping from them. No. There was no forgetting that.

An air of awkwardness settled between Connie and the soldier, and they sat in silence as the train pulled out of the station. A light rain had begun to fall, misting up the windows, blurring the world outside.

'I was rather hoping to enjoy the view,' she said, almost to herself.

He kept his gaze fixed to the outside, despite there being little to see, other than rain. His head slumped. He rested his forehead against the glass. His shoulders were shaking. He was weeping.

She stretched her hand across and touched his knee. 'It's all right,' she whispered.

Silent tears became sobs. He pushed her hand away. Shook his head.

'I...perhaps I should leave you in peace,' she said.

He reached out and snatched her hand back, caught between a need for solitude and a desperation for company. Soft, gentle company. 'No. Stay. Please stay.'

She moved to sit beside him. 'May I?'

He nodded. 'Please.' He fell against her, his head on her bosom, his tears soaking through her blouse.

She wrapped her arms around him and held tight.

There was such an awful pain emanating from him.

He was a man. He was a stranger. This wasn't how a lady should behave. But times were changing, and she would do as she saw fit, not what was expected, certainly not what she was told. That person was becoming a distant memory, and she was glad of it.

Chapter 33
1919

~

Andy's boat ran aground on the pebbly shore. He didn't deserve to be here, to be the one who had made it home. Robbie should have been the man to have survived. That would have been fair. That would have been just. He would never have made it this far had it not been for Robbie. Hell, he would probably have been one more body trapped on that barbed wire. There was no joy in this survival. Only grief. And he didn't know where to put that grief; how to deal with it.

What did he want now? Where did he want to go? He barely knew who he was. The cold was becoming unbearable and there was no warmth to this sun. A harsh glare. Nothing more. His body was quaking uncontrollably. His mind was leaving him, such as it was. A terror began to fill the spaces. And that was all there was. Blind, raging terror. He had to move if he were to survive. Find shelter, warmth, food. Those instincts remained, even if the man himself didn't.

The crunch of pebbles under his feet seemed to be unbearably loud. With each footstep, a thumping that reverberated in his head. Gunfire. Explosions. He wanted to scream. To drown it out. Then they came. The memories. The visions. The tearing of flesh. The screaming of men. The stench of terror. Now he did scream. He clasped his hands to his head, pushed so hard that it hurt. That was what he wanted. Pain. That was what he deserved. He fell to his knees and screamed like a madman.

Voices. A buzz that he was aware of but couldn't make any sense of. Movement. His body being lifted. And then nothing.

He came to in a hospital of some sort. That smell—unnatural, harsh, biting—only existed in hospitals. Through blurred vision he glimpsed strangely distant people in white, heard hushed voices. Someone screamed. Not him. No, that wasn't him. A needle in his arm. Sleep again.

'Do we know who he is yet?' A doctor asked.

'He was in a British uniform, so we must assume he's one of ours. There were no papers, though. Only a photograph of a young couple. There was no writing on the photograph. Nothing to point to who he might be. Who she might be. We'll just have to hope he gets his senses back, poor love. So many of them just don't,' the nurse said. She was a plump woman. Unruly wavy brown hair was tied back in a tight bun. Her hazel eyes had seen so much pain, so much suffering, but they still held a sparkle to them, a confirmation that there was something good out there. Something to fight for. Her full lips smiled at every opportunity. Especially in here. This place, these men needed it.

'Right. We'll transfer him to the sanitorium. They know more about how to treat people like this.'

The nurse winced at the insensitivity of it all. The brusqueness. *People like this!* She would want more for her brother if he were to end up this way. She stayed by the soldier's side after the doctor had completed his rounds, took his hand, squeezed it. 'You just hang on, love. Hang on and I'll see you right. My name's Beatrice, but friends call me Bea. You can, if you want. Bea. How about you? I would love to know your name.' She waited, holding his hand, looking for confirmation that he had, at least, understood.

Nothing. Silence. Eyes staring. No recognition of anything that she could sense. She had seen so many young men like this. Brains wiped by the horror of it all. Shells of humans. She had survived it by keeping her distance, like everyone else. Getting too involved, too emotional, would make it all so much more difficult. Her job was to make her patients as comfortable as possible during their stay here. That was it. But there was something about this particular soldier. Something that pulled at her more than the others.

She should ignore it. Fight against it. Rise above it. But she wasn't sure if she could. Not this time. This felt strong and somehow connected to her. She was due leave. That would help. And by the time she returned he would have been moved on to the sanatorium where they knew a bit more about how to help *a man like this.*

Chapter 34
1919

∽

Lizzie busied herself sorting shelves, dusting her precious books, lingering over her favourites, but there were so many. So many wonderful stories that could lift one away from wherever one was; whatever situation had settled and made life more difficult; more complicated. Her fingers flitted across the spine of The Vagabond. She pulled it out, stroked the cover. 'Oh, why not?' She had read it so many times that it was like an old friend and that was what she felt the need for right now. Mhairi imprisoned, Connie off to visit her. She should have gone too. Of course she should have. To hang with having to stay here for the shop. Yes, it was an important hub in the greater scheme of things, and yes, she needed that income, small though it was. But Mhairi was such a close friend, she was as good as family. And that little girl. Oh, how Mhairi's heart would break when she heard. 'I should have gone!'

The gentle chime of the bell above the door made her break from that dirty guilt, and smile. A lover of books, or a fellow activist, were always welcome! She turned, expecting pleasant conversation. A request for something outlandish, perhaps. Or something for a young woman to raise her expectations in life. Or a gentleman to give to his love—poetry perhaps—a means of expressing what he could not. What foolish beasts we are, unable to put words to the most wonderful of feelings, to that unique emotion. Love. Why is it so very difficult? Why do we hide that which sits within us? We are so very peculiar!

She lifted her eyes to greet her customer but the smile on her face became fixed and false. It was him! Connie's father Edward Fotheringale! She would not, could not, let him see beyond the smile. A quick panic rushed through her as she wondered if anything could be seen that was evidence of Connie living here. Thank God she was away! But what on earth was he doing here? A coincidence, surely.

'Good afternoon, sir. How can I help?'

'Good afternoon!' He motioned tipping his hat. 'I sincerely doubt if you can help,' he said, his eyes casting up and down her body, as if appraising, sizing her up. 'I have it on good authority—'

She gulped. Had he noticed? No. Keep smiling. Be professional.

'That these—' He looked around disdainfully. 'These premises once belonged to my family.'

Oh my God, I hate you. I hate you so very much more than I ever wanted to hate anyone. Get out of my shop!

How she would love to have been able to say what was in her heart, to dismiss the rank air he breathed from her shop, but she knew better. It was best not to unnecessarily poke one's enemy. 'I am so sorry. Your journey has been a wasted one. This shop has always been in my family. You appear to have been misinformed.'

'I see.'

Clearly, he didn't. She could sense that there were more questions coming. As if by sheer magic the bell chimed again. A customer. Someone she didn't know began browsing her shelves.

'If you will excuse me. I must attend to this customer.'

She bowed slightly, hating it, but enjoying the fact that it was entirely fake. This cretin of a human being was of less worth than a gnat! She strode off. 'Madam?' she said breezily. 'Can I direct you to anything in particular?'

'No, I—'

Lizzie took the woman's elbow and guided her towards the window. 'This,' she said, with excitement, 'is quite wonderful.'

Fotheringale stared, his mouth slightly ajar as if a word were stuck in it.

'Good day, sir,' Lizzie said, not looking his way.

The impudence of her! He wondered what the world was coming to with women like that behaving so appallingly. Did she even know who he was? Quite unbelievable! He strode out and left the door open.

Lizzie shook her head. 'Manners maketh the man, eh?' she said with a laugh, as she closed the door behind him.

The customer raised her eyebrows and smiled.

'Men like that!'

'Yes, indeed!'

'Now, where were we? Ah yes, the wonderful James Joyce. Are you a fan?'

She had managed to annoy Fotheringale, and that was victory enough, but she doubted his excuse for coming into her shop. Something didn't sit right, and it left her on edge. She would have to be more careful for a while, perhaps warn Hannah and the boys. And with that came the image of Robbie. Poor young Robbie. Such a waste.

Chapter 35
1919

~

The officer sat up with a jerk. 'I am so sorry. I don't—I don't know what came over me.' He shook his head, stretched for his kit bag, and rushed out.

'It's all right. Really it is,' she called after him.

The train was pulling into Waverley station, Edinburgh. Connie straightened her skirt, her blouse, wrapped her coat around her and walked out onto the platform. She would need to ask for directions or hail a cab of some sort. It had been so long since she had visited a railway station, and never on her own, nor Edinburgh. She hoped she would find a means of transport outside the station.

The air was cold and damp, a heavy mist sitting on everything, blurring the street, the buildings. It really felt rather miserable. A perversely perfect accompaniment to her mood. Thankfully a horse-drawn cab was just dropping someone off at the station. She hurried across the pavement, raised her arm, and called. 'Taxi? I say! Over here!'

The driver grinned and waved in reply.

He lifted his flat cap from his head and nodded. 'Where to, miss?'

'A hotel, if you would be so kind?'

'Did you have a particular one in mind, or just any?'

'Something near to the Calton gaol would be preferable.'

He pulled a surprised face. 'And what would a fine young lady such as yerself be wanting to be near a place like that for?'

'Oh, I have my reasons.'

'Right then, well, you cannae go wrong wi the North British Station hotel. It's right there.' He pointed to a grand looking building on the corner of Princes Street. 'I'm doing myself out o a fare as I speak.' He laughed. 'But why don't I just help you along wi yer, bag an we'll say no more about it?'

'Oh, I couldn't possibly! I shall pay you, of course!'

'Right you are, then. If you insist.'

'I do!'

Everything was shrouded in mist, and night was drawing in. It was best to be safe. That soldier had unsettled her. A complete stranger breaking down like that and seeking her body for comfort. The hell he must have been through. Who knows how unstable he might be, and others. So many strangers. So much unknown.

The taxi pulled up after no more than a minute outside such a grand affair. Arches and curves and balustrades. It was an immense building. The driver insisted on carrying her bag in for her and guiding her to the check-in desk.

'Thank you so much,' she said. As she thanked him, she squeezed a note into his hand which was far too much for the fare, but this was a strange city, and he had offered her a kindness. To her mind, that should be rewarded.

She checked in and was taken up three flights of stairs to a large room with a view across Princes Street and on to Waterloo Place. Rising in the background, Calton Hill, where the gaol stood. She stared out at the place imagining Mhairi, locked up, alone.

With some difficulty she moved one of the plush

velvet armchairs across the room, cursing her lack of strength, and placed it at the window. She sat for a while, just watching the pulse of Scotland's capital city, as she pondered going down to the restaurant, taking dinner, perhaps even mingling. But she decided against it. The pull of this view, the passing of people going about their business, kept her transfixed. Besides which, her anxiety about what tomorrow would hold had eaten away any appetite that she might have had.

One solitary figure held her attention and she stared as the young woman walked briskly along Waterloo Place, pushing a pram. The woman leant over regularly, as if chatting to the baby, comforting it with soft words.

It was late and Connie wasn't sure how easily sleep would come so she held on for as long as she could. There was so much importance to what she had in store for the next day. Dear Mhairi. Locked up. There. Her life should have been like that of the young woman. Mother and child in blissful harmony. Their own world. Mhairi's situation was so very far from that. So very far from anything that made sense.

She lay in bed, tossing and turning, as anticipated; what the day ahead might hold spinning through her head, not allowing her to call sleep. Did Mhairi know that Rosie was somebody else's child now? She doubted it. What an awful thing for a mother to learn. How was she going to break it to her? Were there even any appropriate words? She didn't think so. It was going to be horrendous. And this was all on account of her father! Her own flesh and blood.

Connie's legs were tangled up amongst twisted sheets. She threw the covers off in frustration at her inability to switch her thoughts off. Perhaps a few minutes watching the outside world again. She sat at the window once more, but now it was deserted. Nothing but the quiet of sleeping buildings, the low, flickering glimmer of streetlights. She opened the window and listened to the heartbeat of the city. The endlessness of it. It was a comfort, and she relaxed into it.

Chapter 36
1919

~

Bea came back from her short break, refreshed, but strangely keen to see that soldier again. That wasn't what was meant to have happened. She hadn't forgotten him, let him go, at all. Her shoes squeaked on the highly polished floor as she walked briskly to the ward. That familiar smell that was home to her. The cleanliness that signified care and help and all of the things that were important in this world, her world. But his bed had someone else in it. She scanned up and down the rows of other beds. No. He wasn't there. Such a mix of emotions. Sadness at his departure; joy that he had been well enough to move on; relief at her escape from whatever it was that she had been harbouring. It had been wrong and now she could get back to being her. To giving all of her attention to nursing; to these poor souls. What had she been thinking? She shook her head at her unprofessionalism; sent it away.

'Nurse?' another soldier called softly from the bed beside her.

She turned, switched on her well-practiced smile.

'Yes, my love. What can I do for you?'

Her day was filled with tending and comforting and reassuring. 'Yes, you'll be fine. We'll have you right as rain in no time. Just you wait and see.' Most of the time she was lying. The men in there would never be right as rain again, but words of comfort were a great healer of the mind, and by that miraculous connection, if fortune were smiling, the body.

At the end of her shift, a photograph poking out from under a bedside cabinet caught her attention. She bent down and carefully picked it up. It was the one belonging to that soldier. He must have dropped it, or someone else had not given due care and attention to their patient.

She went against her better judgement and checked the register of patients. The occupant of bed number 37 had indeed been transferred, and he wasn't so far away. She would return the photograph, if nothing else. It might be important; a key to unlocking some good memories for such a tortured soul.

A brief ten-minute tram-ride and she was at the sanatorium. She stood up, walked to the exit, and stepped gingerly onto the pavement. A slight hesitation. No. She had made her decision. This was the right thing to do. The return of the picture, at least.

The sanatorium was large and cold-looking. It had the feel of somewhere unwelcoming. Austere. This wasn't what those men needed. Not to her mind. They needed tenderness and love. A confirmation that there was good in this world. They could get better and enjoy it. Live their lives again. But she was just a woman with no power, no sway, and no influence. And the country was in such upheaval anyway. So many broken lives. Such turmoil. That damned war!

She walked up the steps to the entrance, took a deep breath, drew on the strength that she had been trained to use and walked through the heavy doors.

'Can I help you, nurse?' a woman called from behind her desk in the entrance hall.

Bea smiled, walked across to the desk. 'Yes. I'm looking for a young soldier who arrived from the Royal

Victoria yesterday. He left something behind that is important to him.'

'Oh, I see. Well now, if you just hand it to me, I'll make sure that he gets it.'

'No, no. I can't do that. I promised him, you see, and I am a woman of my word.'

The woman paused, her mouth open, about to say no, but something softened. 'You know what? Let me just see what I can do for you.'

'You are very kind. Thank you!'

Row upon row of men were crammed together on narrow beds. White everywhere—walls, beds, sheets and covers. Peculiar noises. Groans and mumbles. Faces full of fear, confusion, an unknowing that didn't belong in the mind of a human.

'Here we are, now.' The nurse who had been working on reception leaned across the bed, straightened the sheets and blankets. 'You've got a visitor, Andy.'

'He has spoken to you, then?'

'He has that. Just a few words, but once it starts, as I'm sure you know, more often than not, it just flows back. There's no injury, so I reckon he'll be going home soon enough.'

'Wonderful!' Bea sat down on the edge of the bed. 'Andy, do you remember me? I nursed you at the hospital.'

He turned to face her, managed a weak smile. 'Yes. I remember your face. Yes.'

'Wonderful.' She took his hand and squeezed it. 'Do you remember this?' she said, as she held the photograph up to him.

He swallowed hard. Stared intently at the water-stained picture. Something jarred deep down in his stomach. Tangled around his heart. He gulped, sat upright, snatched the picture from her, stared. Visions, memories, clicked through his fractured mind. *Oh my God. Robbie. The picture was of him and his wife.* And as if that photograph had been a key, it unlocked his memory. All of it flooded back. They were terrifying; those pictures in his head, those memories, if that's what they were. It would be easier to take if they were just figments of his fragile imagination. Something made up. Inconsequential. But as they joined up, made sense, he knew that they weren't. This was his history. His doing.

'There's no rush,' Bea said. 'You just take your time. Get well.'

He gripped her hand, almost painfully. 'I've. Done. Something. Awful,' he said in gasps, as if the words themselves were painful to speak.

'Every man in here feels the same way. The best thing you can do is talk about it. Share it. And I'm listening.'

'No. You don't understand. It could be the end of me.'

'Andy, I'll not tell a soul. Shall we start with the photo?'

In his head he had the story. Fragments of it. Robbie hoisting him up, their flight. Fear. So much fear. The soldiers, an execution. Fear of that. That could be them. But then the water. The oar. Robbie gone. The blackness of it all. But the words wouldn't come. Only tears.

She smiled in that way that the best nurses have. That soft understanding. No judgement. Just a smile. A receptor for the pain that she could see was there as she dabbed his tears away.

Chapter 37
1919

~

With a last desperate snatch from beneath the water, Robbie's hand had met the oar; his fingers curled around it. He clung on tight. His face broke through the water. At last, a deep breath. Oxygen in his lungs. Survival. He would do this. He would survive. The oxygen fed his body. He could feel it pulsing through him as he searched through the blackness for the little boat, for Andy. But there was no sign of it. He spun around and again, treading water as best he could. No, nothing to see of it. He called. Listened. Nothing but the lurching of the sea.

He knew that if he were to have any chance of survival, he had to focus on getting himself to safety now, to land. It was there, in the distance, tantalizingly close, but so far away. He kicked as hard as he could, swimming towards land. He was exhausted and cold, but the thrashing of his legs kept the worst of the chill out. Kept his heart beating. Only the land didn't seem to be getting any closer. It was agonising. He could see it there, in front of him, but it wasn't being kind to him.

There was a wind in his face, water rising up in swells, so that the land, momentarily, disappeared and fear gripped at his belly. He rested, treading water, for a count of ten, then pushed on with all of his might for a minute. Ten then sixty, ten then sixty. Thank God for his gran teaching him to swim way back when.

What a memory that was! He allowed himself to drift with it. The water of the loch as cold as ice even though it was a summer's day. His gran was up to her thighs in the waters, cajoling, encouraging, holding his weight in the flat of her hands. Slowly, slowly, releasing him, letting go. He could feel it. The loss of her support, but he was still afloat. He was swimming. And it was the very best feeling in the world. His gran whooped and clapped. 'On you go, son. On you go!'

But now it was taking him, the sea, taking him home. Not to his home, to its. He could feel it calling and pulling at him. He didn't look down for fear of being sucked into its dark depths. It would have been so easy to give in to it, but that wasn't who he was. He shouted, 'I'll be damned if it ends now!' Water filled his mouth as he called. He choked and spluttered. Swam to his Gran.

A light! There, glinting on the swell. There and gone. There and gone. It was drawing closer, the beam of light widening, getting stronger. The sound of an engine shouting above the deafening cry of the sea.

He desperately waved his free arm as best he could, the other gripped the oar for all that he was worth. 'Over here!! Over here!!' It didn't matter now who it was, or what it was, other than an escape from this watery hell. *Mother of God, please see me!*

He didn't allow his gaze to drift from the boat, nor his voice to stop calling. The boat was coming his way. A shout. 'Hang on there. Just hang on.'

Oh, what a feeling, as they dragged him on board, soaked, bedraggled, hoarse, a shadow away from death. But he had been saved.

It was a fishing boat. A small affair. But it was immense to him. The gratitude he felt couldn't be expressed as he coughed and spluttered some more. A blanket was wrapped around him, and he was taken below deck. A tiny cabin, but an absolute sanctuary.

'We'll have you onshore in no time.'

'What the devil are you doing away out here, anyway?'

'I slipped, fell off the boat. Thought I was a goner, for sure, so I did. But, by Jesus, I caught hold of that oar and clung fast. What were the chances of you finding me in all of this, eh?'

'Someone's keeping an eye on you, I reckon.'

'Or I have the luck of the devil,' Robbie said with a grin.

'Yes, or that!'

'Where is it you're headed?' Robbie asked.

'We'll drop you off at Folkstone, then be on our way.'

'If you're going further north?'

'No, son. We're off eastward.'

'Folkstone it is then. Thank you.'

Before they bade him farewell, they handed a few coins to him—a collection they had made to help him on his way. He grinned at them, shook each of their hands. 'God bless you, each and every one.'

~

Robbie didn't know what to do when he stood on solid ground once more. His body swayed as it tried to find its land-legs again. Soldiers carrying kitbags, civilians walking to and fro. Everyone with a purpose, it seemed. But as he looked more carefully, focused in on individual people, rather than a mass of humanity, he could see others like him. Lost. Unsure. This was an entirely different world from the one he had left. A place busy with quasi normality. Yes, there were signs of what had happened—scarred buildings, debris, scarred people—but it was so different to everything

160

that had consumed him over the past two years.

He felt a kinship towards the other soldiers, but it wasn't one he wanted to pursue, to get involved with. Better to watch from a distance; to make sense of it all, but there wasn't sense to be made of any of this. He knew that. It sickened him. That it had happened at all, that he had been a part of it, that he had taken human life.

Snap out of it, man. This'll do you not one bit of good! He listened to himself, lifted his head and his demeanour. Smiled, because that was what he did. Smiled at the world. Even now.

Chapter 38
1919

~

Lizzie was on tenterhooks. She kept her eyes peeled, her step firm, as she made her way to Hannah's. A small part of her enjoyed the sneaking, the playing the part of a spy, a criminal. It was just her, Lizzie, who, other than distributing some leaflets and going on marches, had never done anything untoward. And here she was, checking for a tail. It was all quite exciting. Well, it might have been if the situation hadn't been so dire.

She took a final surreptitious glance left and right before dipping into Hannah's stair. Again, she paused and listened, just in case. No. There was no tail. She hurried up the three flights of stairs and knocked on the door.

Hannah answered and grinned. 'Well, come away in, why don't you?' She paused, listened, before closing the door.

'I was careful,' Lizzie said. 'No tail.'

'It's not that I don't trust you, it's simply a habit. Come, come.' She led the way to the kitchen and put the kettle on the stove. 'You'll have tea?'

'Yes please.'

They sat in silence until it was broken by the whistle of boiling water. That peculiar time in between thought and expectation. A time when nothing seems appropriate but silence and patience.

'Brian, Dave? Tea?'

'Aye, grand.'

They sat around the kitchen table, listening with

interest to Lizzie's tale of Fotheringale's visit.

'He doesn't know, does he?' Hannah asked.

'It felt like he had an idea; that he was checking up on me, on the shop. But would it really matter now? I mean, Connie's cleared and safe, isn't she?'

'Yes. To all intents and purposes. But that man is a law unto himself. The way he marched in here and rifled through my things. Outrageous!'

'You know, I reckon it's nothing. Just a bully being a bully,' Brian said.

'So, I can relax, then?'

'I wouldn't say that. Be on your guard, but don't worry!'

'How is that even possible?'

Hannah shrugged. 'It's just a way of life these days. You know, if you want out; if you want to step back a bit, that's just fine.'

'I'll be damned if I'll let him intimidate me like that! No! There's such a buzz about the place now. I can feel it. Revolution!' she called, raising her tea.

They lifted their mugs in reply. 'To revolution,' they called in unison, and it felt so very good.

'Right! Work to be done!' Hannah declared as she started the printing press up again.

Lizzie laughed. 'I'll be getting back to the shop.'

'Can I give you a new supply?' Hannah asked, shuffling some leaflets into a neat bundle and looking expectantly in Lizzie's direction. 'God, I miss Robbie. For this,' she said, raising the leaflets. 'And for that smile, that way of his that refused to allow anything to dampen his spirits, to dampen anyone's spirits. So wrong. So very, very wrong!'

'Yes. He leaves a gaping wound.'

'And Mhairi?'

'I don't know anything, but Connie should be there by now. I don't expect much. Mhairi must have been going through absolute hell. And now the news about Rosie. How is she meant to cope with that?'

Chapter 39
1919

~∾~

Connie had to be at her best for this visit with Mhairi, if a meeting in gaol could be called such a thing. The connotations around visiting a friend were joyous, expectant, a gathering of people, a celebration. This was as far from that as one could imagine. But still, an effort had to be made. A sleepless night hadn't helped, but she did her best. A smudge of foundation, some powder and blusher, a layer of lipstick. She grimaced at the reflection staring back at her.

It was peculiar how the scar had changed with her perception of life. It had diminished alongside her growing confidence, and that was all down to Mhairi. She no longer saw a face to keep hidden, to be ashamed of. No. This was a sign of survival, and she was proud of it. She held her head high as she walked onto the street. A light drizzle made everything grey and bleak; the buildings, the sky, even the very air itself. It felt fitting. She opened her umbrella and headed up the hill.

She had been expecting what she thought was the worst, but her expectations were shadowed by such a very long way. Mhairi looked like a different person. Her skin was grey, her face gaunt, her hair cut in a rough style more befitting a man, her eyes held no sparkle.

'Oh, Mhairi, what have they done to you?'

Mhairi stared, cried silently. She wiped at her face with the sleeve of her prison dress. It was coarse and stained. 'Connie? Is this real?'

'Yes. Yes, it is. How...how are you?' What a stupid question! Clearly her beloved friend was in an appalling condition.

Mhairi managed a sardonic smile. 'Aye, grand. Just grand.'

'You should never...he should...oh my God, how I loathe my father!'

'He's no my favourite the now, either.'

Even now, Mhairi held on to that caustic sense of humour. It made Connie smile.

'You have quite the reputation now. Comrades are demanding your release, at least your transfer to Glasgow. We have marched for you. Placards and everything!'

'That's good, but it won't come to anything. You know that, right?'

'Times are changing. You never know.'

'And Rosie? I was hoping, maybe, to see her, at least.'

Connie's head dropped at those words; at the painful look of tense, desperate, expectation written on Mhairi's face.

'What? What is it? What's the matter?'

'I'm so sorry. I hadn't wanted to tell you. Not like this.' Her words spilled onto the floor with her gaze.

'Tell me what, Connie?'

Connie lifted her head up slowly, until eyes met eyes. 'She's gone, Mhairi. Adopted.'

'But...but naw. How could they? They can't do that She's mine! Mine an Robbie's!'

'I'm so sorry. We tried everything. Well, Hannah did. She knows so many people. But there is nothing more to be done.'

'Oh, aye there is! I'm getting out of here, and I'm

166

fetching her back! My wee wean. Mine!'

'There is no way to find her, Mhairi. She has a new family now. She belongs to someone else.'

'How could you let it happen? You're her godmother. You're meant to protect her!'

'I'm so sorry. I—'

'Get out! Leave! Now!' Mhairi screeched. Something had changed in her. Something had fallen from her soul. She clawed at her face. Droplets of blood.

The guards came, restrained her, dragged her back to the cell.

Mhairi could hear the screams of her tormented soul echoing against the cold concrete walls. But they were distant somehow. Separate from her. Dissipating now. Silence.

Connie waited; her mouth open, unsure. She had known that it would be awful, but there were no words for this. She turned and left it all behind her; walked out to the street and looked up at the prison feeling utterly useless. No, feeling like a criminal.

Despite the drizzle seeping through her clothes, she walked on through streets she didn't know. On and on, until darkness fell. She was so cold, soaked through, despite the umbrella, and now far from anything that she recognised. She had walked around Arthur's Seat and found herself sitting by the still dark waters of St Margaret's Loch. She sat there, hugging her knees, in the coldest, most desolate mood she had ever encountered. The city seemed far away now. The night was swallowing everything. It didn't matter. It suited her mood. *No. I shall not give up like this. There must be something I can do. I am free. I have contacts. This has not ended!*

167

She stood up and walked to the edge of the water which seemed to sink vertically down to something far below. A darkness. She paused, stared out at it all, beyond it all. She wondered, briefly, what had become of that soldier she had met on the train. He seemed to be such a tortured soul. A shiver crept up her spine. She turned her thoughts back to Mhairi. 'What am I to do?' she said into the nothingness.

'Nothing drastic, I hope.'

She jumped in alarm. Looked behind her to where the voice had come from. It was that soldier! How the devil? He stepped forward and stood beside her, no longer in uniform.

'We meet again,' he said, his voice low and distant.

'I—um, sorry. I didn't recognise you.'

'Easily done. No uniform. Ditched it as soon as I could. Anything that drags me back to that hell—' He shook his head, dismissing the images, the thoughts. Words and feelings that he didn't want to share. 'It seems that you have problems of your own.'

'Huge insurmountable ones. Yes!'

'Come, let's talk, you and I.'

'But I—'

'Please? By way of an apology for my previous appalling behaviour.'

She didn't know why, but she was drawn to this stranger. There was a feeling to him. Something almost familiar, but not. It was very peculiar but intriguing. She went against everything she had been taught, every warning given to a girl, to a young woman, and walked off with him into the night.

Chapter 40
1919

∾

Andy might not have been fully recovered, but he was deemed well enough to be released and his bed was required for someone in greater need.

'You'll be looking forward to that then. Getting home,' Bea said. 'You make sure and leave a note of your address and I'll pop by if I get the chance.'

He hadn't told her that he had no intention of going home. Not yet. He didn't feel ready in his head to slip back into that normality. And he had no idea of what might be waiting for him there. Of what his family might have been told. That he was dead? That he was a deserter? That they should report him to the police should he return? No. Not yet. He had to know more first, be something of the man they knew. Be safe. And he had to try and find that girl, Mhairi, and her and Robbie's child. He had made a promise, and it had to be kept. Tomorrow, at dawn, he would leave and make his way to Glasgow.

He woke before dawn and readied himself. Bea had brought him some civilian clothes. A skin shed. And it felt good. He could breathe again in this skin. In the pocket of his new shirt, she had slipped her address. Yes, it was against the rules, but she didn't care. Not this time. There was something about this young man; something deep and troubled. Perhaps she could help somehow.

A voice trickled through the silent ward. Someone he recognised. No, that couldn't be. He pricked his ears.

Nothing. It must have been a trick of the mind. He found himself wondering if it would ever stop; that blurred line between reality and imagination. Would he ever just be normal again. A functioning man who could cope with the world. Who could step out without fear.

He had folded his old uniform up and tied it with his belt. It would be ditched as soon as he walked through those doors. He nodded his farewell to the matron on duty.

'You look after yourself now,' she said.

'Thank you.'

The blast of cold morning air that hit him as he walked down the steps was quite wonderful. It might have been polluted and smoky; a fog wrapping itself around the streets, but it was a freedom of sorts. An escape from it all. So far, he was okay. Nothing untoward had happened. Surely it wouldn't now. He shoved his old uniform into a litter bin with more effort than was needed. It was another cleansing. A final act. The war was over. He was a civilian.

A shout broke through the morning hush. 'Andy? Andy man, is that you?'

His instinct was to run, but he knew that voice. He turned and was met by the most wonderful grin. Robbie!

They ran to each other and bounced chests, embraced. It didn't matter if it wasn't the done thing. It didn't matter that they were drawing stares from the few souls out on the streets.

Andy thumped Robbie on the back, over and over. He pulled back. They held each other's shoulders, each other's stares.

'By Jesus man, is it good to see you?' Robbie said.

'You were dead...'

'Aye, well, it'll take more than a wee bit water to put an end to me.'

Andy laughed. 'How did you find me?'

'A few questions to the right people. It wasn't that hard, although I wasn't thinking it would be this easy either! Only tried a couple of other places for sick bastards before I got to this one.'

Andy laughed, louder this time, his head thrown back in a wonderful release. The tension that had been strangling him seemed to be letting go, his shoulders freeing. He slapped Robbie's shoulder.

'Aye, well—'

They strode along the pavement in their own private bubble. No-one else was there. Nothing else was going on. It was just them. Arms around each other like a couple of lovers. They stopped at the riverside.

'We need to be getting you some civvies,' Andy said, tugging at Robbie's uniform.

Robbie looked down at himself, laughed. 'Aye. Best get rid, eh?'

There were returned soldiers everywhere. Men with awful scars, both visible and not. There was little or no help for them. No jobs to come home to. No support. It felt like they had fought for nothing. They had certainly returned to it. Nothing!

Robbie had persuaded Andy to come with him to Glasgow, not that much persuasion had been needed.

'There's plenty folk up there who'll put up a fight for us. You'll see.'

～～

It was a wonderful thing to climb those tenement stairs, to knock on that door, to have it opened by

171

Hannah. A step back into that old life. That old person.

Hannah screeched, with an uncustomary loss of cool, and threw her arms around Robbie. 'We thought you were dead. My God. Is it really you?'

'Aye, Hannah, it's me all right. A bit the worse for wear, but me!' He grinned the way that only he could. 'And this here is my old mate, Andy.'

'Delighted Andy!'

Robbie and Hannah locked arms and huddled close together. 'Robbie my wee brother who's come back from the dead! I can't—' She sniffed. An uncharacteristic swell of emotion took over. For once she didn't try to hide it, didn't swallow it down. She allowed herself to cry.

'Oh, look at you, now. There's no need for that,' Robbie said.

*Oh God, Robbie. Yes, there is...*She wiped the tears away with the sleeve of her shirt and ushered them into the kitchen. He would ask, and she would have to tell him. It would be awful. So very awful.

Andy's eyes took in the posters, the feel of the place. It was like nothing he had ever experienced.

Robbie's eyes and ears were straining. His stance said it all. That expectation but a creeping fear. Something was wrong. 'Where are they, then? My bonnie lassies?'

Hannah closed her eyes, her head fell. 'Oh Robbie.'

'What? What the hell has happened?'

Hannah fought to get the words out. It was so very hard.

Robbie listened as the story unfolded. A darkness crept over him; threatened to smother him. 'I'll kill that bastard!' he whispered.

'Oh, Robbie.'

'It's nothing to me now. Killing. It's as easy as breathing. He's mine. I'm killing him.'

'And I'm helping!' Andy said.

'I understand but think about this. Mhairi is still here, and she needs you now more than ever. Killing that excuse of a man might be a pleasure, but it would be wrong. Right now, it would be wrong.'

Chapter 41
1919

∼

Mhairi came-to strapped down to a cold metal bed; her arms wrapped tight around her in a straitjacket. She was quiet now. Her brain was silent. Numbed. The world was a cold black hole in which she was existing. But she was nothing.

'That's more like it. You hush now. You don't want things to get worse, do you?'

The guard untied her, set a bowl of porridge down. 'You eat this, and behave yourself, and I'll take you back to your cell.' He stood against the door; arms crossed in front of a puffed-out chest and watched.

Mhairi's hands were trembling. She gripped one with the other in an attempt to control the shaking; to lift spoon to mouth. Too much was spilling. It had to be done. She fought for control of her body. She had to get through this. Minute by minute, day by day, she had to find a way to get through this.

I'll come find you, my sweet angel. Yer mammie'll come an find you.

Connie had seldom met a man with whom she could relax like that. She had always been wary, withdrawn. Perhaps it was down to her father and his dominance. His bullying. Of course, there were Robbie and the comrades, but no-one on a personal level. Not like this. This stranger had taken her hand, and she had allowed it. She imagined the chastisement of her father. *"Most unbecoming! Whatever will people think?"* She smiled at the thought of his expression, his distaste.

They had walked slowly and carefully back across Holyrood Park. There was scant light there and each step had to be carefully placed.

Little had been said between them but there was a quiet easiness. It was such a relief for him to feel that silence was all right. It didn't matter that he could find no words. Sometimes he simply lost the power of speech these days. His head swarmed with such awful visions, such appalling memories that he shouldn't have allowed. That he should have prevented. So much guilt. And sometimes it was impossible to rise above. To do anything else. He had to let it be, to wait until it had passed. Still, he wondered, *what must she think of me?*

When they reached the bottom of the Royal Mile, he forced himself to speak. 'You know, I don't even know your name,' he said. He wanted to add, *'and yet, I feel like I have known you all of my life,'* but the words remained silent, dormant in his head.

She smiled up at him. 'Connie.'

His reply should have been *'Of course it is! If I had to guess I would have said "Connie" right off the bat!'*

She would have smiled and said, *'Silly!'*

'No. God's honest truth.'

'What is?'

Somehow his reply had crept out, as if the words had lives of their own. They were a being. A thing apart from him. He felt himself blush, but it was dark. She wouldn't know.

'Nothing. I didn't mean—my apologies.' He squeezed her hand and hoped it would be the end of the matter.

Thankfully it was.

'I think that you should tell me yours. It's only fair!'

'Yes, of course. Charles. Charlie to my friends.'

'Then, as we are now firm friends, I shall call you Charlie.'

The man in his head said, *'I do hope that we are a little more than that. Do you believe in love at first sight? No. Don't answer. It would spoil everything, absolutely everything, if you were to say no, and I couldn't bear it. I really couldn't!'*

'Splendid,' he said. He pulled her gloved hand to his mouth and kissed it. 'Dearest Connie.'

He stopped. Took a deep breath. She was still there. Really there, and he had spoken to her. This had been real. All of this was real.

She didn't quite know what to make of any of this, of him. He was, well, peculiar. A part of him seemed to be missing, but there was a feeling between them. Something that gave her butterflies and made her swoon ever so slightly.

Perhaps he was simply as damaged as she, and they had found each other for a reason. Were such things possible? She had read about them in her books. An immediate love that transcended everything else. That bound two people together in the most unlikely of ways. It made her think of Mhairi and Robbie. That unlikely meeting, a series of coincidences, or fate, or this wonderful thing for which we have no words. This magic.

Dear God. Poor, poor Mhairi! Here Connie was having this wonderfully flirtatious encounter with a handsome stranger. And there was Mhairi. Locked up in that awful place. Her husband gone. Her child taken. Her life torn apart by Connie's own father.

The wave of guilt made her step falter. A tear

escaped.

'Whatever is it?' Charlie pulled her close and she didn't resist. 'Tell me,' he whispered.

She told him through a quiet, broken voice as their footsteps echoed along the empty cobbles of the Royal Mile. Her words were swept between the tall grey tenements and into the night. An easing of her pain.

∼

Mhairi lay in her cell, trying to tune out the noise of her fellow prisoners. It was never quiet in that place. Always someone crying, or cursing, or whispering. The coughs and wheezes of strangers. The harsh steps of the guards. The jangle of keys.

The clouds had suddenly parted. A sliver of silver moon cast itself across the wall of her cell. She reached up, felt it on her fingers. Felt it in her soul. 'You and me are under that same moon, Rosie. Can you feel me? Can you?'

Chapter 42
1919

∽

Lizzie was pottering about in her shop, not doing much at all. Her mind was far away, but she deemed it best to at least try and keep busy. Connie would have seen Mhairi. Mhairi would know about Rosie and her heart would be broken. Lizzie was distracted by a familiar tap at the back door. She held her breath. No-one else knocked like that! A friendly rat-a-tat-tat-tat, rat-a-tat-tat-tat. Almost a song.

She ran to the back door and opened it, hoping but not truly believing. The feeling that swept through her when she saw it really was him was wonderfully overpowering. 'Robbie!' she cried, as she threw her arms wide and wrapped them around him. That familiar laugh. That lightness.

'Lizzie, if you don't unwrap me, you'll squeeze the life out of me, so you will!'

'Oh, I make no excuses. None at all!' She squeezed even tighter, before letting go and stepping back, her hands still on his shoulders, as if she were frightened to let go. 'Is it really you?'

'Aye, none other.' He grinned. 'Lizzie, this here is Andy. My fellow deserter.' Both men laughed, albeit sardonically.

'Well, good for you!' She shook Andy's hand. 'Good for you. The pair of you look like you could use a proper bowl of soup! Or a drink? Which is it to be? Come in, come in.'

'Soup would be just grand, but I'm keeping a clear

178

head until this is put to rights. There was no believing it when Hannah told me. What a piece of—'

Andy sat quietly and took it all in. These people. This place. It was hard to believe what his world had been like just a few days ago, and now this was his life. He would do anything for Robbie, and, by proxy, for his people too.

Bellies full, and stories told, a tiredness swept through the room and took hold of Robbie and Andy. Lizzie could have sat up all night, wallowing in this wonderfulness, but she could read them.

'You'll stay here, of course,' she said. 'The both of you,' she added, glancing from one to the other. 'And tomorrow we'll start to put your world back together again.' She stood up, straightened her skirt, smiled. 'Mhairi was sleeping in my old room. You'll take that, of course.'

'I'd just as easy curl up on the couch,' Robbie said. 'The places we've slept, or, at least, lain down to sleep. Mud and grime, death and—' He stopped mid-sentence, shook the memory out. What use was it now? None at all.

'Nonsense! I won't hear of it! Besides, I couldn't quite bring myself to move back into the bedroom after the arrest. It just felt...wrong. So, you'll do as you're told in my house and take the bedroom! There are two mattresses on the bed. We can slide one onto the floor for Andy here. Will that do?'

'That will more than do. What a woman you are! If I hadn't met my Mhairi...well.'

She slapped his arm, softly. 'You fool, you. But I love you all the same.'

'See? The woman, she loves me,' he said to Andy,

grinning.

'Off to bed with you!'

There was no silence, even at this hour. Night had long fallen, folk off to their beds, but still the creaking of this old building, the rattle of its pipes, the whistle of the wind, the patter of some stranger's footsteps out on the pavement, a shout, a whisper, a cry.

Robbie peeled back the covers. Breathed deeply. Inhaled the scent of Mhairi, surrounded himself in the essence of her. He stroked the dent where she had once lain, lay softly in it. He was desperate to see her, touch her, hold her. But that had to wait until he had arranged a visit. He didn't know how easy that would be. Pieces of her rocked him to sleep, and it was achingly beautiful.

Andy's head was full of a confusion. An awful confusion. Daytime wasn't so bad. He could mostly control it then—this madness—but at night, when there was nothing else, it took over again and he was unable to do anything about any of it. The visions, the sounds. They were all so real right there in his head. The sound of his own scream woke him up. He scratched at his head, his face, and called out. 'Robbie!'

Robbie jumped out of bed, crouched down beside Andy, took a hold of his hands, pulled them away from his face. 'Andy, lad, it's okay. I'm right here and you're safe. It's okay.'

The door opened a crack. 'Are you all right in there?' Lizzie asked.

'Aye. As good as,' Robbie answered. 'It's the terrors. They still visit him of a night.'

Andy was rocking back and forth now, crying. Calmer. Stilling.

180

'The poor soul. Can I do anything?'

'He'll be right. You go back to your bed.'

She stood silently watching the outline of them in the moonlight. Two men wrapped as one. The constant whisper. 'It's all right. You're all right, Andy son. You're all right.'

She couldn't imagine the hell they must have been through, and she was selfishly glad of it. What was wrong with people? How could they do this to each other?

Chapter 43
1919

∼≈∼

Mhairi felt herself hardening, becoming someone else. If she were to be of any use at all she had to pull herself together. She had to be strong for her Rosie. There was no point in fighting against any of this. She could see that now. *Bide your time, Mhairi. Bide your time.*

There was no relief in this hellhole. The place stank, as did the inmates; lice crawled and fleas bit. It was peculiar, because outside it was quite beautiful. The building looked more like a castle than a gaol. Turrets and towers on a site so spectacular as to look out upon all of Edinburgh. Perhaps that was just another layer to the punishment? The beauty of what they could no longer be a part of. Beyond was Arthur's Seat standing monolithic and grand like a beast in the centre of the city, the castle itself, the cobbles of the Royal Mile, Holyrood Palace and its gardens. So much beauty, and all denied.

She had wanted to at least read, to keep her mind alive and somewhere else. But even that had been denied her. The worst thing she could do was dwell on memories. They hurt too much. Until she was able to do something about them, they hurt too much. And that's where madness lay.

And now she had given herself another layer of guilt. Connie, who hadn't deserved that outcry. She wanted to apologise, to hold her hands and say that she didn't mean it. But no, that would be cast aside as well. No regrets, no dwelling on past mistakes. She had to be strong. She had to get through this. It was everything.

～

It was almost dawn by the time Connie and Charlie reached the hotel. A distant glinting glow in the sky as the sun attempted to break through streaks of grey cloud. They stood in the entrance. He took her hands in his.

'I would be so very happy if you could stay for just one more day. We have such a lot to learn about each other. It feels to me like parting now would be nothing less than a sin,' Charlie said.

Connie smiled. 'I would like that, and I have unfinished business up there.' She nodded towards the gaol standing cold and dark in the distance. 'It simply cannot be left like this.'

'Oh, so it is not me that keeps you then. My heart is breaking!'

She laughed at the puppy-dog face he had pulled. 'It is a little bit you, but somewhat more, Mhairi.'

'Of course! I was only teasing. You are staying, then?'

'I shall book one more night.'

'Wonderful.'

'Now, I need to sleep, as do you.'

'I am not sure that I can. At what time shall we meet? Perhaps you will allow me to take you for dinner.'

She smiled up at him. 'Yes, I would like that. Shall we say six o'clock?'

'I will be here at six then. Goodnight. Or rather, good morning!'

Connie fell back onto her sumptuous bed feeling quite wonderful. Sleep came instantly.

Charlie paced his room trying to fight off the demons which visited him. He poured himself a large whisky,

183

and another, and another. It dulled the pain, but didn't take it away. He slumped down on his bed, his head in his hands, and wept. 'I am so very sorry. Forgive me. Dear God, forgive me!'

Connie had used her best charms to secure another visit to the gaol. A smile and a slip of a note. A raised eyebrow. Another note. A nod.

'On you come then. This'll get you ten minutes. No more.'

'Thank you. I am indebted to you.'

'Aye.'

~

'Connie! I'm sorry. It was...it was too much for me,' Mhairi said instantly on seeing Connie.

'Of course it was. No more need be said on the matter. What we do need to talk about is getting you out of this place.'

'That's no gonna happen, is it? Best face up to that.'

'It is not only my father who carries some sway. And I am not afraid to face him!'

'But he might—'

Connie held her hand up. 'I will not be afraid of my own father. Not anymore.'

They hadn't been able to come up with any solutions, any way out of this, but their friendship had been confirmed once more. That was enough for now, at least it was for Connie. Mhairi needed more, but she knew that she would have to wait.

~

'How did it go?' Charlie asked as they sat down to dinner.

'It was awful,' Connie replied, her head cast down as

if a great weight sat upon it.

He stretched across the crisp linen tablecloth and lifted her chin with his finger. The silver cutlery chinked beneath his outstretched arm. His head cocked in question.

She managed a smile. 'Well, our friendship has held strong, but this—' She gestured around the grand dining room with its oak tables and immense windows draped in velvet, the fine porcelain plates and exquisite silver cutlery. The dignified hustle and bustle of upper-class life. 'It feels so wrong that I am here and she— well, she is there, in hell.'

'Then we shall go elsewhere!' He took her instead to a small tavern where they drank beer and ate homemade pies. There was a boisterous revelry about the place. 'Better?' he asked.

The soft smile that had returned to her face was all the answer he needed.

Chapter 44
1919

〜

Connie and Charlie parted company the following morning at Waverley Station with heavy hearts and promises of future visits. How peculiar that in two short days her world had changed so completely. Was she being foolish? As irresponsible as her father believed her to be? Perhaps, but it didn't matter. Charlie made her feel happy, complete, and it was quite wonderful.

As the train back to Glasgow rumbled along the tracks Connie's thoughts flitted between Mhairi and Charlie. Such a contrast. Pain at completely opposite ends of the spectrum. One awful, from a place so dark as to be previously unimaginable; the other of such promise, unexpected, beautiful.

As the train pulled in to Glasgow she was full of mixed emotions. This was her home, and she was happy to be here, but her heart had been left behind. She hailed a cab that took her to Lizzie's. On the way she passed some posters demanding Mhairi's release. Insisting on her innocence, the treachery of her accuser. *My father. Dear God. My father!* Connie's family was now a chosen one: Mhairi, Lizzie, and Hannah her sisters, if not in name, certainly in heart. She didn't yet know what part Charlie would play in this family, but it felt significant and very exciting.

She stepped out of the carriage, refusing the help of the driver. 'I can manage quite well myself, thank you,' she said, politely enough, but with a slight edge to it. An insistence. *I will not be what is expected of me.* Glasgow was grey and dreich, but it wasn't the weather that made the place. She scooped her leather bag up and hurried down the steps, then along the little path that led to the back of Lizzie's shop. She paused, her hand on the doorknob. Her heart skipped a beat at the voice she heard from the other side. That was Robbie! That unique mix of Scottish and Irish, that hint of laughter to each word. There could be no doubt. None at all! She threw the door open, almost causing it to bounce back off its hinges.

'Dear God! Is it really you?' Connie squealed.

'Aye, it is, that!'

They embraced briefly. There was a tension. An expectation. A need to know.

'So?' he said.

'We were expecting you yesterday. What happened?' Lizzie asked.

Connie sat down with sigh. 'Oh, that can wait. It was quite wonderful, but it can wait.' She turned to Robbie, took his hands in hers. 'I won't lie to you Robbie. Life has not been kind to Mhairi in your absence.'

They all listened intently, as Connie explained as well as she could.

Questions exhausted. As many answers as possible given. A final calming sentence.

'But she has you now, Robbie, and that will be quite wonderful for her.'

'Aye, she always has me, right enough. But she's there an I'm here an it's all wrong.' He shook his head, turned away. 'So wrong,' he whispered to the floor. He stood up, brushed himself down. 'I'm off out for a bit. Work to be done. Andy?' he said, as he scooped up a pile of leaflets

187

and slipped them into his satchel.

Connie waited until the door had closed behind them and Robbie and Andy's footsteps could no longer be heard, before she told her story about the new man in her life. It would have been wrong to be talking of such happiness when Robbie was so distraught.

'You'll meet him soon, of course. He has promised a visit before the end of the month.'

'It really is serious, then?' Lizzie asked.

'Totally, completely, and utterly. I am in love!' She pulled her hands to her chest and grinned like a schoolgirl. 'Can you believe it?'

'I think it's quite wonderful, but so quick. Are you sure?'

'Oh, don't spoil it for me. Who knows what might happen, but for now I am quite giddy with love, and it is delightful!'

'You deserve it, Connie, my love. Just—well, just be careful.'

Connie stared, bit back the disappointment she felt at being spoken to like that; like she was somehow less capable than everyone else. Would it ever leave her?

～

Robbie and Andy sat themselves down on a bench in George Square. This was still the meeting place for political discourse, for stopping and chatting and raising awareness. Raising hope. There were always eyes on: spies, infiltrators. Moreso now since Bloody Friday. That wasn't going to be allowed to happen again if the government could prevent it. Officialdom lurked, trying not to appear so to the general populace. But experience had taught Robbie how to spot them easily enough and Andy was learning fast. Lingering looks

188

broken by an abrupt glance away, their attention drawn by nothing. Clothes a wee bit too smart, too clean, like they'd been hanging in a decent wardrobe, in a decent house. *Aye, we see you!*

Robbie and Andy would veer away, casually; their attention caught by that same nothingness. They would exchange meaningless chatter, empty laughter.

Chapter 45
1919

~

A letter had arrived for Connie. It was from Charlie, and it told of how he felt, how his world had changed since their meeting, how much he missed her, and the confirmation that he would visit the following weekend. She was beside herself with excitement.

'You will adore him, I am sure,' she said to Hannah, her eyes holding that new sparkle, that zest for life.

'I have yet to meet a man I adore,' Hannah said disdainfully. 'Robbie, I love, of course, and I have the greatest respect for Brian and Dave and our comrades, but adore? I think that is beyond me, Connie!' She threw her head back and laughed.

'Just you wait! You'll see.'

~

Connie had spent all morning making herself ready, then rethinking it; stepping in and out of clothes, trying different hats, different shoes, different pieces of jewellery. Too much. Too little. Finally, she settled on a plain, but pretty, two-piece suit in a soft purple—the skirt fashionably just below the knees—with a cloche hat to match. She wrapped a string of pearls around her neck, clipped a subtle brooch to her lapel and twirled in front of the mirror. She had decided that she should appear normal. Not dressed up like somebody she wasn't. This was perfect.

She had hummed and hawed about whether to meet him at the station on her own, or with company. Company would be nice, but, again, not the right thing to do. She was becoming a strong independent woman, and that was how she would present herself.

By the time she stepped into the taxi carriage her nerves were ablaze. The journey was almost intolerably fraught. She stepped into the station with her lambskin coat wrapped tightly around her—a feeling of security—her head held high, her breath as controlled as she could manage. He would be arriving right there, any minute! The clamour of the train as it drew into the station. The hiss of the steam. The screech of the brakes. Inside Connie was squealing too, but she kept it deep down as she scoured the heads descending from the train.

He wasn't there, and he wasn't there, and she began to think that he had changed his mind. Her shoulders slumped with her disappointment, but she forced her head to remain high, confident.

It seemed that everyone had alighted and there was no sign of him. She walked along the length of the train, peering in the windows, just to make sure. Perhaps he had become embroiled in a conversation. Perhaps he was awaiting luggage. She waited until it was obvious that he simply wasn't there. What a fool she was. What an absolute fool!

She turned to leave, a scowl for the passengers who were hugging and being hugged, crowding the station, getting in her way with their smiles and suitcases. She wished that the platform could swallow her up. It must be so very apparent to all and sundry what had happened. She had been stood up, let down, made a complete and utter fool of.

She kept her head down now as she left the station and all of its bustle behind her. A cab was sitting waiting, but she ignored it. A slow walk home would give her time to rid herself of this horrible feeling. A chance to cast it off into the grey skies.

When she reached Lizzie's, it was uncommonly empty. She made her way up to the little box room that had become hers and tossed her bonnet onto the bed, stamped her foot. 'Am I not allowed one tiny piece of happiness? Is that too much to ask?' she said to the mirror as she unclipped her hair and shook it free. She stared at herself, focused on that scar, ran her fingertips across it. 'Why would it be any different?' she whispered.

Lizzie returned soon enough with Hannah. They had been handing out leaflets to the Saturday crowds. Celtic had been playing at Parkhead and that meant thousands of possible sympathisers. A working-class sport and a working-class struggle. It was always a good bet. As soon as they saw Connie they sensed that nothing should be said.

'I don't know about you, but I feel in need of a gin. To hang with the early hour!' Lizzie said. 'Hannah? Connie?'

Hannah kicked her boots off and slumped into the armchair. 'I could murder one! But there is work to be done. I'll have one and then be off.'

'So could I,' Connie added, her voice quiet and subdued, a scowl to her face.

Hannah and Lizzie had settled into stories of whom they had chatted with, the reception they had been given, the enjoyment of being in amongst such a throng of people of a similar mindset. It helped that Celtic had won!

Connie was glad of the distraction and of the

empathy of her family. Nothing was said, but the feeling was there. They cared.

'Did you hear that?' Hannah asked.

'No. What?' Lizzie said.

'It sounded like a knock at the shop door.'

'Well, it's the wrong door for anyone we know to be knocking at. Best ignored, I think,' Lizzie said with that customary shake of her blond curls.

'Unless—' Connie leapt up.

Hannah and Lizzie exchanged concerned glances.

'Refills anyone?' Lizzie asked.

There was little point in any attempt at distraction. Connie was gone. She rushed through the shop, almost tripping over her own feet. There, through the glass of the front door, that distinctive figure. It was him! Charlie! She was quite sure of it. But her hair was a mess. She was a mess. To hang with it! The bell chimed as she opened the door, her heart in her mouth.

'Darling Connie! I am so very sorry! I missed the blasted train. Am I forgiven?'

She threw her arms around his waist and held on for all that she was worth. 'I thought—oh, it doesn't matter what I thought.'

'Can I breathe? Please?'

She laughed, released him, stepped back. 'I look absolutely frightful!'

'You could never!'

She took his hand and led him through the rows of books. His eyes scanned it all briefly but returned to her. He felt like he was the luckiest man alive.

Hannah left through the back door, a hug for Lizzie, and a call of farewell to Connie, that went unheard.

Chapter 46
1919

Robbie, at last, was to have that visit with Mhairi. As he walked up the hill to the gaol his heart was full of so much anger towards the man who had put her there; his head thumping with the hurt he had caused. But he was about to see her. His Mhairi. And that had to be pulled to the fore. He had to be full of nothing but love. Hard as it was, he swallowed it all down, picked his head up, and smiled at the world. As he walked in, the horror of the place made him wince. *Hide it, Robbie.* The stench and the misery bit at him. *Hide it deep down,* he told himself. And there she was. His beautiful girl. She could never be anything else to him. Beautiful.

'Robbie,' she whispered through a stream of tears. 'You were dead. They told me you were dead.'

He wrapped her up in his arms, his tears falling on her neck.

'It'll take more than an army to kill me, so it will.'

She smiled. Robbie.

'Break it up, now! None of that!' the warder said. 'It's against the rules.'

They pulled apart and stared at each other, both seeing the person they had been before, untouched by the horror, the pain, the awfulness of their recent lives.

'I'll get him, Mhairi. I promise you that,' he said when the all too brief visit came to an end. 'But first we have to get you out, get our little Rosie back. Get it sorted.'

The pain of parting was gut wrenching and deep for both of them.

He had visited Mhairi as often as was allowed, despite the difficulty, despite the pain he felt when he left her there. But it was something so hard to come to terms with. To rise above. He buried himself in work, helping Hannah, shouting about injustice, about Mhairi. Petitions were delivered, and finally, a change of prison had been agreed upon. Mhairi had not been released, but she had been moved to Glasgow. That was something, at least. The conditions were slightly better, the visits easier, more frequent. It felt as if they were, at least, breathing the same air. Whispers could be carried from one to the other.

Robbie and Andy spent most of their days at Hannah's or out leafletting. Keeping busy was the way to get through for both of them. They picked up odd jobs when they could, though they were few and far between. If it hadn't been for the kindness and help of Hannah and her friends, they would not have been able to support themselves.

'And how is Mhairi?' Hannah asked.

'Ach, you know her. She could put a smile on a paper bag, that one, but there's no disguising what's sitting there behind her eyes.' He shook his head. 'I feel like such a failure.'

Hannah nudged him. 'And that smile of yours can open a thousand hearts. Come on. We have work to do.'

Andy had learned the art of the printing press and was churning out copies of their paper. Stories about the shameful housing, the lack of jobs, the poverty of this place and every other town and city across the country. And, of course, Mhairi. Sometimes just a line or two, but she was mentioned in every issue, alongside

195

every other wrongly imprisoned activist, desperate parents, hungry children. What were they to do other than steal? And Mhairi hadn't even done that!

It was good to see Andy working like this; his mind taken off his own internal horrors. He was walking taller, talking that bit more easily. Sleep remained broken by nightmares. He had less control over that. The demons would creep back in when his guard was down, but that aside, he was doing well.

'Almost done, Robbie. I'll be with you in a minute,' Andy said.

'No rush on my part. This place is like a piece of my soul.' He could have added that it was easier here for him as well. More to focus on, less to miss. The place was always alive, buzzing with hope and expectation. People coming and going, banter and chatter. *Come the revolution!* Aye, that too! That fed him. Fed them all.

Robbie and Andy were walking back to the shop through the city centre. Night was falling and the city was quiet; so quiet that the sound of the rain falling on the cobbled streets filled the air. It was settling. A gentle peaceful rhythm made by nature. A little girl skipped by with her father. They were hurrying to escape the rain, smiles on their faces. Robbie followed their path, a smile of his own for the joy of it, but his also held sorrow, regret. That emptiness of Rosie's loss bit at him hard.

'You know, I wonder, every time I see a wee girl like that, I ask myself, is that her? Is she mine? My Rosie? It's all I can do no to walk over and ask.' A couple of tears had escaped unbidden, but it didn't matter. Those sorts of pretences had left him back in the fields of France. What was the point in pretending when it could all be snatched away in an instant? He didn't think there was any. A man could cry, and plenty did now.

'You can't hurt yourself like that, man. It'll kill you,' Andy said, his arm on Robbie's shoulder.

'Aye. Maybe.'

~

Robbie opened the back door to the shop. Listened. Stopped dead in his tracks. He turned to Andy with a stare that held a mixture of terror and hatred. Andy felt it too. That voice. There could never be any forgetting of that voice! *'Get up there and fight, you damned cowards!'* They stood there, hearts pounding. What on earth were they to do now? So many connotations. Were they even safe? Damn the man! Even now, here in their home, he was threatening them just by his very presence.

'I don't know about you, but I'm not letting it in anymore,' Robbie whispered. 'I'm not letting him step on our lives.' He took a deep breath, straightened up, his head high, and walked on in.

Andy paused, hung back. That fear grabbed hold of his shoulders, filled his head. That hell should not be here. He didn't know what to do, logical thought was so very far away. They walked through to that little room that held so many memories; that had been a place of friendship and safety. How quickly it could all be taken away from you. That safety, that security, that sense of belonging and love. Yes, love. For that was what it had held. Now it lay broken and shattered. Something terrible had set foot in this place; stood there in front of them. Their own demon in the flesh.

A silence heavier than death fell down on them all. The women sensed it. The men knew it. Life had changed.

'You,' Robbie whispered with venom.

Charlie gulped, stared. He had no words.

'I don't understand,' Connie said, her hand draped through Charlie's crooked arm. 'Do you—do you know each other?'

'Oh, you could say that, eh, *Captain*? *Sir*? What is it you're having folk address you as these days?' As the words escaped, Robbie could feel the need to temper it all. This could play out any number of ways, and he wasn't sure if he was safe anymore. But the force was too strong for it to be held back. It was too late now anyway. Enough had been said. If there had been any doubt, any thoughts of misrecognition, he had driven them away with that outburst. Deep down inside he would like to have done more. He would like to have killed the man.

Andy stood as if rooted to the spot, his mouth open, his eyes fixed, as his head filled once again with horror. With the memory of it all. He wanted to let it out. To scream. To just let go. His legs were threatening to buckle, alongside his mind.

Robbie felt it. Took hold of Andy's shoulders. Held his gaze. Tried to break it. To get through. 'You're all right,' he repeated, again, and again.

'I do apologise, Connie,' Charlie said, making a hasty exit through the shop.

Connie snatched at her coat, cast a departing stare at Robbie and Andy, at Hannah and Lizzie, and ran after Charlie as he hurried down the street.

She caught up, tugged at his arm. 'Charlie?'

He didn't look her way. It was as if his vision were fixed on a distant point. Something far away. A place that only he could see.

Again, she tugged, stronger this time. Her voice insistent. 'Charlie!' The question now a statement. A demand.

He slowed, turned towards her. 'You should go,' he said, his voice strangely cold, distant. He uncurled her fingers from his coat. 'Just go.'

She stood and watched as he walked away. *No! Confound it! I shall not be dismissed like that!*

Chapter 47
1919

A peculiar wake had been left behind. Something dark and foreboding was brooding in Lizzie's little shop. It needed clearing.

'Robbie, my love,' Lizzie said, 'I don't care about the time of day, nor your desire. You shall sit, alongside Andy, and take a drink. Then you have something to say, I believe.'

'It was him, wasn't it?' Andy mumbled, looking at the floor.

'Aye! I'll never forget that face, or that voice. Not as long as I draw breath, I won't.'

'Boys, sit down. Come on,' Lizzie insisted.

They shuffled onto the settee and quietly sipped at their gins. Both with so much to say, but neither wanting to go there again.

Robbie finished his drink, slammed the glass onto the table.

'Another?'

'Aye!'

Robbie's tongue had loosened with the drink. He stood up, motioned towards the shop with his head, intimating that Lizzie should follow.

They huddled in the corner beside the window. Rain splattered against it, creating a curtain, the steam of their breath adding to it. Rivulets of clarity clouded.

'Andy can't hear this. Not yet. It's taken so long to get him this far. Hearing of that bastard and what he did will send him right back again.'

'Okay.' Lizzie reached out her hand, squeezed Robbie's arm. 'Okay.'

'He was our *Captain*.' Robbie spat the word. 'You don't need to know it all, and God help me, I don't want to tell it. But it was him that saw Andy run out of one hell and straight into another. So many men. They couldn't take it, see? The horror of it. They ran. Andy ran. That bastard? He ordered me to shoot him. "I'll have no deserters on my watch," he shouted at me with that posh voice of his not caring one bit about the men inside the uniform. He said I'd to shoot Andy or be shot myself. Can you believe that? What kind of a human—'

Lizzie took his hand, squeezed it tight. 'Oh Robbie.'

'I wouldn't. Course I wouldn't. I told him that and I bolted too. Didn't think I'd make it to the first row of barbed wire, but I did. And the one after. And then I found Andy flat out in the mud. I dragged him on and somehow, we made it.' He shook his head. That was enough. Too many visions. Too much pain.

Lizzie sensed it and they stood in quiet togetherness until feelings settled and the air lifted, as much as memories would allow. 'We should go back in.'

'Aye. What is *he* to Connie, anyway?'

Lizzie took a deep breath. 'It seems that she has fallen in love.'

'Oh aye? Like to like I suppose?'

'Meaning?'

'They're cut from the same cloth, no? When it comes right down to it, there's them, and there's us.'

Soft mutterings drifted through the bookshelves. Andy, talking to himself. It sounded like gibberish. No sense to be made of it. They walked back through. Andy was sitting there, rocking back and forth, his knees held tight to his chest. His hands flexing in spasms.

'Christ!' Robbie whispered. 'Is there to be no end to this for him?'

Lizzie shrugged; no words offered themselves. This was so unknown to her. To all of them. A sickness that wasn't a sickness anyone knew anything about. A sanatorium in London was experimenting with electric shock treatment. Another in Edinburgh was arguing that talking through the horrors of the past would help alleviate the pain; would help the men to work their way clear of it. Both had a modicum of success; both had their decriers. But there were so many men carrying these scars. Shell shock, they called it. Shell shock sounded gentle somehow, nothing like as bad as the sickness was.

'Should we just leave him be? Let him work through it?'

'Naw, I reckon he needs taking outside. Fresh air. Normal folk doing normal things. He needs to see that it's all okay, even if it isn't.'

They took one arm each, held him up. Held him together.

Andy looked skyward as the evening breeze washed his face, filled his lungs. A softening.

They headed for the park. It was almost dark now, but there were still some children playing in the warmth of a spring evening. Innocent laughter, so welcome, but so unfitting to what was in their heads. The hell of it all. They walked on and on, twisting between trees and shrubs. The call of evensong drifted above everything else.

Andy stopped. Stared from Robbie to Lizzie and back again. 'Where am I? What—?'

Robbie squeezed his arm. 'You're all right. Just out for a wee walk. It was a bit stuffy in there.'

Andy closed his eyes. Tears fell. 'I'm not all right, Robbie, man. I'm as far from that as I've ever been.'

'Perhaps we should head home?' Lizzie asked.

'Aye. Aye maybe we should.'

When they reached the shop, it lay in silence. No Connie. No-one at all. Robbie prayed that it would stay that way. Lizzie's head was full of questions, full of concern for both Connie and Andy. She would bury them for now, but this had to be resolved one way or another. That was what she excelled in, offering suggestions, solutions, spreading positivity. But this? This felt beyond her.

Chapter 48
1919

~

Connie had taken Charlie to one of her favourite tearooms. The walk there had been awkward and silent, but she thought it best to allow him to talk when he felt like it, not at her command. She knew that he had suffered during the war, but he had never expanded upon it. That was fine. It wasn't important to her. The past.

They sat at a small table by the window and watched Glasgow go about its business. An easy distraction should it be needed. The waitress brought them a pot of Earl Grey tea and a selection of cakes, cupcakes, shortbread, sponge cake.

'Thank you,' Connie said to the waitress, smiling up at her. A polite nod as the girl stepped away. That had been Mhairi, once upon a time. How foolish of her to forget. They had shared laughter here, raised eyebrows at the behaviour of other customers. The entitled clicking of fingers as if calling a dog. That shared laughter had made it a much better place to work. Mhairi. Her imprisoned friend. The woman to whom she owed so very much. All of this. This freedom. This confidence. This joie de vivre.

Charlie stared, wondering where Connie's thoughts had strayed to. He reached for her hand. 'Connie, I don't want to talk about then, the war, but it seems to have been thrust upon us somewhat. There are things you should know that I would rather you didn't.'

She held up her hand. 'Then don't tell me. It truly is

of no importance to me. We talked about this. The past is the past and that is that.'

'Yes, but I wasn't expecting—I wasn't expecting him. Of all people.' He closed his eyes briefly as if trying to shut out the memories. 'Him.'

'But Robbie is one of my dearest friends—'

Charlie wrapped her hand in both of his and looked intently at her confused expression. 'You must trust me on this. It is something quite insurmountable. I think, perhaps, it is best for us to part.'

She started, leant back, eyes wide. 'What are you saying?' Her voice rose in desperation with each syllable.

'That this is too much for us to overcome. There cannot be an us. Not anymore. Don't you see?'

'No, I absolutely do not, and I have no intention of letting you go. Not now. Not ever!'

'Connie.'

'Hush now. We shall have tea and allow everything to settle.'

She was having nothing else. He would stay. It had taken her a lifetime to find someone. To find him. This would not end!

He was not the sort of man to cause a scene, to upset, so he smiled politely at her and agreed. For now.

The soft chatter of the other customers, the tinkle of porcelain cup upon porcelain saucer, the swirl of a silver teaspoon, the breath of others. It was enough to fill one's head, to allow one's silence. And that was what they did. A sip of tea, an unwanted but expected mouthful of cake, keeping up appearances, blending in.

Connie wanted to visit the restrooms, but she was afraid that he might take the opportunity to slip away;

to disappear from her life. She would wait.

Charlie motioned for the waitress and paid the bill, keeping his composure, smiling and polite, as expected. He rose and walked around to Connie's chair, pulled it away to facilitate her standing. The bellboy held their coats for them as they slipped arms into sleeves and fastened their buttons.

The evening air was bracing, uplifting, as it washed against them. A light rain began to fall.

'Connie, I—'

The tone of his voice was warning enough.

'No! I refuse to hear it! We shall act as if it were earlier today, as if nothing untoward has happened. You and I shall survive this, whatever this is. Nothing is more important than you and me together, right now.'

She slipped her arm through his and squeezed. There was no reply, physical or verbal, but it felt horribly as if something were lost that could never be found again. She had gone back to his hotel with him, no argument would be taken. This power that she had found, this strength, was altogether new, and she relished it. It grew on her as if it were a living thing. An ivy wrapping around a tree, but not leeching, not taking life and stealing strength; giving it. She brought that strength to the fore as they walked through the entrance of the Grand Station Hotel, her head held high.

He began to speak, to protest.

'Hush!' she commanded. 'Key?' she insisted, holding her gloved hand out.

He laughed nervously. This was outrageous, but it was also quite thrilling.

They took the stairs to the second floor. She unlocked the door and motioned for him to enter in front of her.

'I am nothing if not a gentleman,' he said pointedly. 'After you.'

She nodded and entered the sumptuous room. A vase of flowers on the walnut table filled the air with their heady scent. Roses and lilies. A peculiar combination. She wondered whose choice they had been as she crossed to the windows. The city outside was darkening, leeries walked the streets lighting up the lamps. That familiar soft glow. The clatter of trams, horses' hooves, mixed with the hum of the odd motor car. The curtains swished weightily, as she drew them across the windows, securing their privacy, cocooning their intimacy.

She untied her bonnet and hung it on a hook, slipped off her coat and tossed it across the back of a wingback chair, kicked off her shoes.

Charlie stared in disbelief, his mouth open. She should leave! If they were to maintain any modicum of decency, she should leave!

Instead, she sat on the bed and ran her fingers across the candlewick bedspread, patted it.

'Come. Sit with me,' she said, smiling up at him.

Was there any point in protesting? He thought not. The man hidden inside didn't want to. For the first time in his life, he felt utterly powerless in the company of a woman. But this was no ordinary woman.

Lovemaking had been slow and gentle and completely unforeseen. Of course, this went against everything that was expected of a woman of her standing. She giggled at the thought of it as she lay with her head nestled on his shoulder.

He turned his head, stroked her messed hair. 'I must

say, that wasn't quite the reaction I was anticipating. Did I amuse you?'

'No, no.' She rolled on top of him, kissed his nose. 'It was quite wonderful. You were quite wonderful. We have been very bad though, haven't we?'

'Marry me. Make it all right and marry me.'

She laughed now. 'Whatever will they say?'

'I don't care two hoots what *they* might say, only you,' he said.

'I have never felt so right about anything. You, what we have just done, all of it is my destiny.'

'One little word will do.'

'Yes, silly! Yes!'

He blew out an exaggerated breath, rolled her over.

'But there is something you must do for me,' she said, pushing his body away from her.

'Anything, my darling. Anything.'

Chapter 49
1919

~

Robbie had taken Andy to Hannah's flat. That confrontation had left both men with a darkness and Lizzie's shop had lost its charm; its sense of safety. It would be difficult to walk away from what had been Mhairi's home, but a change was needed. And this too had been their home. There had been no hesitation from Hannah.

'This is always your home. You know that. And the same goes for Andy here,' she said in greeting.

The chatter, the buzz of activity. It was the better choice, and a weight fell from Robbie's shoulders.

'You all right with this, Andy?' Robbie asked, putting his hand on Andy's shoulder. A squeeze in confirmation of a good choice.

Andy smiled. 'Yes.'

'Right, that's decided then,' Hannah said. 'Why don't I go and see Lizzie and explain things. You two can—' She swung her arms around the room— 'Settle in, I suppose!'

'I can't deny that a quieter house won't be entirely unwelcome! And it's for the best. For the boys, I mean,' Lizzie said. 'The effect that *Charlie* had on Andy was quite dreadful. Robbie, it seems, is made of stronger stuff.'

'What is going on in that department anyway? Have you seen Connie at all since?'

Lizzie shook her head. 'Not at all. She didn't come home last night. I don't know if I should be worried, or not.'

'I think not. She is a capable woman these days.'

Hannah swung her feet up on the little wooden stool and opened the newspaper she had picked up from the seller on the corner. She tutted and made disgruntled noises as she flicked through the pages. Nothing changed. The same stories, different words.

Connie arrived soon after, flushed, breathless, a grin on her face the likes of which neither woman had ever seen before. She was positively glowing. 'I've come to ask you a favour.'

'Hello Lizzie and Hannah. How are you?' Hannah said, sarcastically.

'Yes, yes. My apologies! But I am so very excited!'

'Okay...'

Hannah and Lizzie exchanged concerned glances.

'It is the most wonderful thing! Charlie and I are to wed, and we would be so very happy if you could be our witnesses. Can you do that for me; for us? Please, can you?' She clutched her hands together and held them close to her chest as if in prayer.

'Slow down,' Hannah said. 'What do you mean?'

'I mean I am to be married, and I would like both your approval, and your help.'

'Connie, my love,' Lizzie said. 'Have you really thought this through? You barely know the man. And—well, it seems that he has done some awful things.'

Connie stamped her foot in frustration. 'Don't you think I know that? Don't you think he has told me all of it? The man I love has asked me to marry him and, by God, I will, with or without you. It would mean so much if you could support me in this.'

She looked pointedly from Hannah to Lizzie and

back again. 'So?'

Hannah frowned, then raised her eyebrows. 'If he is truly the right man for you, then yes, of course!'

'Splendid! Lizzie?'

Lizzie opened her arms and welcomed Connie in for a confirmatory hug. 'I would be delighted!'

'That's more like it!' Connie said. 'Charlie has bought one of those beastly automobiles and is waiting a little further along the road. He thought it more prudent to keep his distance in case the boys were here.'

'Yes. Poor Andy was completely distraught after their meeting, and I wouldn't trust Robbie not to be violent in some way. He hates the man, and I don't use the word lightly. This is Robbie we're speaking of. The man who loves everyone.'

'Apart from the upper classes!' Connie said, cocking her head.

They laughed. 'Well, those who wield their power like an entitlement, yes. But he does love you!'

'And I him. Dear God, I hate what this war has done. Good men destroyed, maimed, hatred and distrust sitting in their bellies. I only hope that one day they can rise above it. See through circumstance to the soul of those who they believe have wronged. It was never the men. It was the war and what it makes them.'

'Amen to that,' Hannah said, 'but I won't be holding my breath.'

'But we are friends?'

'As if anything could come between us. Of course we are!'

The three women hugged again, and Connie left.

∽

Charlie held the car door open for Connie and

offered his hand in assistance.

'Charlie, darling, I need no such help. In fact, I resent it. Deeply!'

Charlie tossed his head back and laughed. 'The habits of a lifetime cannot simply be swept away, my darling.'

'Oh, but they must!' She pushed his hand away and climbed aboard, beaming at him. 'And next I shall learn to drive this monstrosity.'

He started the engine. 'And am I to teach you?'

'Well, of course!'

As they drove along George Street Connie tensed. Her father was walking along the pavement. She hadn't seen him since he had had her locked up. She shrunk down low in her seat.

'What the devil?'

'Just drive, Charlie. Just drive.'

'Connie?' Charlie said.

Chapter 50
1919

~

Hannah opened her door to find Connie waiting expectantly.

'I see marriage suits you,' Hannah said. 'Come in!'

'Are you alone?' Connie asked.

'Am I ever?'

'I mean Robbie and Andy. Are they here?'

Hannah's expression changed to one of concern. 'No. They picked up a day's work at a building site. What is this about?'

'I come with such wonderful news. Charlie has friends in the right places. Before the war he was a barrister. Well, he is again now. I don't suppose one ever stops being such a thing.'

'Connie? Can you just get to the point?'

'Yes, well, his father is a judge, and, you see, Mhairi's release has been secured! The petitions, the upset, the whisper of words in the correct ears, debts to repay. She is to be freed!'

Hannah swallowed hard, stared. 'And you are absolutely certain?'

'Yes! I heard it from Charlie, who heard it from his father, who, in turn heard it directly from the Lord Advocate, or some such! I can't quite remember.' She shook her head, a slight scowl on her face at her lack of memory, of accuracy. A return of the excited smile. 'But it is absolutely confirmed. Robbie can collect her from the gaol. Or I can. I can drive, you know. I could drive

213

Robbie and have Mhairi collected in style. Wouldn't that be something?'

'Slow down, Connie. I don't think, given the circumstances, that that would be the best idea. Kind though it is.'

'Because of Charlie?'

'No. Well, partly, perhaps. But you must remember who Robbie is, who Mhairi is. That sort of flamboyancy would be frowned upon.'

Connie looked crestfallen. 'Of course. And Robbie has yet to speak to me. I do so want to make amends. I had hoped that this might begin reparations.'

'I wouldn't count on it, but the gesture is a splendid one. We shall see. Do we have a date yet? For her release, I mean.'

'I don't think so, but I have been assured that it is imminent. Oh, and you must come to our new house for tea, or drinks, or some such. Charlie is such a darling that he packed up and left Edinburgh just for me! I can't quite believe my luck, at times. Say you'll come. Do!'

'Yes, of course!'

Connie left in a whirl of excitement, if a tad disappointed that she wouldn't get to be a part of the actual release itself. Ah well, she had at least done her bit as best she could. Charlie had been true to his promise.

∽

Hannah chewed on the news and decided to await confirmation before mentioning anything to Robbie. She didn't have to wait for long. One of her contacts at the gaol confirmed that a release date had indeed been set. Mhairi was coming home!

When Robbie and Andy came back that evening

214

Hannah's normal cool had evaded her.

'What's up with you, then?' Robbie said.

She grinned, her face lighting up in a way Robbie hadn't seen before.

'Robbie, you need to sit down.'

'Eh, naw, I think I'll stand, if it's all the same to you.' It felt like news was coming his way and he would rather stand tall and face whatever it might be. Good or bad.

'Sit!'

Andy sat, Robbie shrugged and followed suit, his brow furrowed, his heart pounding. 'And?'

'It's Mhairi.' Hannah choked on a tear, clutched her chest. 'She—she's coming home.'

Robbie's mouth fell open. Words were an impossibility. The wave of emotion that was swallowing him left him powerless.

'Tomorrow! She is to be released tomorrow!'

He gulped, forced words through. 'Straight up? For real?'

'Yes! I have it confirmed through a reliable source.'

Robbie leapt up, pulled Hannah close. Tears dampened her neck. He stepped back, swiped at his face, embarrassed and thrilled in one monumental wave of emotion. 'By Christ, is that not the best news in the world? Who? How? Can I go and get her? I mean, do we know the time?'

'We do. Nine a.m. pronto.'

'Christ! That's—that's not enough time to...'

'To what? It's not as if she hasn't seen you recently. She knows what a miserable wretch you are.' Hannah laughed.

'Aye, but it needs to be perfect. The place, me, we

215

need—.' He glanced down at his threadbare trousers, his patched jacket, the shoe with the flapping sole. 'I look a state!'

'You look just fine.'

'Naw. And I need to get back to Lizzie's. To clean it all up. That's assuming she'll let us move back in. She will, won't she? I mean, a place of our own just isn't possible, what with all the homeless, and the soldiers with nothing but their kitbags.' He shook his head. 'Shameful, so it is!'

'Of which you are one.'

'Aye, well, sort of. But I've got you!' He grabbed her shoulders and pulled her so close again. Kissed her hard on the lips. 'By Christ, I love you lot, so I do!'

'And we love you, which is why Lizzie will welcome you back in a whisper!'

'Aye. Aye, course she will.'

Andy stared at the floor. This wave of emotion that was sweeping between Hannah and Robbie didn't belong to him. It felt like these were no longer his people; this was no longer his place. He felt like an intruder, and it screamed at him. His brain buzzed. He could feel himself slipping away again. *No! Get a hold of yourself, man.* He stood up slowly, quietly, and retreated. He would not ruin this for his friend. He would be a man.

Chapter 51
1919

～

Andy didn't think anyone had even noticed that he had left the room; that he had gone. They were so wrapped up in themselves, in the news of their friend's release. It was peculiar. This woman, Mhairi, felt like she had been a part of his life since Robbie had first given him that photograph. He had been desperate to find her when he thought that Robbie had drowned. He would have found his way to Glasgow. He would have searched for Mhairi and tried to comfort her. He would have been there for her; for Robbie, or rather his memory. But now she had come between them. Pushed him aside.

He packed his knapsack with the few belongings he had acquired, slung it on his shoulder and slipped out of the door. As he walked down the tenement stairs Robbie and Hannah's excited voices drifted away. Became a memory.

Perhaps it was time, anyway. This wasn't him, his home, his history. His family wouldn't even know of his survival. What kind of a man does that? What kind of a man was he? Was he even a man at all? Was there any point to him? Black thoughts swirled around his head as he walked along the grey street, unaware of the people around him, a buzz of voices that made no sense, the clatter of trams, the breath of strangers.

He stared across the heads of unknown people. The bustle of coming and going. Existence a blur. The sudden clatter of summer rain pelted the trees and tumbled down in rivulets; streams of the unknown

217

taunting him. He stood under a gathering of trees and looked skyward. The rain collected on the branches, on the leaves, and dripped through in huge droplets. Little shelter was offered, but he found a bench and took a seat anyway. He stared at the ground, watching each droplet hit the earth and break apart. Patterns. Circles. Tiny streams swelled, became significant. Pushed on. There was a peace to it. A silencing which blocked the noise out, the fear out, thoughts out. There was just him and the rain. It was okay. He was okay.

∾

'Christ! Have you seen Andy? His bag's gone. He must have—.' Robbie bolted out of the flat, a sickening ball of guilt knotted up in his stomach.

There I was, so damned happy, so wrapped up in me and mine that I never even thought. Andy, man, I'm so very sorry.

He pounded the streets, trying to imagine where Andy might have gone. Maybe Lizzie's.

'Has he been here, Lizzie?'

'I'm sorry. No.'

He slumped against the wall. 'How could I be so stupid. So thoughtless!'

'You weren't to know.'

'Aye, I was. I should've seen this coming a mile off. If he does turn up, grab him. Don't let him go, right?'

'Of course. Good luck.'

'Aye.'

He ran off again, jumping on and off trams, checking all of the places they had spent time in together. George Square, Parkhead stadium, the streets they had pounded handing out leaflets, the park. His chest was burning, his legs about to give up. But there, slumped on a bench, a lonesome figure. He had passed many like that. People destitute and lost. But the shape of that man. The particular way that his back curved, that his head hung.

'Andy?' Robbie called.

There was no response. He reached through the darkness, touched the man's shoulder. 'Andy?'

The man's head lifted slowly. His eyes didn't meet Robbie's. No. This wasn't Andy.

'Sorry, pal. You look really like a friend of mine. He's gone missing.'

The man mumbled something incoherent.

'Sorry?'

The man pointed through the trees. 'Over there!' he shouted. Laughed. Cried. He clasped Robbie's arm. Squeezed tight. Pulled him close. 'Hundreds of them. You'll see. Hundreds and hundreds.' Spittle flew as he spoke. He started to cough, his chest heaving.

Robbie did his best not to pull back, not to feel revulsion at another man's phlegm on his face, not to be terrified of the disease that might be being forced upon him.

'Right,' Robbie said. 'Thank you. You take care now.' He was about to turn away, carry on his search. He paused. He should do something. Help in some way. But there was nothing he could do. Not right now.

He walked methodically up and down the paths that twisted through the trees, checking and double checking, anywhere a man could hide, but Andy wasn't to be seen; no-one was to be seen, and it felt like a part of himself had also upped and left. The only person who knew, who had lived it, was gone from his life. He felt hollow.

Andy had taken his things. He would be leaving. Leaving Glasgow. *Of course!* Robbie bolted down to Glasgow Central. Noise and clamour. Excitement and tears. The ear shattering blast of the whistle. "All aboard!" The belch of steam blasting up into the ceiling. The grind of metal upon metal. He stared at all of the people, hoping. Just hoping. But Andy wasn't there. Robbie's head drooped with the weight of it all. Such a failure. He scoured everywhere. The waiting room, the platforms, the toilets. Nothing but strangers.

He hunched his shoulders as he walked back out into the interminable rain. As he walked, he still checked every face, every shadow. He cut through the park. Perhaps he had missed something. Someone.

'Andy, man!' he called. 'Where the hell are you?' He stopped, swept the rain from his face. 'Christ!' He was about to give up; head for home, when another shadow caught his eye. 'Andy?' He was waving, not caring about the spectacle he might be making of himself.

The man didn't move, didn't respond at all. Had Robbie made a mistake? Shouted at another stranger? No. It was him all right. He looked to be in a state. Confused and scared. His hands were trembling, jerking. Tears were falling, disguised by the rain.

Robbie sat down beside him. 'It's me, Robbie.' He waited quietly for some semblance of recognition to work its way into those dark spaces in Andy's head. So many of them. So much darkness.

Finally, Andy took notice of the place, the time, the man next to him. 'Robbie. How did you—?'

'You and me, we're tied together. You know that. Don't be thinking you can ditch me that easy!' He nudged Andy in the ribs. 'Come on. Let's get you out of here and home.'

'But—'

'But nothing. I'm no gonnae argue with you, man. Come on.'

He pulled Andy to his feet, slapped his arm around his shoulder, pulled him close. 'All right?'

Andy smiled weakly in return; his brow furrowed. He nodded his agreement.

They were met with relief and smiles at Hannah's.

This felt right to Andy. Whatever had he been thinking, leaving here, like that? He was a danger to himself, but these were good people. They cared.

'Out of those things, the both of you. Look at the state of you!'

Dried and dressed in fresh clothing they sat at the table, their hands hugging their mugs of tea. That tingle of heat that was almost painful but too rewarding to be.

∽

'Right. I'll be off then.' Robbie said. 'I need to get Lizzie's place arranged. The perfect place for my perfect lass.'

'What you need to do is sit down and eat, then rest. Look at the state of you!' Hannah said.

'Aye, but—'

'Aye, but nothing! The boys have been round to Lizzie's. It is all...perfect.'

'What are you lot like?' He managed a grin and took a seat.

'That's better. And yes, we are quite wonderful!'

'You are just that, so you are.'

His breath calmed and his belly full, Robbie still couldn't settle. He paced the room, mumbling as he did so. A few words for Hannah. Some more for Andy. The

221

majority for himself. He couldn't remember ever having felt like this. The excitement, his nerves; he was about to explode.

Andy sat quietly, listening, watching. An immense tiredness washed over him, and his eyes didn't want to stay open any longer. 'I need my bed,' he said quietly.

'Aye, on you go. I'll be there soon enough.'

Hannah and Robbie waited until they heard Andy's footsteps stop, the door close.

Hannah leaned closer to Robbie. Her voice low. 'It's as well you found him. Who knows what could have happened if he'd been picked up by the police? I was writing a piece today about a local lad, a deserter. They caught him and he disappeared. His parents are frantic. We're trying to raise awareness. Trying to help find people. Connect people. It's awful!'

'Aye. You know, they're sending deserters back to France or Belgium if their units are still over there. And you know why? So as they can execute them. A firing squad made up of others just like them. That's how they get you. That's how the fear spreads. Utter bastards. The lot of them. And that *Captain* of Connie's? What's to stop him, eh? What's to stop him telling his pals about me and Andy? Christ! Maybe I should leave too? Just get away. Leave Mhairi in peace.'

'He hasn't said anything, Robbie. My contacts check the lists that the police get. You're not on them. Neither you nor Andy. You're not registered as a deserter, just missing in action. You're all right. And after what he's done for Mhairi, I do think he's trying to make amends. To say he's sorry in his own way. You know it was mostly his doing; the release?'

'Aye, well, that's as maybe.' He downed his gin,

slammed the glass down. 'To hell with them! The lot of them!'

'I'll drink to that!'

They stayed up too late, drank too much, but both felt the need. Sleep would have to be alcohol induced if it were to come at all.

Chapter 52
1919

~

Robbie was up before the dawn. 'Christ, my head,' he muttered to his reflection in the window, wishing that he had been smarter, drunk less, gone to bed earlier. *Eejit*! He crept out without waking Hannah, or Andy. It had to be just him. Just him stepping his Mhairi out to freedom.

~

Mhairi was led the wrong way along the corridor. She stared, confused. 'What's going on?'

The guard grinned.

'I wasn't expecting a visitor. No the day.' Thoughts spun through her head. Were they moving her again? Somewhere worse, further away. Had she done something wrong? Was she going to be punished? But it didn't feel like that. No. She was sure she'd know. 'Are you not going to tell me, then?'

'Oh, I think ye'll like this, Mhairi!'

They reached the front gates. The key was turned, and she was suddenly, gloriously free! The air had never felt sweeter, the summer breeze a magical elixir. To her it was the brightest, most beautiful day. She stood there just taking it all in.

The sound of pounding feet resonated along the cobbles behind her. 'Mhairi!'

She knew at once who it was. That voice still sent shivers of anticipation through her. Even now. She turned to see Robbie running breathlessly towards her, his face red with the exertion.

She squealed and ran towards him. When they collided, they almost fell to the ground. It wouldn't have mattered if they had. Nothing was going to ruin this moment for them. Their bodies touching, their breath twisting together, their lips meeting. The most wonderful feeling in the world wrapped them up and took them away to that place that was theirs and theirs alone.

They walked slowly down the hill, arms wrapped around each other, stopping every few steps for another kiss.

'You sleep in a brewery?' Mhairi asked, her nose wrinkled in distaste.

'Sorry.' He grinned, almost sheepishly, but far too happy for that. 'I was that excited I couldn't sleep. The drink helped pass the time.'

She laughed. 'Can it no just stay like this? Just me, an you an nothing, no-one?'

'There's folk desperate to see you.'

'Aye, well, maybe I'm no that desperate to see anyone but you.'

'I'm a wee bit desperate myself, like,' he said, his eyebrows raised suggestively.

'Is that so?'

'Aye! Christ, it's been that long, my wee man's about to burst.'

She threw her head back, laughed raucously, in a way she hadn't done for so very long. This was the woman she had left behind all those years ago. A stranger now, but that would change. With a bit of luck and good fortune—with the return of her daughter—it would change. She had buried those feelings of loss, of being wrenched from that connection which was the strongest in the world, so far down, just so as she could get through her time in prison. But not now. This was all about her and Robbie, and she wasn't going to spoil it all by allowing that sadness to crawl back up.

As they walked past the graveyard she nodded towards it; asked the question.

He grinned, grabbed her hand, and they ran through summer grass and dancing leaves until they reached a quiet secluded corner hidden by immense gravestones. They fell to the ground. 'It shouldn't be here, like this, amongst dead folk,' Robbie said.

'Robbie, it's just me, an you, an I'm no waiting a second longer.'

It was over in under a minute. He grimaced. 'I'll make it up to you.'

'Aye, you will that!'

They straightened each other out and walked back to the street, hands linked, heads high. For now, this was as close to heaven as they could be.

Chapter 53
1919

Connie snuggled in to Charlie, her head on his shoulder, his arm around her waist. She knew what was happening; Mhairi being released. That joyous moment that they had all been working so hard towards, not least her Charlie. He had been the one to secure her release yet here they were, apart from it all, and it hurt. She understood that it should be Robbie to meet her, to spend those first minutes with her. But they were as good as sisters, and it bothered her.

'Why the sad face?' he asked, stroking her cheek.

'Oh, nothing.'

'I do not believe that for one minute. How can I help if you won't share everything with me?'

'Charlie, my darling, I doubt there is anything that you can do. I would so love to see Mhairi; to hug her and welcome her back. But I am forbidden. What could be so very awful that makes you such a pariah in their eyes and by default me? What went on? Can you tell me?'

She felt his body tense, a tremor run through it. He pulled away from her, only slightly, but enough.

'Charlie?'

He took a deep breath. What happened over there had never been shared with anyone. Not really. Not the specifics. Faces to the men. Names to them. No. Not that.

'I was following orders. Nothing more. It was my duty, do you see? I had no choice in the matter. None whatsoever.'

'Oh, Charlie. Please tell me. There should be no secrets between us. None whatsoever.'

A heavy silence fell on them. An awkwardness that was painful. It had to be put to bed.

'Charlie?' she whispered, stroking his cheek as softly as a feather.

He turned to face her. 'Promise me that it will change nothing; that you will still love me as you do now.'

'Of course. You must know that. I adore everything about you. Everything!'

There was a peculiar distance between him and his words as he told her about the constant bombardment, the desertion, the need to put a stop to it, the command, the further desertion. It had been happening to someone else, and he was merely reporting it. How else could he speak of such things?

'And Robbie escaped?'

'Yes. I didn't imagine that he would. Escape from that was nigh on impossible. And when I saw the two of them standing there, I couldn't quite believe it. And that you should know one of them? That was quite unimaginable.'

'It makes no difference to me. I love you for who you are now.'

'Oh, but it does make a difference. Now there is a rift between you and your friends, and it is all of my doing. And I am so very sorry.'

'It is an irrelevance between us. In time it might heal, and if not, so be it.'

He pulled her close and kissed her head. 'You are quite the most wonderful woman.' He took her hand and kissed her fingers, her wrist, the inside of her arm.

She squealed with pleasure. He groaned as he moved

228

across her body as slowly as his desire would allow. Nothing existed now but this. Them and this.

Chapter 54
1919

~

Mhairi and Robbie had walked all the way back to the bookshop. It had been a walk of few words, for few were needed. Being wrapped up in each other was enough for now. At the back of Robbie's mind sat Connie. Mhairi would find out soon enough who Connie had married, why Robbie couldn't tolerate being in her presence, and it would be devastating. When should he tell her? Should he at all? It could come from Lizzie, from Hannah. But she would ask straight away. She would need to know.

Not yet, he decided. This was one of the most beautiful days of their lives and he didn't want it sullied by that; by *him*.

Lizzie heard their footsteps approaching the back of the shop. She jumped up and pulled the door wide open, a grin stretching across her face. She squealed her excitement. 'Mhairi! Oh my God! Mhairi!'

Mhairi let go of Robbie and fell into Lizzie's embrace. The two of them held tightly on to each other before stepping back and taking in the person who stood in front of them.

'I have no words!' Lizzie said in a choked voice, fighting back tears. 'Just none!'

'Can we get in the door, then?' Robbie said, a chuckle to his words.

'Yes, yes. I am so sorry. Come! Come in!'

'I would kill you for a bath. Wash that place right off o me.'

'I thought as much and have the tin-bath all ready and waiting to be filled. Pots of water sitting on the stove.'

'You are an angel.'

Mhairi stayed in the bath until her skin was wrinkled and the water cold. Robbie stroked her skin dry, wrapped her up in clean clothes, whispered over and over again. 'I love you so much.'

'Is that right?'

'Aye.'

Despite the exhaustion that both of them felt, they made love through the night, until the crack of dawn.

'That's my wee man done,' he whispered, nuzzling in to her neck. He laughed softly. She was already asleep.

It was uncanny how easily they settled back into their previous normality, as if the past years had been a nightmare. An awful thing that had happened to someone else. He didn't ask about gaol. She didn't ask about the war. It was done and they were alive and together. They did talk about Rosie. That would never be done. Never be consigned to history.

~

Hannah had organised a small party in honour of Mhairi's release. It was only fair considering the work that everyone had put in. And it was right that there was a celebration to lighten the air, to lift the fugue of what seemed to be political apathy. So much had happened. Some successes, but few. Nothing life changing for the majority of the working class. Hannah and her compatriots could feel it slipping away. The excitement, the enthusiasm, was waning. That fight for survival, to earn a living, to keep a home was all consuming. It seemed that life would carry on as

231

always. The workers being used to create wealth. The wealthy thriving on it.

Talk soon turned to Rosie; to the unfairness of women having their children taken from them; to the lack of a voice, the lack of rights.

'There must be more we can do,' Mhairi said. 'Someone else to ask. Some more doors to chap.'

'We have done our very best, Mhairi,' Hannah said.

'Aye, I'm no doubting that, but I'm her ma, Robbie is her da. She should be home wi us, where she belongs.'

'Connie did her level best, we all did.'

'Aye. Where is she though? Connie? I thought she'd be here.'

Chatter quieted; an awkwardness swept through the gathering. Glances slipped between Hannah and Robbie, Lizzie and Brian, all of them.

'What is it you're no telling me?' Mhairi asked, a tinge of anxiety clinging to her words as she felt Robbie tense up behind her. She turned to face him. 'Robbie?'

He shook his head. 'It's not her, it's the man she married.'

'I didn't even know. Why didn't you say that she was married? If it wasn't for her, I wouldn't be here. I wouldn't know any of you. She's my best pal. I should know!'

'Aye, you should,' Robbie said. 'I was waiting for the right time. I guess this is it, then.'

Chapter 55
1919

~

Andy was preparing to leave as the party was taking place. He had talked it through with Lizzie. Robbie was the closest person in the world to him, but perhaps too close. His judgment would be clouded by fellowship, by their history. No. Lizzie was the better option. A kind and compassionate woman who would understand this for what it was; a man's need to be a man. He had to allow Robbie to focus on his own life now. Him and Mhairi, as it should be. This really was no place for him anymore. A destiny was waiting for him back where he came from. Home.

There was no rush this time. No running away. A planned and thought through leaving. He had decided to leave a note for Robbie. Words could change his mind again, and he didn't want that. Neither did he want to confront the pain he would feel in saying goodbye face to face. He wasn't man enough for that. Not yet.

He reached Glasgow Central and boarded the train to Edinburgh. His thoughts were clear, his heart still. This was the right move. No looking back. At Edinburgh he found the train to Galashiels quickly enough. There was barely a wait. No time to think. He stepped onto the train and made his way along the carriage looking for a quiet compartment. There were none. He wouldn't panic. No. This new man would step right on in and take his seat without hesitation. He smiled at the man opposite as he settled himself into the seat by the door. His smile was returned. That was enough. He didn't feel the want for chatter, for pleasantries. A smile would do.

The closer the train drew towards Galashiels, the more familiar the countryside, the towns and villages, hills and forests, rivers and burns. This was a place of softness, and he was a part of it, his blood flowed with it. Finally, the train slowed as it approached Galashiels station. He closed his eyes momentarily to gather himself. The whistle of the train, the thumping of his heart. But this was good. This was excitement. A welcoming. It was under his control. He stepped onto the platform and felt like a different person. The man he used to be.

It was only a ten-minute walk to the family's bakery shop, but he took his time, breathing in the familiarity of the narrow roads, the shops with flats above. How was it possible for nothing to have changed when a generation of young men had been decimated? The horror of that.

'No,' he said, too loudly.

He glanced around anxiously. Had anyone heard? Was he making a spectacle of himself again? His heartbeat increased; he could feel his mind beginning to muddle. *'No!'* he chastised himself. *'No!'* He clenched his hands into fists, felt his nails dig into the soft skin of his palms.

He reminded himself that all of that was gone. The trenches, France, gone. It was from a different time; it had happened to a different man. This was a land of perfection and peace and beauty. He was okay. It was all okay.

He walked down Channel Street, Park Street. The air here was so different from Glasgow. It was clean and pure and fresh. Nature was there to be breathed, with

234

little intrusion from man. This was as it should be. This was healing. He paused at the bridge. Snippets of his childhood. More. A film of it spreading out before him. The river, loud and gurgling, almost smothered by trees. A rope tied to a heavy branch, a stick strong enough to hold his weight at the other end. What a feeling that was! The thrill of swooping out over the deep, dark water, the air whistling through his hair, until the decision was made to leap into the river. The shock of the cold. The shriek of an excited surfacing.

There was always that chance of a mistimed jump, a fall into shallower water, at least bruises, at worst broken limbs, and there had been a few. He and his friends would lie about how it had happened, where it had happened. That pact of silence held strong.

'Mind and not play by that river, son.'

'Yes ma,' as he ran out knowing full well that her warning would be ignored.

He walked on to Stirling Street and stopped, took a deep breath pretending to adjust his knapsack. There on the left, that soft, warm home. A two-storey house of traditional rough stone, the lower floor fronted by the bakery. That smell that set his stomach grumbling. Freshly baked bread. The number of times that he had run out with a sneakily snatched bread roll clutched in grimy hands. Or, better still, a pie! 'Oi!' his mother had called. But there was a laughter to it. 'You wee besom,' she had muttered with a chuckle to her voice.

He looked up at the top floor windows from where he stood on the street opposite, sparkling clean, as always, and smiled. A jingle broke through the quiet as the shop door opened. Someone stepped out with a paper bag in their hands. Andy stared, pulling back more memories. Mrs. Crannock. He laughed to himself remembering her refusal to give him his football back until he promised to be more careful. To play further away from other folk's houses. He turned quickly away, not wanting to be recognised before he had stepped inside and announced himself to his family.

He decided to go in through the back entrance. The family's way. The alleyway was empty, apart from a cat prowling through the overgrowth. She stopped and stared at him, then mewled and twisted herself around his ankles. Had his family taken on another cat? He stroked her briefly and walked through the alleyway, into the back garden. She followed, still mewling away. He hovered at the foot of the stairs which led up to the flat, unsure whether to go up or show himself to whoever was serving in the shop. The cat now led the way, her tail tall and erect, wriggling in excitement, as she trotted into the shop.

'You know fine you're not allowed in here; you wee scamp. Off with you!' his mother said.

Andy coughed softly to alert her to his presence.

She looked up. 'Oh my God! Andy! Is it really you?'

She brushed her hands on her apron, swiped at the tears streaming down her face, and ran towards him. 'Son! They told us you were—' She threw her arms around him and squeezed.

'Hello, Ma,' he whispered into her neck. This was right. This was good. He was home.

Chapter 56
1919

~~

Connie and Charlie knew little of each other's previous life. Family, childhood, that sort of thing. Neither had thought it very important and Connie had always managed to steer any conversation that was heading in that direction to somewhere else, somewhere more comfortable.

'Charlie, my darling, you know how I hate to talk of such things. My family are nothing to me, and that is all there is to it. Nothing!'

'Very well, but mine are important. My father did help to secure your Mhairi's release, after all. And he is yet to meet you.'

'Yes, but they were in India.'

'And now they have returned, and I think it only right and proper that you meet. That you thank him face to face.' His stare was intense, probing.

'Yes, and I am grateful. So very grateful. Forgive me.'

'Again?' He grinned at her.

She hit him with the pillow. 'Yes, again!'

They fell back on the bed and did what they did best. Loved each other with such fervent passion that the world outside simply did not exist. Breathless and sweating they lay in that beautiful post coital afterglow, breathing in each other.

He kissed her head, slipped his leg across her, locked eyes with her. 'Darling Connie.'

'I don't think I can, Charlie. I am simply too exhausted.'

'Lie still.'

This was a telling she would take.

~

They sat together at the window-seat, sipping Earl Grey tea, connecting with the outside world once more.

'I shall arrange a visit. Tea at my parents', Charlie said.

Connie sighed. 'Very well. If you insist.'

'I do.'

'And now we shall go and see Mhairi. I simply will not allow anything to stand between us.'

'Are you quite sure about this?'

She frowned at him.

'Very well,' he said, a tinge of hesitancy to his words. 'But I shall wait outside. There is no point in causing further distress.'

'Oh Charlie, you are such a sweetheart, and I love you more than...more than anything!'

~

They pulled up outside Lizzie's shop. He moved in preparation to get out of the car and open her door.

'Sit!' she commanded. 'I may be a woman, but I am perfectly capable!'

He laughed and sat back in his seat.

She stepped out of the car slowly—her movements exaggerated—and swirled around to offer him a self-accomplished grin. With her head held high and proud, she walked to the rear of the building and tapped lightly on the door. A feeling of unwelcome anxiety crept up her spine and clung to her despite her best efforts to cast it aside. She blew out a breath and waited.

Mhairi opened the door, and a darkness fell across

238

her face. She moved to close it, but Connie slipped her foot in between door and jamb.

'Mhairi, please? Can we at least talk?'

'I've got nothing to say to you.'

'But I have to you. Plenty. This must be resolved, Mhairi.'

'Your man there aimed his gun at mine; would have had him lying dead in that mud if he could have shot better. I guess that comes from having others to shoot for him, eh?'

'Oh Mhairi, it wasn't personal. He was simply following orders.'

'Aye, that's some excuse, that!'

'You do know it was him who secured your release.'

'Maybe he did, maybe he didn't. There was plenty other folk working for that, but I guess, because he's the rich, important person, he gets to take the credit.'

'Mhairi. Please! This is torture for me. You mean so much to me. I would still be there, in my own prison, if it weren't for you.'

'Well, I guess that makes us even, aye? Oh, and say hello to your *father* for me. Why don't you.'

Connie stepped back, a sick knot tying up her stomach.

Mhairi took the opportunity to slam the door shut and lock it. She slipped down the wall and silently cried.

A queasiness had come over Connie. She felt faint and disorientated as she pressed her hand against the wall to steady herself. She took deep calming breaths and waited for it to pass, as it surely would.

Chapter 57
1919

~

Despite Andy's protestations his mother switched the sign on the shop to 'Closed'. She took him by the hand and led him up the stairs, as if he were six years old again. He smiled.

'Your father's asleep, but he'll be wanting woken up for this!'

'And Julie?'

'Oh, your sister's off out with her young man. Nice lad. She thinks he's *the one*, but they all are, for a while.' She laughed. 'Now you wait here. Give your father a chance to ready himself. You know how he doesn't like folk to see him any other way. And as God is my witness, he'll be beside himself with this!'

Andy stood gazing out of the window. That view. Trees crawling up the gentle hill. It was like an old friend. A very dear old friend. Although it couldn't be seen he knew what was beyond. The fields and forests of his youth. Wild places. Peaceful places. Adventures and mishaps. Skinned knees and scratched arms. Innocence. It was wonderful.

He was broken from his reverie by a roar from his father.

'By God, son! Come here!'

His father stood with his arms wide, his grin wider still. It didn't matter that he was in his vest and underpants. Nothing mattered but the feel of his son's skin against his. His wife couldn't stay apart from this. She squeezed in and widened the embrace. What joy!

'Where have you been? Why did we not hear anything? They just left us in a horrible hell of not-knowing but fearing the worst. Missing presumed dead, they said, and that was that!'

That confirmation that they hadn't been told he had deserted was the last thing he needed to allow himself to relax. To feel safe, here, in his home. 'Well, there was nothing more that they could say.'

'Come away and sit down and you can tell us all about it.'

A look flashed from mother to father. They had seen others return to the town, broken in body and mind. Stories had been shared of their difficulties. Tread carefully, gently. That was the word. Tread carefully.

His father heeded the warning. 'If you've a mind to, that is.'

'I'll just put the kettle on.'

'I reckon the lad'll be wanting something a wee bit stronger. I know I do! Let's get the good stuff out of the cupboard.'

Andy would have said, *no, tea's just fine*, but he hadn't the heart. This would be done his father's way. He told the outline of his story as vaguely as possible, and they understood that there was no need for more. It had been hell, and he was safe. That was all that mattered now. He did tell them about the shell shock; about having to stay away until he felt better, stronger; about the night terrors.

'Son, you should have come straight home,' his mother said. 'We would have seen you through it.'

'I know that Ma, but this wasn't about you at all. This was about being with folk who had been there. Who understood.'

241

'Well, one thing's for sure. You need a good feeding up, so you do. Look at you! Skin and bones. I'll have no son of mine looking like he doesn't get fed right! Your father and me can get some fat on those bones of yours soon enough.'

They laughed. The air lightened. This was going to be okay.

There were more squeals when his sister came home; more history to tell.

'Leave him be love. He's been through it all once today. The laddie needs to let it lie.'

She smiled. 'Fair enough!'

'And what about you, little sis? Boyfriends by the dozen, I hear! Just you tell them that your brother is home from the war, and he won't stand for any nonsense towards his sister.'

'Don't you go frightening this one away. He's a keeper, so he is.'

'And does this one have a name?'

'Roderick.' She blushed.

'Not Roddie McKenzie?'

'The very same, and I'll not hear a word against him!'

Andy lifted his hands in surrender. 'Not a word from me. Is he still a skinny wee thing?'

'No, he is not! I'm warning you. Leave him be!'

Their father laughed. 'It's like the two of you were never separated!'

And that was it. It really did feel like he had never been away. He took his place in the bakery without complaint. Quite the opposite. He felt whole again. There was still guilt about Robbie whirling through his thoughts and he spent days composing a letter. It was so hard to explain, to put into words. But in the end, he

242

decided that he was fretting over nothing. Robbie would understand. Of course he would! The letter was simple and upbeat. He confirmed that they were the very best of friends and always would be. Yet again, he thanked him for saving his life. Robbie would laugh at that, shake his head. *No need, pal. No need.* He was home with his family and life was good.

As he walked back from the Post Office there was a lightness to his step. Everything that needed to be done had been, and life could now unfold gently. He paused at the bridge and watched the flow of water switch and swirl its way downstream.

He turned as a voice he recognised called out.

'Andy?'

The man was walking with crutches. One of his legs was missing. He stank of alcohol despite the early hour. He lurched towards Andy. This wasn't wanted. It really wasn't wanted, but he knew he couldn't walk on past. Ignore the man.

'Good to see you, Johnnie.'

'Aye. Give us a pound, can ye? I'm skint.'

Chapter 58
1919

Something was wrong. Connie seemed in some distress, her hand clutching at her belly, her steps uneven. Charlie leapt out from behind the steering wheel and ran to her side. He scooped her up in his arms and carried her to the car. She made no protest which confirmed that this was something serious.

Cramping spasms snatched at her stomach. She winced at the discomfort.

'We shall be at the hospital in two minutes. Hold on my love.'

'Just take me home,' she whispered.

'No. I insist. You are going to the hospital.'

'Charlie! Take me home.'

'But—'

'Confound it! Take me home! This happens. It is just nervousness and upset. Nothing more.'

'Oh, my darling.' He reached for her hand. 'Was it so very beastly?'

She stared at him. 'Well, of course it was. I am cast out of her life, and I cannot quite believe it.'

'Perhaps in time?'

She threw her head back and looked up at the sky.

They decided that they should travel abroad. There was nothing to hold them to Scotland. Not now. A clean break in a warm climate with beauty all around could only help. His family had a villa in the south of France. It remained pristine, untouched by the war. It would be perfect.

They had decided to drive. The freedom it gave them to explore, to go wherever they pleased, whenever they felt the desire.

As they closed the door on their Glasgow home Connie held her hand out for the car keys.

Charlie raised his eyebrows in question. 'Are you quite sure that you are up to this?'

'I shall drive. I am not to be treated like an invalid. Are we agreed?'

'Of course. I shall treat you with utter disregard and cruelty!'

She laughed, and it was the best sound to his mind.

～

The scent of the pine trees, the gentle Mediterranean breeze causing a flicker of palm fronds, the lapping of azure waters. It was quite heavenly. They sat on the pebbly beach at the bottom of the small cliff that dropped away from the walls of the villa, their toes in the cooling water, and breathed it all in.

'You are a very clever thing, Charlie. I do feel so much better out here.'

'And I am glad.' He squeezed her hand.

'Let us go into the village and take some of their healing waters of the alcoholic kind.' She cocked her head and grinned at him.

'What a splendid idea!'

They had climbed back up the steps that twisted across the cliff and collected the car. It was only a five-minute drive along the winding coastal road. Connie leaned her head back, lifted her arms into the breeze, let out a squeal.

Charlie smiled.

He pulled into a small café just outside of Monaco. They settled themselves at one of the rustic tables and spent the rest of the afternoon sipping Bordeaux and nibbling olives, cheese, and a crusty baton, in the shade of a gently flapping umbrella. The sound of the waves crashing against the rocks below was quite mesmerising. Cormorants jerked along in the blue, swooping down for unsuspecting fish, surfacing only to be chased and harried by gulls.

They watched the white sails of boats flutter and disappear beyond the horizon.

'I wonder where they might be headed,' Charlie said.

The sun slipped into the sea, casting an orange hue across the water. Gulls swirled and swooped, shrieking their presence to the world as they pecked at the last of the day's offerings. The deep turquoise sky fell into dark blue. A chill with it. The chirrup of crickets filled the night air.

Connie reached for the wine bottle and tipped it towards her glass, but nothing ventured forth. 'Oh bother! It seems that we have drunk it all!'

'Then we should head for home.'

'Oh, I think not! Waiter! Another bottle if you please?' She held the empty bottle aloft and wiggled it at him.

Charlie winced inside but smiled at her.

'Aren't you drinking, Charlie?'

'I fear that my driving skills might become lessened. A couple of coffees to straighten me out will be just the ticket!'

She finished the second bottle and was becoming loud. Other customers were casting disapproving glances her way.

'We really must leave now. Come Connie!' Charlie said with conviction as he stood up and took her arm. 'Up you come. There's a girl!'

Her body had become light, wobbly, as if her skeleton were made of rubber, not bone. Thankfully, she didn't put up any resistance as he led her to the car. He felt sober and quite capable of driving safely.

They had just turned a sharp corner, beneath them the waters swirled and crashed. Connie leaned across to Charlie, trying to rest her head against his shoulder. She hit his arm with too much force, forcing the car to swerve onto the gravel shoulder. He lost control of the car as it skidded over gravel and towards the edge of the cliff. 'Connie!' he shrieked, as he tumbled out of the car.

Chapter 59
1919

~

Hannah had dropped in at the bookshop and was scanning the papers, as usual. She scoffed at much of what was written, but it was important to keep informed. How could one fight if one didn't know what one's enemy was saying? 'Sometimes I wonder if it's worth it,' she said, tossing the paper aside. 'So much fight, so little change.'

'Oh, I could list a few major ones. Fairer rents, shorter working weeks, the vote for women.'

Hannah raised her eyebrows at that one. 'Yes, but not for you and me until we are thirty. Thirty! For goodness' sake. What they are saying is that we are not yet wise enough to cast a vote. The damned cheek of it!'

'Which is precisely why we can't give up. Little victories lead to greater ones.'

'I know, I know. It's just—well, tiresome sometimes.'

'Aye, but you'd die without it,' Mhairi chipped in. 'I mean, why would you get out o your bed of a morning?'

'Mhairi! I didn't hear you sneak in.'

'Quiet as a wee mouse, me!'

Lizzie filled the kettle and set it on the stove. 'Tea?'

'Lizzie? Are you ill? It's past morning and we've got a visitor and you're offering tea!' Mhairi said with a laugh. 'Out of gin?'

'I'm not a complete alcoholic! Besides which, Hannah counts as family.'

'Right enough. Sisters to the end!' Mhairi said.

Lizzie filled the chunky red earthenware teapot and

248

set it on the table with three mismatched cups.

'Speaking of sisters, has anyone heard anything of Connie?' Lizzie asked. 'I know she isn't quite the sister she once was, but she has been out of touch for some time.'

'Probably down to me shutting the door on her,' said Mhairi.

'You didn't!' Hannah said.

'Aye, well, she was being all let bygones be bygones and I'm no up for that. She made her choice, and I told her that.' She shrugged dismissively.

'Perhaps she has a point? It was war and it was awful. Men—many, many men—committed atrocities under orders. Forgive and move on?'

'That's what Robbie says too. I just don't have that in me. No yet.'

'I don't believe one can help who one falls in love with.' Lizzie glanced across at Hannah.

'Indeed,' Hannah said. 'There is more than enough hatred in this world without...well... forgive me Mhairi, but without needless animosity.'

Mhairi stared. 'But he—'

'God knows I am no supporter of what was going on over there, but it's over. All of it. And it should be put to bed, where possible.'

'And this is possible?'

'Yes, Mhairi. I believe so.'

The discussion continued with little purchase being given until Robbie came back, covered in grime, that smile on his face. He had found black work at a nearby building site. The work was hard, the pay low, the conditions awful, the hours long. But it kept food on the table and a small sense of pride in his heart. He was

249

building back. Making good again. That felt like a worthwhile thing. A decent thing.

'I'll just have a clean-up and I'll be with you.'

He withdrew to his room, stripped off his work-clothes, washed away the day, ran his finger along the scars on his leg. That constant reminder of what he had run through. Where he had been. He knew that he was fortunate though. He was alive. A functioning man. He had a home and a wife and a job. Yes. He was one of the lucky ones.

'What's that atmosphere all about? You could cut the air in here with a knife, so you could.' He leant down and kissed Mhairi on the forehead. 'How's my princess?'

She smiled at him. 'We were talking about Connie, again.'

'Were you now? Any tea left in that pot?'

'It'll be a bit cold.'

He shrugged. 'That'll do me fine.' He poured himself a cup, added a splash of milk and three teaspoons of sugar, and sat down beside Mhairi, wrapping his arm around her neck.

'Oh, Robbie!' Lizzie jumped to her feet and picked up a letter from the windowsill. 'This came for you. I almost forgot!'

There was always a slight trepidation tripping through his veins when he received a letter. That fear of being summonsed, of facing court martial, still lingered. Even now. And with that fear, memories that he didn't want to surface any more tried to sneak through into this new life. Things that belonged in a deep dark place. He sighed in relief when he saw that this letter was personal, handwritten, in a friendly white envelope. He slipped his finger along its seal. 'It's from Andy.' He swiped the hair back from his face. A smile grew as he read on. What a relief! The man sounded solid and grounded and perfectly well.

'What does he say, then?'

'Just that he's well. Back with his family. So pleased for the lad. Happy endings, eh? For the both of us.' He squeezed Mhairi into him and kissed her again.

That night as they snuggled up in bed, he whispered to her. 'Life's too short, Mhairi. Let it go. I have. You should too.'

She sighed. 'It's hard, Robbie.'

'And it'll not get any easier. The longer you hold on to that grief, that pain, the deeper it settles, and then there's no shifting it. Get rid, Mhairi. Get rid.'

He spooned her, held her tight, all through the night.

Lizzie and Hannah waited until there was silence. They smiled at one another. Lizzie patted the space next to her on the settee. Hannah settled by her side and they kissed softly, tenderly. The necessary secrecy made it all the more delicious, if frustrating.

'You can't help who you fall in love with,' Hannah whispered, as she stroked a piece of stray hair from Lizzie's face and tucked it behind her ear.

Lovemaking was secret and silent.

Chapter 60
1919

∿

The car tumbled down the cliff-face, exploding on the pebbly shore far below. Charlie's head buzzed, his stomach lurched, his skin felt like it was on fire where the gravel had scored through it. He sat up, slowly. The pain of it. He was coming to his full senses, understanding what had happened. *Connie!*

The crashing of waves far below echoed through the night. Everything else was silent, as if the world knew. A desperation that he had never felt before had seized him. This would be the end of him. He closed his eyes again, dared not move, dared not look. *'Oh Christ.'* The breath of a breeze on his cheek carried the scent of jasmine, of thyme, of beauty, and life. But it couldn't be. Not for him. This was done. He was done. But he had to know for sure. He knew he had to see it with his own eyes, or there would be no believing of it.

He slithered across to the cliff-edge, peered over, but could see nothing but a sense of the swell of the sea. His vision was blurred by his tears. He swiped at them, but didn't want clarity. This emptiness was enough. He rolled onto his back. His head swarmed with loss, with his awful history. The soft thud of explosions. The screams of his men. His! The blackness of it all. Black and swirling madness. She was gone. This was his life once more. He would end it. Roll the other way, tumble down the cliff and be gone. Be with her. There was no-one to miss him. The world would be a better place without him in it. So many men, dead, because of him, and now Connie. That wonderful woman, killed, because of him.

Something rustled behind him, scratched at the ground. A murmur of life. Perhaps he had also hit some poor creature. He crawled across to the scrub of dried bushes, felt around, ignoring the stabs of thorns. Something was there. Something substantial.

Connie's chest heaved as she gulped in precious air. By some miracle he must have held on to her; dragged her clear of the car; they had both survived. He stroked the hair from her face.

'Connie, are you—are you all right?'

She opened her eyes to the haunting light of the full moon, as if this were a dream. The hazy outline of him became clearer as she focused, her brain still fuddled from the drink but sobered somewhat by the scare. 'I— yes—I think so.'

His heart thumped. He felt that he could live again because she was still here. Dear God. He was alive again.

They sat in silence making sense of this, breathing in each other.

It was late at night, the road empty, nothing but quiet and the ocean. Even the crickets had silenced themselves. The sound of the waves lapping on the pebbly shore was soothing, calming, mixed with absolute terror at what had almost happened to them. Their car, down there, far below, nothing but an obliterated mess. That could have, perhaps should have been, them.

'Can you move?' he asked.

She eased herself up, pushing on her arms. Winced. 'Yes, but by God, it hurts!'

They stayed in silence for a few minutes more, just

253

taking in the fact that they had survived when their car lay in pieces far below. They couldn't see it, but they knew.

'Charlie. We nearly—I nearly—' She wept.

He slithered closer, wrapped his arms around her.

She crumpled into them, and he held tight until her tears subsided. The shame of it.

He kissed her head. 'Do you think something is broken?'

'No. No,' she sniffed. 'It just burns all over.'

'Right. We shall help each other.' He let go of her, stretched himself up burying the pain of it, ignoring the trickle of blood that he could feel slipping down his back. He bent forward, held his arms out to her, slipped his hands under her armpits. 'Can you stand?'

'I—I think so.'

He pulled her up slowly, and they stood there, arms around each other, the soft breeze drifting around them. The lap of the sea far below. The squawk of a bird high above, swooping through the blue light. The serenity of a night which had almost ended them.

'Ready?'

'Ready,' she confirmed.

They hobbled down back towards the villa. It wasn't far and it was all downhill, but their progress was painfully slow. A step, a pause; a step, a pause. At last, the red tiles of the villa peeked through the cypress trees, the white walls glimmering in the moonlight beckoned them.

The walls swallowed their fear and breathed out relief as they stepped inside.

'We should bathe and then remove any beastly stones that have embedded themselves into our flesh,' he said.

'I fear there may be many. My skin is on fire. First, I need a drink.'

'Do you—'

Her stare was warning enough. She limped across to the drink's cabinet, reached for the brandy, filled a glass for each of them. 'It is medicinal.'

His serious drinking had been done in the depths of night when she was asleep. She didn't know, and he wanted it to remain that way. Quite how he had managed to conceal it from her, he wasn't sure. She must have smelled it on his breath of a morning. Perhaps she was simply too kind to mention it. Perhaps she just didn't care. It was how he got through the terrors, when they came. They had lessened considerably since their wedding, as if she had cast a magic spell upon him. That was what this whole relationship felt like. A piece of magic cast by the woman he adored.

He filled the bath with hot water and added a healthy dose of salts. 'It will sting like hell, but it is healing.'

They climbed in together and winced in unison as they sank into the water, almost too hot; almost painful, but somehow soothing. A release of the pain. They sat and picked at pieces of gravel and detritus until they had done their best, each clearing the other. He stepped out of the bath and stretched for a towel that was folded on the chair. He draped it across her shoulders. 'You wait right there while I fetch your robe.'

There was no complaint from her now.

～

She awoke to the sound of a tray being placed on the bedside table. The chink of porcelain, the smell of fresh coffee and croissants.

'Good morning, my love,' he said with a sympathetic smile.

'Oh God! My head feels as though it might explode!' She turned to face the breakfast tray, but the sight of it made her feel sick. On his insistence she managed to swallow a few mouthfuls.

'It really is the best thing. A lining for the stomach.'

'Did I really drink so much?'

'Well, quite a lot, but the change in temperature, a strange country, that can also have an effect. Make one feel quite beastly.'

Chapter 61
1919

~

Andy kept himself to himself as much as he could. It wasn't that he wanted to, but right then he didn't feel comfortable bumping into other former soldiers. The men he had signed up with. The men he had gone to training camp with. The men he had fought with. What could he say about how he got back home? There would be tales of battles he knew nothing about. Soldiers who had been killed. So many of them. Then there was that missing year.

He could say that he had been captured, held prisoner by the Germans, but he didn't want to lie; to pretend, as he had done with Johnnie. The man had been so far gone that he hadn't been taking any of it in anyway. It was just the drink that he was interested in. Escape. And Andy understood that. He knew that he was lucky. He'd had Robbie to see him through the worst times, and now his family to prop him up; keep him from falling down again.

His family didn't question or probe. It was as if they knew that there were places he didn't want to go to, histories he couldn't share, and that was just fine with them. He learned his father's trade, staying in the back, kneading, mixing, shaping, baking. That was enough. That was more than enough. His mind focused on a new wholesomeness that was totally absorbing. The feel of the dough, soft and pliable in his hands, the scent of the yeast as it cast its spell, the satisfaction of creating, of doing good for his community, his family, himself.

His mother walked into the bakery where he and his father were sweating amongst the heat of the ovens. 'Andy. I was just hanging your kitbag up in the garden for a bit of an airing, and this fell out of one of the pockets. I thought it might be important, like,' she said, handing him a slip of paper, a questioning smile on her lips.

He took it from her, read the name and address, Bea Cummings, Applestead Farm, Selkirk. He stared at it, a blank expression on his face. 'I've no idea, Ma.' He turned the paper over as if there might be a clue there. 'It's not so far away from here. Maybe it isn't even mine.'

'Not to worry. I'm quite sure that it'll come back if it's meant to.' But she did worry about her son. This man who had returned to her was still struggling with something. She could see it; sense it, but he wasn't talking about it. That was what men did. They bottled things up and carried on. She so wished that he wouldn't. It felt as if whatever he was carrying should be shed. At least shared with her.

She wouldn't judge, and she tried to tell him that; to show him. But any attempt to find a way inside her son's heart was blocked and she couldn't shift it; break the walls down. He would stare briefly, as if thinking about it, and she would think that this was it. At last, he was going to talk to her. But he would turn away and the silence that was left in his wake felt like a knife.

He clenched the piece of paper in his hand and walked up the stairs to his bedroom.

She watched him go with a heaviness in her heart. A tear escaped. 'Oh, son,' she whispered.

He put the piece of paper away in his bedside drawer while he thought on it. It niggled at him, wouldn't let him be. There was something there. Something that didn't want to leave him alone. But he was damned if he could drag it to the surface. He fell into a restless sleep.

He woke up with a start. A memory in his head. That wasn't unusual—the nightmares, the terrors were simply a part of his life, lessening, but still there—but the feeling was different. It was joyous. Happy. The nurse! Bea. She had called herself, Bea. He could picture her clear as day. Hear her soft voice. *'You just hang on, love. Hang on and I'll see you right. My name's Beatrice, but friends call me Bea. You can, if you want. Bea. How about you? I would love to know your name.'*

This must be her address. How he had ended up with it he had no idea. He barely remembered his time at the hospital, or the sanatorium, but he remembered her. Her kindness; her smile. He decided he would write to her. A quick thank you. That was the least he could do, and then, that would be that.

He had been writing regular letters to Robbie and was always glad of the replies, the lightness of the chatter made it feel like Robbie was still with him. This would just be one more letter to write. Only, it wasn't.

He couldn't get the words to sit right. He tried over and over again. Scribbles discarded. Frustration mounting. He should ask a woman for the right way to write this. His sister was too busy flirting away with her boyfriend, but his mother was more than happy to help. It was an honour, a sign of trust, and her heart swelled.

Dear Bea,

I found the address you had given me and wanted to say how thankful I am for the help you gave me when I was unwell. I am sorry I didn't write sooner, but I had clean forgotten that you had given me your address until my mother found it in my kitbag!

Imagine that! I am healthy and happy and trust that you are too. Thank you again for your special care and kindness. I remember it well.

With Gratitude,

Andy

'But Ma, will she even know who I am? She must have looked after hundreds of soldiers. Thousands of them, even.'

'I'm quite sure she will, son. A woman doesn't just give her address out to every soldier she comes across, now does she?'

He laughed. 'I suppose not. But is it okay?'

'It's just fine. Give it here and I'll pop it in at the Post Office for you on my way to the shops.'

That night he tossed and turned again. Had he done the right thing? Could it be picked up the wrong way? What if she replied? What then? He put it out of his mind and the days tumbled along in a pleasant normality. That was all he wanted these days. Quiet. No surprises. Nothing to unsettle his newfound contentedness. He hadn't taken to the drink, as many others had. The night terrors were lessening with each passing day. That awful fear was becoming a distant memory that he had buried far down somewhere unreachable. He was all right.

'Son?' his ma called from the shop. 'There's someone here to see you.'

'Are you expecting someone?' his father asked.

He stared at his father, shook his head, and stepped tentatively through to the shop.

His breath stopped, caught in his fear.

Jesus!

260

Chapter 62
1919

~

Mhairi found it hard to be still, to do nothing, once Robbie had gone to work. It left her head with too much time to spin. Her thoughts were seldom positive. Here was too much historical pain for her to dwell on. Her missing family, her dead brother, her lost daughter and her broken friendship. They seemed to pile, one on top of the other, with no solution that she could fathom. She spent more time at the Salvation Army, just helping where she could. They had been gracious to her when she had arrived in Glasgow with nothing but herself and a missing family, and she wanted to do something to return the favour.

She had asked if they could help find her daughter and was told a very definite *no*. Rosie wasn't a missing person. Mhairi tried to argue her point, but there was nothing doing. It was a dead end; a part of her life that was over, and she would do well to remember that, they said. The child was no longer her concern.

A mother couldn't be told that. You didn't stop being a mother because your child had been taken away. How could they even think such things? She couldn't agree with what they had said—was made angry by it—but still she carried on helping, doing what she could. Searching in her own time.

It had been five years since she had left her family on that cruel day back in 1914. Her little brother and sister would be nine and seven. Still so young, and she hoped, innocent, loved, safe. But if they were, why couldn't

261

they be found? She still scanned every face, both in the refuge and on the streets. She made enquiries at doctor's offices, schools. It was more effective when she said that she worked for the Salvation Army. It was only a small stretch of the truth.

Hannah placed an advertisement in the newspaper for Mhairi to try and locate her family. Anything was worth trying, and Mhairi was grateful. But what of Rosie?

Hannah thought that there would be no point in an advertisement for her. Who would admit to having the child? No-one.

But perhaps a neighbour? Argued Mhairi. A disgruntled acquaintance? An upset boyfriend or girlfriend?

'Please, Hannah. Please! This is killing me.'

'I don't know what to say, Mhairi. You need to start living your life for you, you know? Leave this. Let it go.'

'That's no gonna happen, and you know it.'

Hannah sighed, hands on hips, and reluctantly relented. She wrote a brief story around the photograph Mhairi had given her of Rosie, taken just before they had been separated. She had used the same photographer who had taken her and Robbie's proposal day photo. He had remembered her and Robbie. Asked kindly after him. Hung his head at word of the 'missing presumed dead' notification.

'I am so sorry, my dear. The two of you made such a lovely couple.'

'Aye, well, I'm no believing it. This photo is for him when he gets back, so that he can see how bonnie she was!'

'I truly hope so.'

She had been right not to give up hope; not to accept that Robbie had been killed, and he had come back to her. She prayed that Rosie would be found and returned. Their family complete for the first time.

Robbie always returned home with a smile on his face, but this one felt different. Bigger. More meaningful.

Mhairi hugged him.

He kissed her head, took her hands. 'I've got the best news!'

'She's been found?'

He shook his head.

'My family's been found?'

'No. This is for us. There's a fine wee flat come free, and it's ours if we want it. There's a nice back green. Imagine! Our own wee place.'

Mhairi smiled, tried to hide her disappointment. 'That's—that's great, Robbie.'

Within a week they had moved in. Robbie was barely earning enough to pay the rent and put food on the table, but their friends helped with furnishing the place, making it a home. The bed from Lizzie, table and chairs from Hannah. It was a start. It was theirs.

When Robbie came back from work that first night both hands were behind his back. His eyes were twinkling.

'What are you hiding there?' Mhairi asked.

A tiny mewl answered her question. He held out the smallest scruffiest wee kitten she had ever seen. It could barely walk. Its fur was filthy and matted.

Mhairi reached her hands out and tenderly pulled the kitten to the warmth of her chest. 'Oh, Robbie! Wherever did you find this wee thing?'

'At the building site. It's been there for a couple of days and no sign of its mother. My guess is it's been left behind somehow and it's turning right cold now. It would die on its own out there. Is it not just the cutest wee thing?'

'It will be when we get it cleaned up!'

He felt such a swell of success! Something for her to smile about, to care for. That tenderness to her face had been missing for too long.

'It'll be needing a name,' he said.

'Aye, it will.'

'Whiskers?'

She cocked her head at him. Shook it. 'I don't think it looks like a Whiskers. It's all stripey like a wee tiger.'

He laughed. 'I like Tiger.'

'Folk'll be wondering what's going on if we're out in the back green calling on Tiger!'

They both laughed.

'Tiger it is then.'

They washed him in the sink. He clawed both of their arms.

'He'll hate us now!'

'I doubt that.'

Mhairi rubbed him dry and wrapped him in a warm towel. He was soon taking milk, eating mushed up meat and fish, and making a nuisance of himself. Curtains were climbed, as was anything else he could get his claws into. He would scamper up Robbie's legs when he returned from work and sit on his shoulder, as if taking possession of the man who saved him. At night they would be woken by him scampering around the flat chasing something or nothing.

'He makes a lot of noise for such a teeny wee thing!'

Chapter 63
1919

~

Connie and Charlie pulled into the driveway of their house. The sandstone looked a very dark grey in the rain, leaves swirled in little whirlwinds, shrubs bent as if hiding from the weather themselves.

'I'm beginning to question returning! The weather is simply foul,' Charlie said, shivering to emphasise the point.

'My darling, you underestimate. It is atrocious and all other adjectives that describe very-much-worse than foul!'

He laughed. 'Wait here and I'll fetch the umbrella.'

She didn't protest and watched as he ran up the path, his jacket pulled over his head.

The door was opened by the housekeeper, and she hurried down the path with an umbrella. 'Here you are, sir. Welcome back!'

He laughed. 'Thank you, Maud. If only the weather were a tad more welcoming as well!'

'On you go, sir. The fires are on. I'll fetch milady.'

'I wouldn't hear of it! In you go, Maud.'

He hurried back down to the car and held the umbrella for Connie. 'Is this permitted?' he said, with a cheeky smile.

'It most definitely is! There are times when one must simply bury one's principles.'

They ran indoors and shut the cold greyness of autumnal Glasgow behind their heavy oak door. Once changed and settled they sat at either side of a roaring fire, on their Fairfield velvet wingback chairs, rich burgundy to match the curtains and contrast with the white carpet. Both had relaxed into silk pyjamas; hers peach, trimmed with lace; his bottle green, run through with a fine blood-red stripe. Matching dressing gowns were draped across their shoulders. She had curled her legs under herself, his were stretched out, long and lazy.

'There is something altogether fabulous about being wrapped up in warmth and comfort when it is so beastly outside,' she said.

They both turned to stare at the sheets of rain that lashed the windows, the sway of the nearly naked elm trees, the heavy grey of the clouds.

'One could almost be underwater!'

'One could. It still sends a shiver down my spine when I think of how close we came to ending up as such. Food for Mediterranean fish!' He laughed, threw his head back.

'Charlie, darling. It wasn't in the least bit funny. I nearly killed you. I nearly killed us!'

'Oh, but my sweet, you didn't, and that is all that one should concern oneself with. We are alive and it is quite splendid!'

The thought of her death did still churn up the darkest of thoughts and he wouldn't soon forget the absolute fear of being without her, but he kept it deep. Swallowed it down. He reached for the heavy brocade cord and pulled. A bell rang in the kitchen that called his staff. Within seconds his housekeeper was there.

'Ah, Maud. I think a couple of brandies.'

'Yes, sir. Right away, sir.' She walked briskly across to the drinks' cabinet, set two crystal glasses on a silver tray, poured a healthy measure of Remy Martin into each and returned, offering a glass to her employers.

'I feel uncomfortable with that,' Connie said, her nose wrinkled in distaste.

'With what, darling?'

'Summoning poor Maud to pour a drink when it is just there. We are perfectly capable, are we not?'

'Oh, but she likes to be of use. Isn't that right, Maud?'

'Of course, sir. If that's all?'

He nodded.

She curtsied and left the room.

'I do not like any of it! I do not like having *staff*. I do not like being called milady, or any such thing. I do not like being waited upon, if truth be told.'

'I had no idea. Then we shall dismiss them.'

'Charlie, that would be awful. You cannot be serious.'

'No, of course not. How would we manage?'

She let out a heavy sigh and shook her head.

'But you were brought up with servants. You had your Mhairi, after all.'

'Yes. And I didn't like it then. Well, no. I liked it very much insofar as we became such friends. And I had been so unwell that it was needed. But other than that, I did not enjoy it in the least.'

She paused, lost briefly in thought, a cloud darkening her sparkle. 'Life was so much richer with Mhairi by my side. She taught me so much, saved me, and I have let her down so badly.'

'By marrying me?' he looked aghast.

'No! I do not mean it like that. The misunderstanding between Mhairi and me is horrible, and I should not have allowed it to strengthen. I should not have allowed her to leave my life. I should not have allowed Rosie to be taken like that. She is my godchild, and I did what? I

267

fell in love with you, and I cast her aside. I cast both of them aside as if they were nothing. I am a disgrace!'

He tried to comfort her, but it was such a challenge. He felt little empathy, little appreciation of how she might be feeling. Surely everyone enjoyed being waited upon. Their lives made easier. And this Mhairi was a serving girl, after all. Quite how she had been chosen as Rosie's godmother was beyond his comprehension.

His wife's friendship with such a girl had to be one of circumstance. This hadn't been a true friendship. Such things were not possible. And to his mind Connie was better off away from her influence, and that of her other friends: Lizzie and Hannah were disreputable enough, but Robbie? A deserter. A common traitor. No. She would do well to keep her distance, move in the correct circles.

Perhaps he should do more to introduce her to some appropriate young ladies of standing. Yes! Of course! He had been too selfish keeping her entirely to himself. They should socialise, attend gatherings, luncheons, even parties. He didn't care for such things, but he loved his Connie. This would be done for her.

Chapter 64
1919

～

Andy stood in the hallway between the bakery and the shop, his heart pounding, hardly daring to look. He clutched at the doorframe for balance, for security. His mouth had become so dry that it was difficult to even think about speaking. He stepped forward and his anxiety dissipated into the heady air of the shop. His head became so light and giddy that he barely managed to contain his emotions. Such relief! Such joy and relief!

Bea smiled, walked towards him, took hold of his shoulders, kissed both of his cheeks. 'Andy! Hello.'

'Bea. I—well—yes. Hello.'

His mother was beaming, her hands clasped to her chest. This was quite wonderful! 'Why don't the two of you go upstairs and I'll make you a nice cup of tea. You'll take tea, Bea?'

'Yes. Thank you. Thank you very much.'

His father tugged at his wife's pinnie as she headed up the stairs. 'You mind and leave the two o them in peace, now,' he whispered.

'I'll just—'

'Aye. I know fine what you'll just do.' He raised his eyebrows at her in warning.

She slapped his hand in admonishment and tutted. 'I'll just see them right and come straight on down.'

He gently tapped her behind and grinned. Memories of when they had first met swept into his head. She had been a looker, and no mistaking. God knows why she had chosen him, but she had, and they were as happy now as they ever had been. What a blessing. Would that his son could be so lucky. Christ knew, he deserved it, after whatever it was that he had been through. It wasn't spoken of, but it sat there dark and heavy in his son's soul. He would give anything to have it lifted by something; by someone special.

Andy's mother made them tea, set out a selection of cakes, fresh from the bakery, and put the tray on the coffee table. 'I'll leave you two in peace, now. Just give me a call if you need anything.' She grinned at her son, patted Bea on the shoulder, and reluctantly left.

Her husband was waiting at the bottom of the stairs. 'Well done!'

'Aye, well, we were young once too!'

'If memory serves, we always had a chaperone. Your mother, or your sister, or your aunt, or...'

'Oh, but we did manage to sneak away.'

He chuckled. 'We did. And, I'll not be forgetting that, right enough.'

They grinned at each other.

Upstairs there was no awkward silence. Bea had seen him at his very worst. He wasn't quite sure how much she knew of his time overseas but had a vague memory of baring his soul to her. Of there being no judgement. Only softness.

She leaned forward in her seat. 'I was so happy to hear from you. You've no idea. And us living so close to each other. Who'd have thought it? Perhaps that was why I felt drawn to you.'

'Did you really?'

'I did. I even tracked you down at the sanatorium. Broke all the rules, so I did.' She blushed slightly.

He did likewise and smiled. 'And here you are.'

'Yes. Here I am.'

'Are you still nursing?'

'I am that. Not down there anymore. It was hard, and I was lonely. Homesick. I took a job with the local doctor.'

'Well, I'm glad about that. I almost didn't write, you know. Our meeting was...well, it was from a time I'd rather forget.'

'Maybe we met long ago; passed by each other as strangers up here, walked along the same streets. Let's pretend that we had, that we are old friends, and all of that other stuff in between lies far away. Not even a memory. How about that?'

'You're good at this.'

'Good at what?'

'Making a broken man feel whole again.'

'I see nothing broken in you. Just the same boy I knew long ago, all grown up.'

'Shall we—would you like to go for a walk?'

She smiled, raised her eyebrows at him. 'Along those familiar old streets?'

'Aye. Along them.'

He slipped his father's good coat off the peg. 'All right, da?'

'Aye. On you go son. Don't you be out too long. It's turning nasty out there.'

Andy held Bea's coat open for her and she slipped her arms into the sleeves. He pulled her collar up. 'There now. All snug.'

She slipped her arm through his and they walked down to the river. They stopped on the bridge and watched the wind carry the golden and red leaves down to the tumbling water.

271

His thoughts were with what she had said earlier. They could have passed each other by and just not known. So very many people that could be passing you by when they're meant to be with you. A part of you. How easy to miss them. To lead a different life, less rich, less fulfilled. He pulled her arm closer to him.

'All right?' she asked.

'Oh, I am very much more than all right.'

She stood on her tiptoes and kissed his cheek. 'Me too.'

The clouds had gathered. Angry formations of grey and black. The wind had picked up. She squealed as a leaf blew in her face. He wiped a speck of mud from her cheek. The patter of rain bounced off the pavement.

'Run home or take shelter?'

She shrugged.

He took her hand and led her down the riverbank and under the bridge. There was an odd collection of rocks, large enough to sit on. He grinned.

'This was our den. We would play here, as children. A great place to hide and make ghostly noises from. We thought we were being really scary.'

'And the passers-by were terrified, no doubt.'

'Oh, I'm quite sure of it!'

They listened to the rush of water, glanced up at the river. The rain seemed to be easing.

'Shall we make a run for it?'

'I think so. I'll need to get going soon, anyway.'

He sighed, more audibly than he had intended.

'Why don't you come to mine, next time?'

He felt as if his heart might explode. 'I would really like that.'

Chapter 65
1919

~~

Mhairi had been offered her old job back at the tearoom. It would mean less time for the Salvation Army; less time for her search, but she could see that Robbie was right. She had to live her own life, and what with this new flat of theirs, they could do with the extra income. It felt good to be working hard with little time to think of anything else. Her preoccupations quieter. She had been on her feet all day and was glad to reach home. Her home. As she slipped key in lock and turned it, the security that it gave her was a brand-new feeling.

She gratefully shut the door against the cold wind and the snow that it was bringing with it, soft now, gentle flakes that were quite beautiful as they cascaded down from the sky, but it felt like the clouds were heavy with a lot more of it. A blizzard even.

It still took her by surprise to be greeted by a mewling bundle of fur wrapping itself around her ankles. Tiger was growing into a handsome young cat, despite his rough start in life. His fur was sleek, his markings quite beautiful, his eyes the most wondrous green flecked with gold. She smiled at him, bent down to give him a welcome stroke. 'Hello, wee one,' she said.

The snowflakes turned to drops of water on her coat as she hung it up on its peg. She kicked her shoes off and rubbed at her icy-cold toes before slipping them into woollen slippers. 'You wouldn't want to be out there. Right cold, so it is!' Tiger cocked his head at her as if he understood. He attached himself to her heels, still mewling, as she walked through to the kitchen. Thankfully, there was a skuttle full of coal in the fireplace and she wouldn't have to go outside again to get more until Robbie was home. She rolled up some newspaper, tied it into tight balls, set it on the fire grate, built up some kindling around it and lit it with a match. It seemed reluctant to catch, taunting her with the beginnings of a flame and then sinking back again to nothing but blackened paper. At last, it caught, and she built it up with coal.

'That'll have us nice and warm in no time.'

Tiger didn't need any encouragement. He stretched himself out and dozed in the comfort of the flames. 'Oh, so I'm second best to the fire now. Is that it?' He was quite oblivious to her now. She thought about the simplicity of that; being able to switch off from everything and just lie in peaceful oblivion. 'It's no a bad life you've got, now, is it?' she said.

She had just filled the kettle to make a pot of tea and placed it on the cooker when a knock at the door startled her. It wasn't the right time of day for a visit from Hannah or Lizzie. She reluctantly left the warmth of the kitchen and hurried back to the hall, wrapping her arms around herself in an attempt to lock the heat in. She tentatively pulled the front door open a crack. There was no-one to be seen, only a package. Quite a large one, in a cardboard box, which already had a sprinkling of snow on it, as did the footsteps leading to and away from her door. How peculiar. She snatched at the package, dropped it in the hall and closed the door to the cold.

She carried the box through to the kitchen and set it on the table. Tiger languorously lifted his head to catch a look before settling back down. Apparently, it was uninteresting. Mhairi was intrigued. It was addressed to her in a delicate script. She gasped. That was Connie's handwriting. An unwelcome intrusion into her new home. Her new life. She put it in a corner, out of sight, but not out of mind. 'Damn you, Connie!' she mumbled.

She poured herself a cup of tea and sat close to the fire, wishing that Robbie were here. That the package hadn't arrived. That the past hadn't happened at all. If she could go back to Robbie signing up, she wouldn't allow it. They would run off to a place far from everywhere, far from everyone, and be a family. A proper family with their own beautiful little girl. They could have gone to Kinlochleven. No doubt there was still work to be had up there. Yes, it was its own version of hell, but nothing compared to what Robbie had been through. She found herself crying again. Would it ever stop?

It was dark out by the time Robbie got home. A blast of cold air extinguished soon enough by the warmth of his smile, the softness of his words.

'How's my beautiful girl.'

She smiled. 'Oh fine.'

He could see that she wasn't, but he wouldn't say, just like every time before. They had settled into this existence; this acceptance of letting each other be, in the hope it would somehow all be right again. The sadness would go of its own accord. And it usually did, for a while anyway. He kissed her head, held his hands out in front of the fire. 'Bitter out there, so it is. Snow up to my ankles!'

His glance was held by the package in the corner.

'You been out shopping?'

'Naw. It came today. From Connie.'

'Oh aye? What is it, then?'

'I haven't looked. I don't want to know what it is. I want it got rid. I would have taken it out myself if it hadn't been so cold.'

'Mhairi, love, maybe take a look?'

'You know fine my thoughts on her, on this. And how did she find us, anyway?'

Robbie blushed. There was no need for words. She could read him well enough without.

'Why would you do that?'

'Because she asked. You can see how hurt she is, how sorry. It's eating her up and it's eating you up too. It needs to stop.'

She was taken aback by his tone. That wasn't the way he spoke to her. No softness, no understanding.

'I'm serious, Mhairi. This needs to stop!'

He strode across to the package, pulled it open, lifted the contents out, placed them on the table. 'Would you look at it, Mhairi? It's top-quality bedding and towels. Look! It's even got our initials sewn on. Yours and mine. Look.'

'Easy enough when you've got her kind of money. I'm telling you I'm not having that in my house.'

'And I'm telling you, we are!'

She got up, pulled her boots and coat on, and stormed out of the flat, slamming the door behind her.

Robbie paused. They had never had a fight like this. He would leave her be. He had just got in after a long day's work. He was cold and tired and hungry. She would come to her senses soon enough.

Chapter 66
1919

~∽~

It was almost Christmas and there were parties galore on offer. Charlie sifted through the invitations looking for something above intimate but less than anonymous. He knew that Connie wouldn't care for something overly grand, overly pompous. This had to be chosen carefully. He decided upon the Baxter's party. There would be a fine selection of appropriate young women for him to introduce Connie to. He knew little of her history and did wonder why she had been kept so isolated by her father. Surely it would have been wise for her father to have more sway on his daughter's companions.

Charles knew that Connie's father was a widower, and he wanted to know more. In the early throes of their relationship, it hadn't mattered to him. She had become his world, and he accepted her for the woman who stood in front of him, not her history. And she had done likewise for him. No questions, just acceptance. And that had been quite wonderful. An easing of the world. Now it irked him that she didn't trust him enough to share her history. He had shared his. Surely, she should do likewise. She kept secrets from him. That felt wrong.

Perhaps it was because of their own brush with death; the accident that could so easily have taken both of their lives. They had survived and now, he wanted more. He wanted to know every bit of her, her thoughts, her dreams, her history. All of it had to be his, and his mood darkened with each turn of her head, each, "Oh Charlie!" She would laugh, toss her head back in that most endearing of ways, kiss him. But now he worried if she didn't let him in, they might lose each other somehow. Drift apart. The magic they shared would trickle into the gutter and be gone. He couldn't allow that.

She had reluctantly agreed to attend the Baxter's party. Stuffy people with stuffy lives and stuffy conversation. It would be monotonous and a bore, but she would do this for him. At least pretend to make the effort. Her thoughts slipped away to Hannah's. The parties she would host were always lively, vibrant affairs full of interesting people with a lot to say about the world, and thoughts on how to put it right. How she missed it. How she missed them.

∽

They stepped out of the carriage and were greeted by a footman. Charlie held his hand out and Connie laid hers on top of his, as expected. She could do this for one night. Pretend that she was like these people. Fit in. Do as was deemed appropriate in such circles, despite her dislike of it all. They smiled at one another and walked to the entrance of the grand house in which the Baxter's lived.

'You look simply wonderful, my darling,' he whispered to her. And she did. Her scarlet drop waist dress was of the finest silk. It was decorated with a variety of sequins and beads, surrounded by the most delicate embroidery. The weight of the trim on the full skirt made it swish and sway with each step she took, swirling deliciously around her legs. Matching gloves stretched over her elbows. A headband finished the look.

She had secretly taken a large gin before their departure—the necessary boost to her confidence, the settling of nerves, and now that she was faced with all of these people, all of this pretence, she was quite desperate for another.

A waiter was patrolling the ballroom, a tray of champagne flutes balanced professionally on his hand.

She stretched her hand out, scooped up a glass, swallowed its contents in one gulp, before reaching for another. She smiled politely and glided amongst the gathering of Glasgow's finest.

As she reached for her fourth glass Charlie whispered, 'Steady on, old girl.'

She stared at him, disappointment carried on her brow. He caught the look, returned her glass to the waiter and pulled her close. 'One cannot dance with a glass in one's hand.'

He led her around the dancefloor, the two of them entwined, as if they fitted together. No. They did fit together. Quite wonderfully. He revelled in the jealous looks cast their way. Such a beautiful couple, despite it all. Old scarrings, cast away. Hidden by that obvious love that they shared.

'Charlie, my darling, I am quite exhausted. I really do need a drink.' She dropped his hand and forced her way through the other couples to the table of drinks. There was a decanter of gin. Perfect!

'Madam?' the waiter said.

'A rather large snifter of gin, if you please.'

'Of course.'

Charlie had been trapped in a brief conversation, with one of his colleagues. Sometimes there was no getting away from such things. He flicked his eyes between his colleague and Connie. Another man joined the conversation. Fotheringale slapped Charlie's back.

'Good to see you, old chap. Settling in all right, are we?' Fotheringale said.

'Yes, yes. Thank you. Glasgow is like a second home to me, so this move was no great hardship. A fine city!'

'Indeed. You have yet to introduce me to your wife. You do have a wife, correct? I believe something was mentioned about such a thing!' He laughed. 'Where is she?'

Charlie turned to scan the crowd. His heart sank as he saw Connie swallow one gin and ask for another. He paused, wondering if it was wise to point her out just now, deciding it was. It would be fine. 'There she is.'

Fotheringale frowned. 'Constance? You are married to Constance?' His voice rose in surprise. An unaccustomed lapse in his controlled demeanour.

'Yes—I—do you know her?'

Fotheringale laughed, but without humour. 'One could say that,' he said quietly.

Connie swayed slightly, two glasses in her hand, a squint drunken smile on her face. Then she saw him, her father, deep in conversation with Charlie. They were talking about her! A wave of fear and confusion made her feel nauseous, unsteady. Her feet got tangled up with each other and she tripped and fell. One of the glasses smashed into her hand. People were staring. Whispering. She was crying. One hand cradled the other, blood dripping onto her beautiful silk dress.

'Connie!' Charlie called.

She pulled herself onto her feet and ran. This was too humiliating. Too awful. Too terrifying. The blast of cold air that hit her as she ran out of the front door did little to sober her up. She jumped into a waiting carriage.

'Take me away. Just—just take me away.'

'Yes miss. Where to, miss?'

'I don't ruddy well care! Anywhere!'

He noticed the blood. 'I reckon we should get you to the doctor's, miss.'

'Did I ask for your input?' she snapped, then regretted it. 'I am sorry. Do forgive my frightful outburst.' She paused, thinking where was best. Home would be unthinkable. Her father might...dear God, her father with Charlie. It felt like her world had just broken, collapsed in on itself. She gathered herself, her thoughts. The bookshop. Yes. She would seek refuge at the bookshop. Again! 'Take me to Virginia Place. Do you know it?'

'I do that. Very well, miss.'

He clicked his tongue and ushered his horses forward. Silence now apart from the clop of the horses' hooves, muffled by the fallen snow, the snuffle of their heavy breath, a soft whistle from the driver.

Familiarity was all that she wanted. An old familiarity. A place of comfort and safety. Lizzie's. Her mood lifted as they drew close to the little shop. She asked him to pull up a little away from the shop itself. But she had left with nothing. No purse. No money to pay the man. The embarrassment. Closely followed by panic.

'I—I seem to have left without my purse. She unclipped her pearls and handed them to him. 'Would these do?'

'That's far too much, miss. I couldn't possibly.'

'Yes, yes, just take them.' She dropped them into his

hand and hurried out of the cab. It didn't matter that she could barely see for the veil of snow that swirled around her; that a trail of blood ran crimson in her wake, that her hand ached, that her head burst with confusion.

Chapter 67
1919

~

Andy and Bea had been courting for two months now. There was no rush to this, no great proclamations of love or dependency. Just a warm glow of something quite special. A coming together of people who worked well as a couple. Souls who could rest in each other. He had told her everything and she had accepted it, without question. It felt as if they had known each other for years; schoolmates who had become something more.

They were having tea at his house. His mother fussing around, his father beaming at them.

'What was he like as a boy, then?' Bea asked. 'I don't see him as being a troublemaker, just a bit of a handful.'

He blushed. 'No secrets, Ma,' he said.

'Oh, yes please. I want lots of secrets.' Bea nudged him, grinning.

'Truthfully, what you see is what we got. A blessing of a boy, and no mistaking.' She squeezed his knee. 'A blessing.'

'Yes. The trouble was all with Julie there,' Andy said staring accusingly at his sister.

'Not true! Not true at all. You were just better at hiding it than me. Now I could tell stories if I had a mind to. Oh yes. I could put a nasty blot on your report card, Andy.'

Andy flicked a crumb at her with perfect aim. It bounced off her nose. She gasped before returning the favour. They were laughing at each other, softly, gently.

'You two just won't grow up, now, will you?' his ma said.

His da flicked a crumb at his wife.

'Oh, it's like that, is it?' She retaliated.

'Aye!'

It descended into mayhem, crumbs flying, accusations made, but all with laughter. With joy.

Bea had been told by her father that you can tell a lot about how a person will be as a partner by the relationship of their parents. 'Have a good look at the parents before you make any commitment. You mark my words.' Bea hoped that this was true. She had seldom been in the company of such carefree love. Such abandon.

Bea still didn't know what had drawn her to Andy back in London, but she was mighty glad of it. That secret bond that no man or woman can make sense of. That whisper of love. A promise of something special.

Andy's mother held her arms up. 'Enough!' she said with a laugh to her voice. 'What will Andy's sweetheart be thinking of us?'

The crumbs stopped flying. Andy and Bea blushed simultaneously and smiled at each other. There it was. Confirmation, as if it were needed, from Andy's parents.

'And because this was all Andy's doing, I vote that he gets the job of tidying it all up,' Julie said. 'You know where the brush and dustpan are kept. Oh wait, you probably don't.' She grinned mischievously at him.

'Fair enough,' he said. 'Why don't you go and play with your dolls, or something?'

She squealed in protest, threw one last crumb at him which settled beautifully in his hair. He picked it out and grinned. 'Good shot, Sis!'

'Off you go, the lot of you,' Andy's ma said. 'I'll have this cleaned up in a blink.'

Bea knelt down to help her.

'No, no,' Andy's ma whispered. 'You do quite enough by keeping a smile on my laddie's face. On you go now. That's your job. This here is mine.'

Andy and Bea took their customary walk down to the river. It was bitterly cold, but that didn't matter. They stood on the bridge wrapped into each other. Snow swirled around them. The river shouted through the silence. Ice had built up along the riverbank and was slowly creeping its way across the water.

'It'll be frozen right the way across soon enough,' Andy said. 'We used to play dare, crossing from one side to the other, the ice cracking underneath us.'

'Dangerous.'

'That's what made it fun!'

'And, of course, your parents didn't know.'

'That they didn't. We'd have been locked in and sent to bed with no supper!'

'I can't imagine your parents doing that.'

'Oh, they would, believe you me. There's right and there's wrong and they made very sure we knew the difference.'

A crack split the air. A gunshot. More. Andy fell to the ground. Pulled his arms over his head. Sense gone.

Bea knelt down beside him, wrapped her arms around him. Felt the shaking of his body. The terror pulsing through him. 'It's just the farmer, Andy. It's just the farmer,' she whispered. 'There's nothing to frighten you here. Nothing.' She kissed his hands, pulled them gently away from his head. 'It's all right.'

It wasn't. He wasn't. Was there no end to this?

She helped him to his feet, took his face in her hands, stared into his eyes. 'It's all right.'

They walked slowly back to his house and waited for the fear to go away. He wouldn't allow his parents to see him like this.

Chapter 68
1919

~~~

Mhairi had trudged through the snow with no particular destination in mind. She just needed to clear her thoughts, to be alone for a while. She had had a fight with Robbie. Her Robbie. That was a first and it hurt.

Her toes had been bitten by the sting of the snow that had seeped through her shoes. Her fingers were nipping from the cold. Her heart ached. But she was still angry with him, with the whole situation. She wouldn't turn back. Not yet.

She looked up to get her bearings, just in time to step back from an oncoming taxi carriage, the horses' hooves muffled by the snow but still loud enough to echo down the quiet street. It was Christmas Eve. Behind closed doors and drawn curtains she imagined the lucky ones celebrating, huddled around blazing fires, wrapped in that warm glow of familial love. What was she doing out here? She should be home with Robbie. Of course she should.

She was about to turn back towards home when something caught her eye. A figure huddled against the cold and the snow. She would never forget her own time in that situation. That fear of the weather taking the life away from you. That pain of hunger in your belly. That feeling of being trapped in the darkest place that seemed to hold no escape, no ending. That place where no-one else noticed you. She walked towards the stranger.

As she drew closer and focussed through the snow,

which was falling relentlessly, thick and blinding, she could make out that it was a woman begging, her hand outstretched.

'Help a poor family, would you? I just need a bit of help, a bit of food.'

That voice. It reached into her gut and pulled it inside out. Her breath was threatening to fail her.

'Ma?'

The woman picked her eyes up from the ground, stared, blinked hard as if to clarify the image in front of her. It was a mirage, surely? A dream. She rubbed her eyes, lifted her hand towards the figure. 'Dear mother of God, is it really you?'

Mhairi clasped the outstretched hand, pulled her mother up and into her, held on so tight. So very tight. Neither moved nor spoke, they just held each other for as long as the cold would allow.

Mhairi was the first to break the embrace, to try to step back. Her mother clung on to her with a claw-like grip, a wild thing that could not release its prey; could not let go of any of this, for fear of it disappearing back into the blizzard, of confirming that this was just another of her imaginings. The desperate wanting of a heartbroken mother. God knew it had happened so many times before, even more since Spanish flu had ripped the rest of her family away, left her alone.

'We need to get you somewhere warm, Ma. Come on.' Mhairi was cold enough, but her mother was a breath away from hypothermia. Mhairi took her coat off and wrapped it around her mother's shoulders, pulled it tight across her chest.

∼

When she opened the door to her flat and felt the

warmth of the place, not just physical, she could have cried. How foolish to allow such an argument to almost ruin this. Robbie was there in an instant, the relief dripping from his face, alongside his tears.

'Mhairi—I'

'Hush. No need. I know. We need to get my ma sorted.'

'Your ma? How the—never mind.' He helped Mhairi walk her mother over to the fire and sit her down. 'The woman's freezing and soaked through. I'll boil some water for a bath. First a wee dram to warm the two of you up.'

'Robbie?'

'Aye?'

'I love you.'

He grinned. No words needed.

Tiger stretched, yawned, and glanced up at these intruders on his sleep. They were to be ignored. The lick of the flames far more important for now.

Mhairi bathed her mother, washed her hair, allowed her to soak until she wanted no more. She dried her and dressed her in the warmest clothes she could find.

Mhairi's mother, Helen, barely took her eyes off her. This vision. This wonderful, wonderful vision that was her daughter.

~

They sat at the table with bowls of homemade broth and crusty bread. After two bowls Helen finally took a breath, slowed down, relaxed. 'By God, I thought I was done for. There's been many a hard day, but that one? that felt like my last. And look what it brought me.' She smiled for the first time in so very long, because now she could. 'You've done well for yourself, then? A home and a fine young man. Look at you! My wee girl, no so wee anymore.'

Mhairi sat on Robbie's knee, her arms around his neck, his arms around her waist, that soft warm place where she belonged. Mhairi and her mother shared histories, stories of what had happened since that awful parting in 1914. Her mother wept at the loss of Jamie, at what her daughter had gone through. Such hardship for one so young. But look at her now!

Mhairi's family had made it to Glasgow. They had shared a room in a house of strangers but were grateful for it. It came along with the work her father had found in a factory. Tied houses that were only secure for as long as the work lasted. It was a home, but it was tenuous. And then that flu from the Devil came knocking on the door of the factory, the house. First one and then all of them. Every person in that house apart from Helen was taken by it. She only fought to stay alive because she hoped that one day this, the unthinkable, might happen.

They talked long into the night until Robbie's yawns, which he had tried so hard to suppress, became almost perpetual.

'I need to be letting you two get to your beds,' Helen said. A bed was made up for her on the settee. She and Mhairi hugged and bade each other goodnight, both still in awe of having found each other again.

'Sleep tight, Ma.'

'Aye. You too.'

Mhairi wouldn't let Robbie rest until they had made love. A slow, beautiful confirmation that all was well with their world, with them. A deep sleep took them all and wrapped them up. Safe and warm and together.

Chapter 69
1919

～

Connie tapped on the back door of the shop, but there was no light, no chatter, no sound of anyone or anything. She wasn't at all sure of the hour, her head muddled with pain, confusion and alcohol. 'No, no, no. I need you to be in.' She knocked again, louder, more insistently. Still nothing. She glanced up at the surrounding buildings. It must be dreadfully late. There was no light to be seen anywhere. The snow was blinding, but light would have shone through. At least she would have seen that!

'Lizzie?' she called. 'Lizzie!' She knew the futility of it. No-one was home. Sometimes one just knew, and she did. It was as if the house itself were saying, *I'm empty.* But desperation can override logical thought.

There was nothing to do but move on. To where, she didn't know, but she would surely die if she were to stay out here all night. 'Damn it, damn it, damn it!' she shouted at the shop, at the ground, at the interminable snow.

She balanced herself against the wall and walked back towards the road. Silence. Anyone with the capability would be indoors, sheltering themselves from this. She had just reached the front entrance and was using it to twist around onto the pavement when a shout rang out, followed by a sharp whistle.

'Stop! Thief!'

A young child was pelting towards her. A brief memory of Mhairi's stories accompanied the vision.

291

That desperation. Connie lunged out and caught the child, almost dragging both of them to the ground.

'Please, miss. Please?'

'Quiet!' she whispered sharply. 'Back there.' She pointed to the path around the shop. 'Go on, now.'

He scampered behind the shop, unquestioning.

She stood tall; tried to look presentable, sober.

The policeman ran towards her, breathless and red in the face. 'Young lad. Thief. Seen him?'

'Yes officer. He ran off that way.' She pointed at the junction ahead. 'Left. He ran left.' There were no footsteps leading in that direction and she hoped that the policeman didn't have the sense to check. She watched as he ran on, and out of sight. She waited for a few seconds, then walked back around the shop, doing her best to tread on the child's footsteps, pleasantly surprised and pleased with the clarity of her thinking.

He was skulking in the shadows, shaking. 'Thanks, miss,' he said. 'I didn't do nothing. Honest.'

'Oh, I think perhaps you did, but that is neither here nor there. I imagine one has one's reasons for stealing. What was it, anyway? Just out of curiosity, you understand.'

He held out an apple.

'All of that effort for an apple. Dear God. This country!'

'Can I go now, miss?'

'Actually, I would like it very much if you could help me find a way in. My friend should be at home, but she isn't, and I'll be damned if I'm going to freeze to death out here!'

He laughed, and it made her laugh too. An unexpected sharing of lightness between two strangers in a dark place.

'Have ye checked the hidey-holes?' he said.

'The what?' She shook her head. 'No. I suspect not.'

He lifted up the doormat. Nothing. He checked under the plant-pots. Nothing. He shrugged. 'Your friend doesnae want just any auld thief getting in now, does she?'

'No, I suppose not.'

He lifted the hatch to the coalbunker, fumbled around, stepped back, stood up tall with a triumphant look on his grimy face. He held the keys out to her.

'Oh, you are frightfully clever! Well done you!'

'Right you are, miss. I reckon that's us even then.'

He turned to leave.

'Young man! Wherever do you think you are going? It is bitterly cold. You are a fugitive. I think it prudent that you come in, at least for a while.'

'You don't half talk funny.'

'Is that so?'

'Aye!'

She unlocked the door and pushed him in. 'You will be on your best behaviour.'

'I will, that.'

'Right. Well. I suppose one really should introduce oneself. I am Connie. Do you have a name on you?'

'Aye. I'm Billy.'

'Right, Billy, I have no idea about such things so could you set about lighting a fire?'

'Reckon I can do that.'

'Splendid. On you go, then. Chop, chop!'

He laughed, shook his head, and set to cleaning the grate. 'Have you got a paper on you?'

'A paper?'

'Aye. For the fire, like. To get it going. A newspaper.'

'Ah, I see. Yes. There are always papers around.'

He set to preparing the fire, not sure of what was happening, but glad of it anyway.

She turned on the kitchen tap and drank as much water as she could bear. Experience had taught her that she would be thankful for it in the morning. She made cups of tea for them both.

They were sitting silently by the fire, enjoying the warmth of the tea, the crackle of the burning coals, the shadows the flames cast upon the walls, the comfort of this.

Voices drew nearer, footsteps. He gulped. Eyes wide.

She listened closely. Hannah and Lizzie.

'Not to worry. It is my friends.'

Lizzie walked in, arm in arm with Hannah. They immediately uncoupled themselves when they realized that they were not alone.

Lizzie stared. 'Connie?'

'Yes. And my little friend, Billy.'

What a sight! A woman in the finest clothes that money could buy, sitting chatting with a waif, dressed in rags. Yet it was somehow right.

Chapter 70
1919

~∾~

By the time Charlie had burst through the front door of the Baxter's mansion, and run onto the road, there was no sign of Connie. His eyes followed a trail of blood—her blood—that had dripped ruby red in the white snow. He felt sick at the sight of it, as if he himself were bleeding. The trail had come to an abrupt end at the roadside. In the distance, the ghost of a trap, that he assumed had taken her away, almost invisible now in the swirling of snow, the darkness of a cruel winter's night. He looked desperately up and down for a cab, for anything that he could follow; something to lead him back to her.

He cursed himself. This had been such a dreadful idea, and he should have known it. Of course she would feel uncomfortable. These were his people, not hers. Of course she would drink. That was what she did now in times of anxiety, in places of strangeness. He should have known! And Fotheringale? What was that all about? There was definitely something amiss there, but he couldn't fathom it out. Was he the cause of her running off like that? Yet more of her history that he knew nothing of. He could think of nothing else; no other reason, other than the shame of falling down like that. Of making a spectacle of herself in the finest society. Now he felt impotent, useless. What kind of a man was he?

His head swarmed with anxiety. Nothing was making sense. That awful buzz in his brain that he thought he had finally seen the back of. He was useless without her. Empty, afraid and useless. He paced up and down, up and down, willing a solution to somehow appear before him.

From that first day they had met she had changed his life so completely, made him feel again; feel good, feel content, feel a future. A wonderful future with her by his side. He should have just let it be; let her be. Why attempt to change something that is already quite perfect? How foolish to alter and twist and mould to a state that he had never appreciated anyway. The sort of women he had been introduced to, the company he had kept, the life he had led, were utterly meaningless vacuous vessels in comparison to Connie. Shallow imitations of a life worth living. He had had it all and it had ridden off into the night.

There was no point in standing there doing nothing. He should follow the tracks left in the snow while he still could. Even now they were beginning to fade as the relentless snow built up on the ground. All that was left to follow were light indentations. He followed as best he could, striding, almost running. If he ran, he feared he might miss something, a crossing of tracks could confuse him, mislead him. No. Despite his desire for speed, he kept his pace steady and strong, but careful, his eyes not wavering from the ground. From those tracks.

Where would she go? Where was it that she felt safest? A heartbeat ago that would have been easy to answer. Home. The home he had built with her, for her. He doubted that she would go there now. Something had changed in her. That look on her face before she fled. Absolute terror and hatred—yes, hatred. Where else? Where would she go? The bookshop? That peculiar collection of a mismatch of people who had somehow slotted together in that jumble of a shop. A peculiar place for peculiar people. But they weren't, were they? They were her people, and he had ruined it all for her. His presence had been a poison which had bled into the hearts of those his Connie loved. Could he even say that anymore? His Connie? Dear God, let this be salvageable.

He was growing more and more desperate as the minutes passed, his heart thumping, his breath threatening to give up on him. Still, he kept focused on those tracks. But as he hurried on another trap's trail had left its marks in the snow, and another. Tracks blended and blurred and became lost in each other. It was becoming so difficult to separate one from the other, to differentiate between them, and when they split up at a crossroads, useless.

He stood, staring at the tracks heading to the right, others to the left, praying for guidance, for something magical. There were no such things left to him. The one piece of magic he had been sent he had destroyed. His Connie. One doesn't get more than one chance at such magic. Such wonder. No. He was finished.

The river Clyde loomed black and threatening in the distance. This felt like the night when they had bumped into each other again at St Margaret's loch. That awful darkness that had taken up residence in his head—his soul—and had made him decide to end it all. He was going to walk into the black waters of the loch and allow them to take him. An end to the pain. An end to his guilt. But she had been there and changed it all. She had saved him. Her presence alone had lifted him out of that hell.

Dark thoughts threatened to swallow him, to drag him away from reality again. He was drawn to it; that deep, deep water called to him again. His body had been taken over by his demons once more and was leading him to the water, the bridge. So much pain could simply be washed away in it. Finished. He leant against the wall of the bridge, stared down at the blackness far below. The quiet. It was beautiful. He turned round, slipped down the wall to the pavement, his arms tight over his head as his world exploded, men screamed. That awful, awful sound. This had to end.

Chapter 71
1919

≈

Helen was up before anyone else stirred. She had found it hard to sleep; so much going on in her head. Had this really happened? Was she dreaming? Did she deserve any of this after having let her daughter wander off into all that danger back then? Besides which, she was quite desperate to make herself useful, to be a mother again. She knew that Robbie would be up before the dawn to go off to his work and she would have breakfast ready for him, the range on. Give him as good a start to his day as she could manage.

Robbie was reluctant to get out of his bed, to uncurl himself from Mhairi. He inched his way free managing not to wake her. Tiger mewled softly then snuggled into a tighter ball at Mhairi's neck. Robbie smiled at his good fortune and pulled his clothes on. 'Christ, it's cold,' he mumbled, rubbing a finger across the patterns Jack Frost had sketched on the windows: forests and leaves and mountains. If you looked closely enough there was a whole other world in there. A magical place of undiscovered beauty.

He tiptoed through to the kitchen knowing, by the warmth and the smell of black pudding and Lorne sausage sizzling in the frying pan, that Helen was up before him.

'Morning,' he said.

'Morning, son. I hope ye don't mind.' She swept her arm above the range, smiled softly. 'Just to say thanks, like.'

'No need for that. You're family!' He walked across to the range. 'Smells great!' He pecked her cheek.

She bit back a tear. 'Sit yerself down.'

She set a plate down for each of them, poured mugs of tea and sat opposite him.

'You look after my Mhairi, don't you?'

'I love the skin off that lassie's nose. There's nothing I wouldn't do.'

'I can see that. So glad of it. No weans yet?'

A fleeting shadow threatened to spoil his mood. He cast it aside. That wasn't his story to tell. If it was to be shared it should come from Mhairi. 'Working on it!' He grinned, wiped his plate clean with a slice of bread, reached for his knapsack.

'There's a wee ham piece in there for ye too.'

'I can see where Mhairi gets her kindness from. You'll be here when I get back?'

'If the two o you don't mind.'

'As I said, you're family.'

He opened the bedroom a crack to see Mhairi still fast asleep. Best leave her be. But he couldn't resist creeping in for a kiss. He hadn't missed a day since her release, and he had no intention of doing so. 'See you tonight, Mhairi, love,' he whispered to her sleeping body. He pulled the door to and walked to the front door.

He tugged his boots on and wrapped his scarf and coat around him. It was going to be as cold as the devil out there. He braced himself, opened the door and closed it again as quickly and quietly as he could. A soft click trickled through the silence of the frosted morning air. Head down, shoulders hunched, he trudged his way

300

into work, but his heart was warm.

∽

Helen was in a quandary. She was quite desperate to be in the company of Mhairi again; to see her beautiful face, to hear her voice. The temptation to wake her was almost too hard to fight against. But, no, the lass needed her sleep. She would have found it easier if there had been tidying to do, but the place was spotless and after she had cleaned up the breakfast things and put them away, she couldn't find anything else to do.

She sat by the range and talked to her husband. A habit that had only increased as the years dragged by. At times she could forget his passing, imagine him there by her side. Not that it had always been easy, their life together. He had been a stern man brought up on religion and righteousness. His ways would be followed. Helen had known that from the start, and it was worth it to have a good strong man to lean on. It was expected of a woman like her anyway. The dutiful wife who obeyed her husband. And, yes, loved him. Loved him dearly.

'Oh, ye should see our Mhairi now! You'd be so proud, so ye would. Or maybe ye can see her. Maybe you're looking down on it all an smiling. Who am I to say? If ye are, ye know fine well how I got here. How there is a wee bit o magic, even for folk like us, just like ye said. For you it was the Lord. Trust in the Lord, ye'd say, over and over. Never could stick wi that, after everything, but you did. Aye. Even then, you did. Maybe he wasnae smiling on ye. Maybe he was too busy. Maybe. But I can hear ye now. "Praise be," ye'd say. "Praise be."'

'Ma,' Mhairi said. 'Is that you talking to yourself?'

301

'Ach. It's just something I took to after yer father—well, I tell him what's going on.'

'An does he answer you back?'

Helen laughed. 'Still got a tongue on ye, then!'

'Aye. You taught me well!'

'Oh, come here an gie yer ma a cuddle.'

When Robbie came home, he had brought a Christmas tree with him. They spent the evening decorating it with homemade paperchains, pinecones and togetherness. Tiger had other ideas and leapt and chased as much as he could. Pieces of paper flew around the floor, pine needles skitted. Robbie tossed him a cone and laughed as it was batted from left to right until it disappeared under the settee. Tiger squeezed himself under it then mewled as he realised he was stuck.

'Come on then, you wee daftie!' Mhairi called as Robbie lifted the settee up.

Tiger stared up at her with blinking eyes.

She scooped him into her arms.

Chapter 72
1919

～

Charlie had become so cold that he couldn't feel it. He couldn't feel anything, hear anything, see anything. Even the noises in his head had left. He was blank, empty, curled into a ball on the pavement. There was no need to jump into the river. It would be over soon enough.

'What have we got here, then?' A policeman said, leaning over, peering at Charlie. It was obvious that this was a person of some standing, not some common drunk; the clothes, the general look of the man, and there was no smell to him other than wealth. He reached for Charlie's arm, gave him a gentle shake. 'Sir? You can't be staying here, now. Catch your death, so you will. Come on now. Let's be getting you up. That's the way.' He eased Charlie to his feet, but there was no strength in those legs. No expression on his face. An empty vessel. 'What's to be done with you?'

He slipped Charlie's arm around his neck and tried to walk, nudging the almost dead weight of the man step by step. This was going to be a heck of a challenge! He managed to drag Charlie over to a bench in Richmond Park at the far end of the bridge. He swept the snow off and sat the man down. 'I need to get some help here. You hold on. I'll be right back. Just hold on, sir.' There was no response, no reaction whatsoever.

He hurried off, glancing back to check on the stranger. The man didn't move. Not a twitch, nor a glance. But he was still upright. That was something at least. The station wasn't far. He would be back in ten minutes at the most. Still, it snowed, and a wind was picking up, drilling the cold right into his bones, the snow right into his eyes. He tucked his head down and pushed on.

The policeman returned with his sergeant and a wooden trolley. They hoisted Charlie up, lay him on the trolley, and wrapped a scratchy woollen blanket over him.

'We should get the man to a hospital, don't you think?'

'Aye, but first the station. He needs thawing out and fast.'

'Right you are, Sarge.'

They sat him by the gas fire and waited, until his complexion began to colour, his lips slipped from blue to pink, and he stirred. A shuffle, a tenuous lift of the head.

He stared at them, at his surroundings. A feeling of panic fluttered in his chest, swelled. No memory of this.

'Where the hell am I?' he mumbled.

'You're in the police station, sir. The constable here found you on the bridge. Damned near frozen to death, so you were!'

This was wrong. He shouldn't be here. The water. He wanted to be in the water. He wanted to be gone. He began to weep.

'Sir? Come now. It can't be that bad. Drink this. It'll help.' The constable wrapped Charlie's fingers around a mug of strong coffee laced with a good measure of whisky. 'Come on, now. Drink.'

Charlie hesitated, wanted to refuse, but did as he was told. The burn of the liquid as he swallowed it down was soothing, breathing life back into him. Still tears fell and embarrassment mixed in with them.

'Can you tell us your name, sir?'

Charlie looked up through blurred vision. 'Charles,' he mumbled.

'Good, good. Charles what?'

'Charles Alexander.'

'The advocate?'

Charlie nodded.

'I thought I recognised you, sir. Right now, let's be getting you home.'

The sergeant urged his constable away. 'Let's be getting a cabbie to take this gentleman home.'

'Right you are, sergeant.'

The sergeant travelled with Charlie to his house. It was best to take no chances with important people like this.

Charlie glanced up at the windows. No lights shone from them. No footprints showed in the snow. Connie wasn't here. He was quite sure of it.

'Right you are, sir. Let's just see you safely inside. Is there someone here to take care of you?'

'Yes, yes. My housekeeper. I can manage quite well from here.'

'If you don't mind, sir. I'd be happier to see you safely indoors.'

≈

Charlie unlocked the door and stepped inside.

Maud was there in a minute. 'What the devil's going on here, Mr Alexander?'

The sergeant answered. 'The gentleman found himself in a spot of bother. Nothing to worry yourself about. I just wanted to make sure that he got home safely. I'll be off now. Goodnight to you.' He bowed slightly and stepped back out into the snow.

'Connie? The mistress? Is she home?'

'No. I haven't seen her since you left. Is everything all right, sir?'

'I don't rightly know, Maud.'

'Well, let's be getting you settled with a wee hot toddy. I'm sure she'll be home soon enough.' She poked at the dying embers of the fire and built it up again with fresh logs. 'Come and sit down by the fire. I'll be right back.'

'No. I must go somewhere else. I must find her!'

'At least a hot toddy before you go.'

'No. I must leave now. Take yourself back to bed, Maud. That's an order!'

Chapter 73
1919

~∽~

For once, Lizzie hadn't reached for the gin. It was obvious that Connie had already drunk far too much for her own good—they all had. Her eyes were glazed, her speech forced, as if words were difficult to form. But she was laughing well enough with this young lad. He stank of stale clothes and poverty, but he had a way with him. A sincerity beyond his years.

They all huddled around the fire. 'Top notch fire-building, Connie,' Hannah said. 'I didn't know you had it in you?'

'Oh, that wasn't my doing. That was young Billy, here.'

'Compliments to you, then, Billy.'

'Aye, well, if ye cannae light a fire, yer as good as deid out there.'

'Right, Billy. Tell us your story and maybe you can stay the night,' Lizzie said.

He stared at her, stared at Connie. 'What are ye meaning like? I got chased by the polis, Connie here hid me, brought me in. Right nice, it is, by the way. Yer house, like.' He grinned.

'I was thinking more about why you are out on the streets, in a blizzard, on Christmas Eve. Will your parents not be concerned?'

He laughed. 'Naw. Got none. At least none that I know of.'

'So, you have, or you haven't?'

His brow furrowed; he stared. 'I'll just be off. Thanks,

and everything, lady.' He stood up, turned to Connie. 'You're the best person I've ever met, but folk that ask too many questions,' he nodded towards Hannah and Lizzie. 'They're no to be trusted. Learned that, see? Bye, and good luck to ye.'

Lizzie stepped in front of the door, blocking his exit. 'No harm meant. We're on your side. It's just good to know who you have sleeping in your house, that's all.'

'Aye, well, that's as maybe. But if you'll step out my way, I'll step out yours.'

Connie got to her feet, swayed slightly, before righting herself and reaching out for Billy. She put her finger under his chin and lifted it up so that their eyes met. 'Just stay the night, at least. We'll not do anything to force you, but it's foul out there, and in here you've got a fire, and food, and a place of safety. Promise.'

He looked from Hannah to Lizzie who both nodded in confirmation. His face softened, as if a weight had slipped off it, his shoulders relaxed. He sat back down. 'Right then, what've ye got for eating?'

They laughed.

'What? Are ye no hungry? Cos I am an no mistaking!'

The lightness that belonged in the shop returned. Hannah cooked up some sausages and potatoes which were wolfed down by everyone.

Connie told the story of her night; of Charlie being in deep conversation with her father; of him pointing her out; of her sudden fear, the breaking of the glass, her tumble, her cut, her escape.

'I don't know what I would have done if young Billy here hadn't happened along. I might well have frozen to death on your doorstep! Imagine coming home to a frozen Connie. That would have been quite something!'

308

'Looks like we saved each other, then,' Billy said.

'Yes. And as such we are bound together for life!' She rubbed his head, took his hand and squeezed it. As she did so, she remembered having said something similar to Charlie. Was that really over? Her marriage? Her heart still flipped at the thought of him, but he had changed so very much recently. And her father. He knew her father and had kept it secret from her. Why would he do that if not for reasons untoward?

'Penny for them?' Hannah asked.

'Charlie.'

'Ah. The falling out was a consequential one then?'

'Yes. I—I don't think I like him anymore. Can one like someone one doesn't trust? I believe that to be the crux of any relationship. Trust. And that whole thing with my father. Well, how can that leave trust in place?'

'Yes, that is a bit odd, to say the least. Why don't you let it settle? Stay here for the night and look at things with a clear head in the morning,' Lizzie said.

'You are an angel.'

'I think not. Just sensible.'

Chapter 74
1919

~

Charlie parked his car one street away from the shop and walked towards it along the deserted pavement. He took a deep breath, tried to compose himself. Doubt again. That awful fear of not being wanted. No. He had to do this. If she was here, he had to speak with her, explain, apologise, although he wasn't quite sure of what he had done to cause her to run off like that.

But it was the middle of the night, and not just any night. It was Christmas day now. At least it would be when dawn broke. He stepped closer and followed the path that led to the back of the shop—the one that those who knew took. Friends. He knew that he wasn't one of their number, didn't have a right to this path, but a step into her life felt like the right thing to do.

A light shone out of the back room and lit up the night. He stood there, as still as the very building, and listened. Her voice, laughter with it. She was in there, with her friends, and she was happy. Happy in spite of what had happened. Happy without him.

Foolish thinking! There was no reason why she shouldn't be. She was safe, in her place, with her people. This was all that he wanted for her. Happiness. But it cut him so deep. Another scar. Did he have the courage to do this?

Goddamn it, yes, he did! But he would wait and listen for a few minutes more.

Charlie hadn't been able to make out much of the conversation drifting through the night's shadows. The odd word; the odd phrase. Nothing that made any sense. No stringing together of anything coherent. His understanding wasn't helped by the cold biting at him. He was freezing, and he knew that he had to make a decision now. Stay here and hope that he was wrong; that this was able to be put right, or must he turn away? He didn't trust himself enough to walk back out there and be in the least bit sensible. His head was still a confusion; a jumbled-up slice of turmoil and darkness. He took those last few steps to the back door, hesitated, lifted his hand to knock, paused once more.

Something else took hold of him, made his hand connect with the door and knock. He stood and waited as if his life depended on it. No. His life did depend on it.

'Who on earth would be calling at this hour?' Lizzie said.

'Perhaps ignore it?'

'No. No, the back door is for friends. I'd better...'

'Maybe the polis?' Billy whispered.

'Hide!' Connie urged. 'Nip back there and hide.'

'Over an apple? Dear God! But, yes, on you go. Hide.'

Billy darted into the bookshop and squeezed himself behind the counter, his heart pounding again. Was this always going to be his life? He couldn't remember much else. Perhaps a mother; a distant form, ghostlike, unidentifiable. More of a feeling than a memory. She must have been real at some point. Someone to give him a start in life. But all his memory held was solitude and that fight for survival. He stole a bit, begged a bit, ran and dodged and kept himself free. Free of what? He didn't rightly know. Free from whom? No, not that either. This was just what he did, what he always had done. An invisible child who found safety in movement.

These people, though. They were peculiar. Right posh folk who he hadn't been in the company of before. He hadn't expected help from any of them, but as it came his way, he was mighty glad of it. He knew it couldn't last and was grateful for the minutes he had had being warm and fed and sharing a laugh with posh folk. Who'd have thought it, eh?

If it was the polis, he would slip out the front door and off into the night as if this had never happened. A dream that would fade and slip away, like his ma. That would be a shame, because he liked it here. He liked these women. The softness of them. It was like they made the world that bit easier. That bit better.

The tap on the back door came again. Lizzie stepped forward and gingerly pulled the door ajar.

Charlie smiled, but there was fear behind it. His brow was furrowed. 'Lizzie. I—I wonder if I might speak with Connie. She is here, yes?'

Lizzie looked back at Connie who paused, open-mouthed, before getting to her feet and walking to the back door.

'What do you want Charlie? There is no space for you here.'

He reached for her hands, but she tucked them behind her back.

'Connie, dear,' Hannah said, 'Can we either have him step in or you out. There is no need to have all of us freeze to death!'

Connie sighed. 'I suppose you had better come in, then. You have five minutes. No more.'

Charlie nodded and followed her through to the shop, tipping an embarrassed acknowledgement at

Hannah and Lizzie.

Connie leant against the edge of the counter, trying to keep her breath still, her heart calm. Why did he do this to her? The loss of control, of rational thought. The damned pounding of her heart as if she were some silly love-struck youngster.

'Well?' she said, with as much bravado as she could drag to the fore. She crossed her arms in front of her chest, tucking her injured hand under her armpit.

'I don't understand any of this. Quite how things escalated the way they did. I should never have taken you there; forced you to be in strange company. I am so sorry.'

'And my father?' She almost spat the word.

'I'm sorry?'

'I saw you quite clearly in cahoots with him. You pointed me out to him. I despise the man, and you pointed me out to him!'

Charlie was silent, his memory ticking back. What did she mean? 'Fotheringale! Are you talking about Fotheringale?'

'Of course, I am.'

'But I had no idea. I swear.'

'Why were you so very chummy, then?'

'He is simply a client, and since my move to Glasgow, I have become his permanent advocate. I work for him, nothing more.'

'Oh, wonderful. My husband works for an absolute monster. He locked me up. Did you know that? If it hadn't been for Mhairi, Hannah and Lizzie I would still be locked up, drugged to the hilt, unaware of anything at all. THAT is the type of client you advocate for? My lord.'

313

'You tell him, lady!' Billy squeaked from under the counter, before slapping his hand across his mouth and trying to make himself even smaller.

It brought a laugh from Connie, a gasp from Charlie.

'What the devil?' Charlie said.

'It's all right, Billy. You can show yourself.'

He crawled out and stood tall beside Connie. She took his hand. 'This lady is the best, and you don't deserve her,' he said, his eyes glaring with dislike. Distrust. Disapproval.

'Thank you, Billy. Why don't you go back with the others. I'll be through in a minute.'

'Nuh-uh.' He shook his head, held on tight. 'Not going nowhere. I don't reckon he's a good un. I'm staying right here to keep you safe, like we said.'

Connie laughed. 'Well, thank you, kind sir.' She squeezed his hand.

'Connie, please? I adore you. You know I do. Things just became so very confused. Please stay by my side. I will do anything you want. I beg you, please, please stay with me. Come home.'

Chapter 75
1919

࿒

Fotheringale stood, somewhat aghast, as Charles took his leave and ran after Constance. The damned girl was still out of control, making a spectacle of herself like that in such company. He watched anxiously as the scene settled again, dancing, chatting, pleasantries. It was as if the unfortunate incident had never occurred at all. There were no glances his way. No embarrassed looks or turning of heads. He smiled and made his way to the smoking room. That pleasant smoke-filled domain that belonged only to the males of the species. Thank God for such places! He took a solitary seat by the window, not in the mood for conversation just now, and lit up his cigar.

So, Constance had married, and married well, it seemed. The Alexander name was a good one and he knew of the bravery shown by their son, Charles. The man had been written about in the newspapers, no less. A hero, they had said, leading his troops into battle, standing with them as they fell, dragging one poor young soldier back to safety, alas too late to save his life. Charles had been decorated, celebrated, although, if his memory served him right, the man had kept away from it all. The hullabaloo of celebration. Something of a recluse at the time, although it didn't appear so now.

Was he offended at not having been invited to the wedding? Yes, damn it, he was! Whatever else had happened between them, he was her father, and it would have been only right and proper for him to have given his daughter away. But at least he was free of her, and of the responsibility that had been his for too long. A man simply wasn't cut out for such things.

Peculiar that he hadn't heard about it. He didn't recall seeing an announcement in the Times, which one would have expected. A family like that had certain responsibilities and keeping the public informed was surely one of them, to his mind, at least. Perhaps he had simply missed it. He was frightfully busy, after all. Yes, that must have been it. But not even a whisper at the club? Peculiar. He dismissed it.

He took a carriage home shortly after, not really being in the mood for chit-chat and socialising, his mood darkened by the peculiar events of the evening, anyway, his own armchair was beckoning. The new girl would have lit fires in all of the main rooms. Yet another girl! Quite why they couldn't follow simple orders was beyond him. Yet time, and again, he had had to dismiss them for some slack work, insubordination, inappropriate behaviour.

That girl, what was her name now? The one that Constance had been so unfathomably fond of. Nothing but trouble, leading his daughter astray like that. Yes. Mhairi. That was it. At least none of them were quite as atrocious as she. But he had taught her a damned good lesson, being the instigator in having her locked up. It would have been even better if he had managed to have her charged with kidnap as well. He had no doubt whatsoever that she had been behind that whole escape nonsense. She and those awful women shouting about this and that. Ruddy nonsense. But one takes what one can. A victory remains a victory even if lesser than one would have liked.

And that child of hers. Well, he had saved her from a life of misery. Women like that had no place raising a child. No. Removing it was the correct decision. Apparently, it had been placed close by. A home of some sort for people of that ilk. Much better for all concerned. He hadn't forgotten that smirk as Mhairi had run off, as if daring him to chase her. He doubted that she would ever forget his as he had her put in cuffs!

He sat by the fire in his favourite wingback chair—soft leather and shining studs—nursing a brandy, swirling it around, enjoying the play of colour as flame mixed with liquor. As so often happened these days, now that he was alone, his thoughts slipped back to Clara. God how he had loved that woman! He would have given her anything, absolutely anything. But she was taken from him by Constance.

If the girl hadn't been there Clara would never have been caught by the flames. Such an irony. He couldn't love that child, but he had to have her at hand. His only true connection to Clara. What a cruel dilemma to force upon a man. A child that one cannot love but neither leave behind. Even now she was there, in his thoughts. That piece of Clara. There, yet unreachable; out of his control. As he dwelt on it his heart ached. An irrational pain. Something caught in his throat. He stood up, threw his glass into the fire; tiny splinters burst into the flames. 'God damn it!' he shouted into the silence of his empty life. 'God damn it!' The pain strengthened. Unbearable now. The life squeezing out of him. He couldn't breathe. Clutched at his chest. Fell into the fireplace. The flames. They licked at him, fed on his body. Spread to the carpet, the furniture, the curtains. Everything consumed.

Chapter 76
1919

∾

Robbie went off to work, as normal, on Christmas day, as did Mhairi. It was one of those beautifully crisp days that Scotland was made for. A deep covering of snow on everything, making the world a brighter, more beautiful place. The sky was sparkling with such clarity, a blueness that held the cold of the season, but the allure of it. It was a day to treasure. Frost had carved itself across everything that stood still in twists and curls so delicate they must have been created by something more than was known. Something quite magical. And Mhairi held her own wonderful piece of magic. There was only one piece of her life missing. Everyone had said, let go, leave it be, but she couldn't, neither did she want to.

Helen busied herself in the kitchen preparing the evening's meal. They would sit down to roast goose, green beans, apple sauce and potatoes. Everything was ready for the cooker when Mhairi came home. She smiled at her daughter standing there in her waitress uniform.

'You're right, it doesn't sit well on ye,' Helen said with a smile.

'Told you. But it's a job, and truth be told it can be a laugh. There's a few good women that work in there. We're all polite an quiet on the floor, but we get a good giggle back in the kitchens, when no-one's listening!'

She nipped back into her bedroom and changed into her dungarees and checked shirt. Her own uniform of sorts.

'Can't say as I'm too keen on that outfit either, but you always were one for dressing like a boy.'

'Aye. Nothing wrong wi that, Ma! I wouldn't have been away wi Jamie, climbing trees and leaping the burn in a pretty wee frock, now, would I?' she said with a grin of memories.

'I think back on those days all the time. Mind the six o us all squashed together in that wee cottage?'

Mhairi smiled. 'I do. You gave us the best life, Ma. The best!'

'Until—'

Mhairi held up her hand. 'You did what you had to do. Life can be hard. No more to say.'

Helen brushed the guilt away again. She knew that her daughter was right, but a mother's heart, once broken, can't easily be put to rights again. The cracks can be held deep—a private, personal pain that sometimes breaks free, unbidden. 'Right. Well, let's be getting the tea ready.'

They laid out plates and cutlery, busied themselves with things that needed little thought, little conversation.

'By Christ, that smells good!' Robbie said as he burst through the door. 'How are my two special girls?'

'Och you!' Helen said, a blush creeping up her neck. It had been so very long since she had heard words like that. She felt them deep inside. It was quite wonderful. Only twenty-four hours earlier she had been destitute, lost and alone in a heartless world, begging for her life. And now this.

They sat down to eat.

'No grace?' Helen asked.

319

'No. We don't,' Robbie said.

'I remember Pa an his prayers. Me, Jamie an the wee ones were desperate to start, get stuck in. Him prattling on an on about Jesus and thanks and God an all the rest o it.'

Helen caught her daughter's eye with a gentle chastisement.

'Aye, well, I know fine well you were thinking it too, Ma!' Mhairi said.

'That's as maybe, but he was yer da, an he's gone. I'll be hearing nothing against him, or his ways.'

Tiger jumped up onto the kitchen table, mewled softly, and crept towards the goose.

'Tch! Off with you!' Helen said, brushing the kitten off the table. 'You wee monkey!' she said, staring down at him, wagging a reprimanding finger.

Mhairi bent down and picked Tiger up, snuggled him into her. 'Was she mean to you?' she whispered to him. She was taken aback by how quickly her mother had taken on the matriarchal role in her little home. She was about to say something but bit her tongue. It wasn't important.

∽

'What's up?' Robbie asked, as he snuggled into her that night. 'And don't you try and say, "nothing". I can read you too well for that!' He kissed her neck.

She turned to face him. 'I've got some news.'

'Aye? And?'

'It's—well—I'm expecting.'

'You're not! Oh Mhairi! That's the best news. The best!' Come here. He pulled her close but felt the dampness of tears on his neck. 'What is it? What's wrong?'

320

'I can't quite get a hold of that happiness. It's like it's settled deep inside of me and won't come out. I just keep thinking of Rosie. It's like we'll be forgetting her, you know?'

'But we won't. This changes nothing for her. I'll never stop hoping. Looking for her.'

'Promise?'

'Promise.'

Chapter 77
1919

Connie wasn't ready to simply forgive, nor to forget. Charlie had brought such hurt upon her. Was it possible to simply cast it aside? She wasn't at all sure.

'I am so very sorry, Connie. I have been foolish and thoughtless. Forgive me.'

'Precisely what am I to forgive you for? A general apology means absolutely nothing. A trickle of meaningless words. Nothing more!'

'Very well. I am sorry for trying to change you into the sort of woman I am expected to marry. You are not that sort of woman, and I love you all the more for it. I am sorry for dragging you to that godawful party, full of people I don't care for, and you have no interest in. I am sorry for being an absolute fool. I care for only one thing, and that is you.'

She tilted her head. 'That will do for a start, but I believe there is a good deal more to be said on the matter.'

'So, you will come back? You will come home?'

'I may, but there are several conditions.'

'Go on.'

'Condition number one involves young Billy, here. He is to be given quarter in our house, where he will live for as long as he likes. To all intents and purposes, he will be treated as our son. Do I make myself clear?'

'Our—but—'

'Do I make myself clear?'

'You do.' There was more to say, such as, have you

thought this through? Such as, who is he? Such as, do you realise quite how much our lives will change? Clearly, she hadn't, but did it matter?

'Billy? What do you say? Are you to become one of our number?'

'I've got no idea what ye're going on about. Can ye no just talk proper?'

She laughed. 'Would you like to come and live with us?'

'You, aye. Him, no so much. An I havnae even seen yer house. An I don't like peas, or cabbage, or any o that green stuff.'

She ruffled his head. 'But you like apples well enough to steal them.'

He laughed. Blushed.

Charlie stared, his mouth slightly open, as he took on board just what he was agreeing to. But that was her. That was Connie in a nutshell. A wonderful impetuous being with absolutely no consideration for what was deemed normal.

'Are we agreed, then?' Charlie said.

'I believe we are.'

∽

Connie pulled Hannah and Lizzie close and kissed each cheek before taking Billy's hand and marching out of the door with Charlie in her wake.

'I'm not entirely sure of what we have just been witness to,' Hannah said, a question to her eyes.

'Me neither.'

The snow had stopped falling and the land lay still as if it were asleep. A heavy silence covered everything. The only sound the crunch of their feet on the fallen snow, the puff of their breath.

'I parked the car just up here. A short walk in the snow,' Charlie said, smiling up at the fluttering flakes.

'It is quite beautiful, don't you think? Quite, wonderfully beautiful.' Connie said, a sigh to her words.

Billy squinted up at them, shrugged, kicked at the snow. Laughed.

～

Billy stood in the hallway of Connie and Charlie's house with his mouth open. Things like this just didn't happen. Places like this didn't exist—not for the likes of him.

Maud hurried up from her rooms in the basement, a frazzled look on her face, her hair loose and unruly. 'I apologise, sir, milady. Didn't rightly know what to do as the hour was so late, so I took to my bed.' She peered behind Connie at the youngster. 'And who would this be?'

'Show yourself, Billy,' Connie said, tugging him gently. 'Billy is to live here, with us. I think the first thing he needs is a jolly good bath!'

'Yes, milady.'

'And Maud, there shall be no more of this "sir, milady" malarky. I am Connie, he is Charlie.' She pulled Charlie to her and smiled up at him. 'And this is Billy.'

'I think, perhaps, that life is about to change,' Charlie said. 'Quite considerably.'

'Right, young man. Let's be having you,' Maud said. 'Come now!'

Billy frowned. 'What? What's going on?'

'You are to be bathed and put to bed. We shall speak more in the morning,' Connie said. 'Off you go now. Chop, chop!'

Chapter 78
1920

~

Hannah's flat was ready for the gathering, not that there had been much to do. She wasn't one for overdoing such things. Informality and a comfortable atmosphere, with enough alcohol to loosen tongues and nibbles to settle stomachs. Her Hogmanay parties had been a given for those in the know, comrades and friends relaxing, celebrating. This year, however, it was to be smaller, more intimate, by invitation only. There was healing to be done, and she felt it was long overdue. What was the point in adding to the distresses of the world when there was a simple solution? Invitations had been sent, RSVPs received. If she had a god to believe in, she would have prayed. Instead, she trusted to the ultimate goodness of the human heart.

If all went to plan everyone she invited was coming. She wasn't one to suffer from nerves but this year there was so much at stake, and she had downed a couple of gins to calm herself.

There was a tap at the door. *Right! Here goes!*

They were nearly all present: Lizzie, Robbie, Mhairi, Helen, Andy and Bea. There was so much to say, untold stories of Helen and Mhairi, of Andy and Bea. It was all very joyous; celebratory. Hannah was pacing, trying not to appear anxious, but failing. At last, another tap. She strode to the door, took a deep breath, and pulled it open.

'I am so very glad that you have come. Welcome. Both of you!'

Connie pulled her close, kissed both of her cheeks, smiled. 'Of course,' she said.

Charlie took Hannah's hand, moved to raise it to his lips, but she twisted it into a firm handshake. He smiled, nodded. 'I should have known,' he said, smiling.

'Indeed! Let me take you coats.'

The chatter from the sitting room had lessened, until there was silence, as if they had all been switched off. An audible intake of breath. The air changed. Charged. A nervous tension had taken hold.

Hannah walked into the room, followed by Connie and Charlie. 'I need you all to hear me out. To behave like the exemplary human beings, I know you to be.'

'Hannah I—'

'Mhairi, I understand that this is difficult but needs must. We have been driven apart by a war. A dreadful thing that has no place in our lives. We cannot allow it to ruin friendships that were so very strong. To do so would be to allow THEM to win, to break us, and in turn break our resolve to change this place for the better. And by God, I won't allow that to happen without a fight.'

Lizzie stepped forward, hugged her, held her hand. 'I wholeheartedly agree.'

Robbie looked to Andy, both of them unsure, on edge, but wanting something different. An end to this darkness that sat above them.

Bea squeezed Andy's hand. 'You can do this,' she whispered in his ear. 'It's for the best. You know that.'

Charlie cleared his throat, gathered his resolve, spoke out as clearly as his nerves would allow. 'If I could turn back time; if I could change anything in this life, it would be that. I would never force men to do such a thing—to turn arms on their brothers. What barbarism! What brutality. Please forgive that man and know that he is not me.' He stepped forward, held an outstretched hand towards Andy. 'I didn't even know your name. Andy, I am Charlie, and I am not him.'

Bea nudged Andy softly and he took the hand, a frown of uncertainty on his face. He nodded. A release of something that had been tied in his stomach.

Charlie smiled. 'Thank you,' he said. He stepped towards Robbie.

'Aye, well, if it's okay with Andy, it's okay with me. Let's get past this.'

Helen wiped a tear from her face, looked to her daughter.

'How can I, Ma? How can I?'

'Bitterness can only eat away at you. You know that. I don't know the ins and outs of it all, but I do know that my wee lassie has a stain on her heart that needs lifting.'

'Mhairi?' Connie said, her arms outstretched, an expression of desperation clinging to her, edged with a hint of expectation.

Mhairi closed her eyes, briefly, took a deep breath, and stepped into Connie's embrace. They held tightly to each other, and a little piece of this damaged world was righted, at least in part.

'This is not the place, but there is so much more for us to talk about,' Connie said. 'In private. Will you come to our house tomorrow?'

'I—'

'Just say yes. Trust me.'

'Aye. Okay, then.'

Chapter 79
1920

~

Mhairi and Robbie stood anxiously at the door of Charlie's grand house, unsure of what this was all about, but willing to try. Robbie was about to ring the bell when the door opened. They were met by a grinning young lad.

'She's all ower the place! The state o her!' he said, excitedly, hopping from one foot to the other.

Connie was close behind him. She put her hands on his shoulders. 'Thank you, Billy. Can we allow them entry?'

Mhairi and Robbie exchanged glances as Billy asked for their coats. Had they taken on such a youngster as staff? Surely not!

Connie laughed, reading their thoughts. 'He's a—a friend, I suppose. A lodger, one might say.'

'No. He's to become our adopted son,' Charlie said.

Connie threw her arms around Charlie's neck. 'Darling! You are quite wonderful!'

'Eh, do I no get a say in this, then?' Billy said.

'Of course you do, Billy. I just assumed. Well. Would you like to become a part of our family?'

'Aye! And some!'

'Splendid. Now, we have important things to discuss.'

~

Maud, no longer dressed in her uniform, brought a tray of tea and cakes. She still had difficulty not addressing Charlie and Connie as sir, and milady, but got there after a stammer and a correction, smiling at her initial mistake.

'Right, well, we.' Connie looked up at Charlie. 'Well, Charlie actually, has discovered something which will balance our worlds again.'

'What are you on about, Connie?' Mhairi said.

'We were discussing this young chap's life on the streets. He told us of a home for abandoned children. A place he had escaped from on many occasions, apparently,' Charlie said.

'Aye. They were mean, so they were.'

'But better than life on the streets, surely?' Robbie said.

'Naw. Better be hungry than beaten to my mind.'

'Anyway. I wanted to see the conditions for myself, as did Connie. Such tales were quite horrifying to us. Connie is quite the philanthropist, and I am enjoying the journey with her.'

'Darling, Charlie, can you just tell them?'

'Of course. We went for a look, on the premise of working for my client, Mister Fotheringale.'

'This was a mistake!' Mhairi interjected, a look of disgust on her face.

'Listen to him, Mhairi,' Connie said.

'We went for an inspection, one might say. The name does open most doors. Quite remarkable. It was, as Billy suggested, quite horrifying, and we can only assume that they had made the place appear more pleasant because of our visit. I asked about where these unfortunate waifs came from and was told, single mothers, women unable to care for their children, orphans. I asked for more information, but they were somewhat reticent. I insisted. Children of the incarcerated, they said. "Women like that have no place caring for a child!"

329

'Well, I know of your story, Mhairi, and I probed further. There is indeed a young girl. A troubled soul who hasn't spoken a word since her arrival—'

'And Mhairi, she is your double,' Connie blurted. 'I swear. Your absolute double!'

Mhairi leapt up. 'Where is this place?'

'It is not quite so simple, Mhairi. They will not just hand a child over.'

'But, if she's mine. Ours!' She reached for Robbie's hand, trembling. 'Christ, help me here. What are we to do?'

'We can steal her! I can help. I know the place right good.' Billy cried. 'The way in, the way out, the ways all around. All o it.'

'Indeed, I fear we may be required to bend the law, somewhat, but there can be no mistakes. I do not believe we will get more than one chance at this.'

'I can hardly believe this,' Mhairi said, her voice breaking. 'You are sure?'

'Quite sure!' Connie said. 'You and Lizzie are experienced in such matters as well!'

Mhairi laughed. The memories of that night, which felt like a lifetime ago, when they had smuggled Connie out of the asylum. They could do this. They had to do this.

Robbie took her face in his hands. 'We need to get this right,' he said, holding her eyes with his. Tears building. 'Our wee girl!'

They fell into each other and wept.

Chapter 80
1920

～

Neither Robbie nor Mhairi had slept for more than a couple of hours over the past two nights. So much longing. So much desperation. They had wanted to go that night when they had learned of the place, of Rosie, but they knew Charlie was right. This had to be planned and executed with military precision.

The snow had mostly cleared, and slush taken its place, grey and dirty. An icy sleet swirled in the wind, making painful stabs at the flesh on their exposed faces. At last, they turned the corner onto the street where the home stood, cold and heartless in appearance. The grimy walls were stained dark, the windows were barred.

Only a faint light seeped into the alleyway that Billy led them along. His step was strong and confident. He knew what he was doing. The feeling of pride that he carried was quite the best thing he had ever felt. He turned to the adults, put his finger to his mouth. 'Ssh,' he whispered, as if it were necessary. 'This is it.' He glanced up at a narrow window. 'You need to gie me a hand.'

'You are so very brave,' Connie whispered.

Billy grinned.

Robbie made a basket of his hands and Billy stepped on. Robbie pushed him up. Billy pulled at the window and slithered through. Now they understood his insistence of going in himself. It would have been impossible for an adult to fit through.

Billy landed on the kitchen cupboard, thankful that it hadn't been moved since his last escape, and slipped down to the worktop, and on to the floor. There was no light in there, and nothing to see but shadows. Shadows that he knew and could find his way around easily enough. It was as quiet as death, as he knew it would be. He slipped off his shoes and padded across the floor on damp socks that made a soft squelching sound with each step. It sounded unbearably loud to him, but he convinced himself it was all right. He was safe enough.

Charlie had told him which ward Rosie slept in. That was easy enough to find. The hard part was to find her without alerting anyone else. To wake her up without frightening her. To convince her to escape with him. All that was assuming she hadn't moved beds, moved ward, just plain moved! Doubt was creeping in. He cast it aside as he tiptoed along the row of little metal beds, little metal cabinets, little sleeping children.

He knew that she was just a young thing, a toddler with little understanding; even less sense. When he reached the cot that he thought was hers he tugged the toy rabbit that Mhairi had given him out of his pocket.

"She'll remember this. Always had it in her wee hands, so she did."

He had to believe that Mhairi had been right. A wee prayer was thrown in as well. He didn't believe in any-thing, but if there was a god and he was listening... He knelt down, whispered, 'Rosie?' Held the rabbit out.

She stirred, peered at him through the darkness with sleepy eyes, held her hands out for the toy.

'Come wi me an you'll get it, right? Come on. Real quiet now.'

She slipped out of her bed, obediently, silently.

332

He held his hand out for her to take, but she stopped. Tugged at the rabbit. 'Aye, all right then,' he whispered.

She snatched it from him and squeezed it tight. A memory. A whole stream of them. Not pictures, not words, but feelings. Such strong feelings of something special. Softness, that's what they were. Feelings of softness.

They tiptoed on past the other sleeping children. Not a sound. Not a stirring. They had just reached the kitchen. Almost escaped. Almost in safety. Footsteps. A flickering light. Someone was coming their way.

Billy gulped, swallowed his fear, and led her to the table. He clambered under, tugged her with him. Snuggled her into him. 'Dead quiet. Dead, dead quiet,' he whispered. The person came into the kitchen, feet walking their way. Shadows creeping along the floor, stretching. Reaching for him. He closed his eyes.

Chapter 81
1920

Outside they waited, none of them daring to speak. He had been so long. This felt ominous. None of them knew where he had landed. It was supposed to have been the kitchens, but what if he had got it wrong? A young lad like that could so easily have made a mistake. What if he had taken a wrong turn, made an untoward noise, bumped into something, knocked something over? So many possibilities.

A dull light flickered behind the window. Oh God. What was going on? Still no sound. No shout of alarm. No scream. Mhairi nudged Robbie. He shrugged. She fell into him. He wrapped her up in his arms. Neither dared breathe.

Connie reached out, gently touched her shoulder. No words from anyone, just a fear, like a dense Glasgow fog, wrapping itself around them all.

The light seemed to be settled on something. Stationary. A softer, still flicker. The clatter of something falling. A whispered curse. Was that Billy's voice? They didn't know. The light began flickering again, growing dimmer, no sounds. There would have been voices if he had been caught, surely? A protestation from Billy at least. Nothing but still silence. The light was gone

All four of them kept their eyes trained on the window willing the figure of Billy to appear.

Billy opened his eyes again as the footsteps retreated, the light lessened and disappeared. He looked down at the shadow of Rosie who simply sat there, staring at her little rabbit. He took her hand, crawled out, and crept across to the counter. Now he had to trust her to be able to understand what she had to do. He lifted her onto the counter, jumped up beside her, pointed to the cupboard.

'We need to get up there, you and me, right?' he whispered.

She nodded.

He hoisted her up and she crawled onto the cupboard. He lent his elbows on it and hauled himself up beside her.

'Now you've to squeeze through there and yer mammie's waiting, right?'

Again she nodded.

Again, he hoisted her up.

Mhairi squealed as she saw her daughter's fingers clenched onto the window frame. Robbie and Charlie hoisted Mhairi up. She stretched to reach those tiny fingers. That touch. A bolt of lightning.

'Come on now, yer mammie's got ye. Come on.' She clasped onto that little wrist and pulled, first with one hand, then as soon as she could, with two.

Rosie squealed. Something was caught. A pain snatched at her knee.

'Billy!' Mhairi whisper shouted, as loudly as she dared. 'A wee shove, aye?'

I'm shoving already!

He pushed a little harder at her feet.

She inched through the open window and finally slipped all the way through and fell into her mother's arms.

Robbie and Charlie eased them down.

Mhairi clinging on to Rosie. Rosie clinging on to her rabbit.

'Rosie.' Mhairi couldn't hold it in anymore. Gulping sobs filled the night air as she breathed in the scent of her little girl. Her hair, her skin. Her. There was no doubt now. Her!

Robbie threw his arms around the two of them.

Billy slithered through the window and down the wall. He landed with a triumphant grin on his face.

'You are quite the most wonderful young man!' Charlie said, rubbing his head, affectionately. 'Splendid! Simply splendid!'

Connie wrapped an arm around Billy's shoulder. 'Indeed, you are. Well done!' She kissed his head.

'Mama?' Rosie said.

∽

The End

If you enjoyed this story you can help other people find it by writing a review on the site where you bought it from. It doesn't have to be much. Just a few words can really help spread the word and make a big difference to its visibility. Thank you!

Acknowledgements

I am truly grateful to my loyal band of supporters. To Jude Mondragon for the eagle eye that she lends to all of my manuscripts, to Shona Grieve for her enthusiasm, support, and appreciation of my work, to Morag Brownlie for listening, suggesting and guiding. And, most importantly, to all of you, dear readers, without whom this magical journey would never have taken place. I am so very thankful!
Much love.
X

About the Author

Fiona was the winner of the Federation of Writers (Scotland) short story competition, 2023. Prior to becoming a writer, she worked as an international school-teacher for fifteen years, predominantly in eastern Europe. She now lives in East Lothian, Scotland, where her days are spent walking her dog in beautiful places and writing.

Also by this Author
BEFORE THE SWALLOWS COME BACK

Perfect for fans of *Where the Crawdads Sing*, by Delia Owens, *The Great Alone*, by Kristin Hannah, and, *Sal*, by Mik Kitson, with its celebration of the natural world, its misunderstood central characters living on the outside of society's norms, their survival in the wilderness, and the ultimate fight for justice.

Before the Swallows Come Back is a story of love, found family, and redemption that will break your heart and have it soaring time and time again as you sit on the edge of your seat desperately hoping.

Tommy struggles with people, with communicating, preferring solitude, drifting off with nature. He is protected by his Tinker family who keep to the old ways. A life of quiet seclusion under canvas is all he knows.

Charlotte cares for her sickly father. She meets Tommy by the riverside, and an unexpected friendship develops. Over the years it becomes something more, something crucial to both of them. But when tragedy strikes each family they are torn apart.

Charlotte is sent far away.

Tommy might have done something very bad

Writing as F J Curlew

THE UNRAVELLING OF MARIA

"What a story. I wanted to get to the end, yet I didn't want it to be over. One of my favourite reads of all time. Thank you FJ."
Two women on very different paths.
Lovers separated by the Iron Curtain.
A chance meeting that will change everything.

Maria's life story is based on a lie. When she washed up on Sweden's shores in 1944 with no memory, she was forced to create her own history. In Scotland, nearly half a century later, she still has no idea who she really is.
But she's about to find out.
Angie knows exactly who she is: orphan, drug addict, prostitute. A waste of space. Her life is spiralling out of control, but people like her don't get second chances, do they?
Estonian freedom fighter Jaak has spent decades wondering what happened to his fiancée, Maarja, when she fled the Soviet invasion of their country. He's always refused to believe she is dead.
Could two women in Edinburgh provide the answer to what happened to Maarja?
When Maria's and Angie's worlds collide in a cancer care centre, neither can predict the profound effect it will have on both their lives, and that of a man thousands of miles away.
This unlikely and unexpected friendship turns out to be life-changing and leads them all on the ultimate journey of self-discovery, but do they have the strength to cope with what they uncover?

DON'T GET INVOLVED

Ukraine, 2001
Three street-kids
A Mafia hitman
A deadly chase

Dima, Alyona and Sasha, three street-kids with nothing but each other, stumble on a holdall full of cocaine. This could be it. A way out.

Leonid, a Mafia hit man who will stop at nothing to achieve his goals, is sent to retrieve the cocaine and dispose of the children. Failure isn't an option.

Nadia, a naive expat is looking for a new beginning. She wasn't expecting this!

As their paths get tangled up in the biting cold of a ferocious winter in Kyiv all of them will need to find more strength and courage than they ever imagined they had if they are to survive.

What do you call on when you have nothing left to give?

Dan Knew
A puppy born to the dangers of street life
A woman in trouble
An unbreakable bond

A Ukrainian street dog is rescued from certain death by an expat family. As he travels with them through Lithuania, Estonia, Portugal and the UK he learns how to be a people dog, but a darkness grows, and he finds himself narrating more than just his story. More than a dog story. Ultimately, it's a story of escape and survival but maybe not his.

The world through Wee Dan's eyes in a voice that will stay with you long after you turn that last page.

TO RETRIBUTION
HE THOUGHT SHE WAS DEAD
SHE WASN'T

Suze, an idealistic young journalist, is used to hiding as her cell tries to keep their online news channel open. They publish the truth about the repatriations, the re-education camps, the corruption, the deceit. New Dawn, the feared security force, is closing in, yet again.

Suze runs, yet again.

This time, however, she is pursued with a relentlessness; a brutality which seems far too extreme for her "crimes".

This is more. This is personal.

When her death is finally confirmed,

he is celebrating it.

Big mistake.

Retribution will be hers!